FAKE
BELIEVE

FAKE BELIEVE

STORIES FROM HAZELAND

by Matt Maxwell

A Highway 62 Press book
highway62press.com

Praise for *Fake Believe*

"Welcome (back) to Hazeland. Matt Maxwell weaves a sun-soaked, star-choked spell in this haunting (and haunted) collection. Slide into a gritty and glittering alternate-LA, where dreams (and nightmares) are just beyond the next horizon."
- Emma Gibbon, author of *Dark Blood Comes from the Feet*

"The weird tales contained in *Fake Believe* offer hypnotic excursions through the interstitial psychic environs of a timeless LA populated by an interacting demimonde of rich freaks, bemused lowlifes, and players on the cusp of an awareness they may eventually regret. More please."
- Jamie Delano, writer of *Hellblazer* and the *Leepus* books

Matt Maxwell operates somewhere beyond classification, in a space where horror, scifi, noir and superior storytelling converge. With Fake Believe he's outdone himself, giving us a collection full of unforgettable characters navigating a reality both darker and more wondrous than our own. These are stories that will make you dream.
- Corinna Bechko, writer of *The Space Between*

FAKE BELIEVE
by MATT MAXWELL
Published by
Highway 62 Press
www.highway62press.com

ISBN 979-8-9929099-0-6

All characters in this book are fictional.
Not a bit of it is real.

Other books in the Hazeland series
The Queen of No Tomorrows
All Waters Are Graves
Fake Believe

Coming in the future
The Missing Pieces
Asphalt Tongues

FAKE BELIEVE

Stories from Hazeland

By Matt Maxwell

DEDICATION

For the the comics writers who rewired my view of what comics could even do and talk about. And on that basis, what I could do and write about.

Chris Claremont
Steve Gerber
Jack Kirby
Pat Mills
Alan Moore
Grant Morrison

And a particular moment of thanks for Jamie Delano, who has offered valued counsel and encouragement, even at this late hour.

A CRATE OF BOTTLE FED GHOSTS
CUT/PASTE
THIRD SATURDAYS
SUICIDE JEWELRY
IN WHAT FURNACE
CLUB CLOSED: PRIVATE PARTY
THE CINDERHAUS

Cait MacReady was a forger of books who wanted to play a trick, so she made a book up. A book filled with secrets and power.

The Queen knew about the book before it happened and wanted it for herself.

The Queen used the book to make a thing that would have destroyed Cait and broke the world. She only ended up destroying herself.

Cait woke up from that broken, then found a creature that tried to drown her with time. She came out of it finally wanting a whole life.

A CRATE OF BOTTLE-FED GHOSTS

The Rookery stood alone on the new-turned earth the color of bloody bandages. The landscape around it was scoured to bland and geometric perfection. No shabby housing blocks. No anemic and withering parks. Not even streets. Nearly perfect. Bunker Hill was nearly erased. Were it not for the single and unmistakable scar of that edifice. Gothic in proportion, gaunt and stringy as a row of weeds yet maddeningly overbearing, it blocked progress. It blocked the cleansing turn of time.

Even today, well-meant citizens were trying to help it dodge the fate it deserved. The house and everything in it had all but outrun that judgment, the doom that had come for Bunker Hill.

The Rookery balanced on beds of railroad ties, themselves belted to the widest semi-trailer that Clyfford Fender had ever heard of, broad enough to make even Atlas envious. It was perched there, daring gravity. The smallest miscalculation could finish it. But there was every chance it would survive the move and that would not be acceptable.

He closed the door of the Ford Falcon and that rattled with an emptiness across the newly-scraped plane of clay and soil. Not long ago this had been the lingering neighborhood that Clyfford had retreated from because he couldn't tame it. Once this place was home to bankers and society. Then it was eaten by the degradation of this century, things becoming upended with the poor and unwanted moving in after rich families fled. The Rookery was the last of those fine old houses, built with refinement and care and elegance. But even those things could become rotted with the movement of years. Bunker Hill itself had become overstuffed and overbuilt, a place of sagging dilapidation and cheapness. Class had been chased out of the place by an ever-growing pack of ever-hungry rabble, scabbing like ticks on a thoroughbred racer. Once sleek and then made withered and emaciate. Eaten.

Every sin and crime in this rotten place had been boiled down, concentrated to its purest essence. All those acts tallied and kept here, inside the walls of the Rookery. And why not? They had nowhere else to go as the neighborhood was eaten away around it. The city fathers had tried even to cut the cancer away, running the new 110 freeway as a defensive wall between the rot and downtown. Even that hadn't been enough.

These deeds had made ghosts of men and women and children, consigning them to a damnation here on earth. Even so, that plague of poverty still threatened to infect anything and anyone within reach. Anyone but Clyfford. He'd come here many times before, to study sin and the ruin that it inevitably led to. Razing Bunker Hill had not reduced any of the evil, only forced it into a smaller and smaller square until the whole of the Rookery all but vibrated with it. That aura cast a negative halo that shimmered invisibly black in the midday August sun.

Only a few were brave enough to even have these thoughts. The developers who'd flattened Bunker Hill hadn't thought of anything more than lining their pockets, but even greed could be directed to a righteous cause. And they had aided Clyfford so so much in his quest.

He still wasn't sure how this concentration of evil had happened. How the essence of things had survived. There had been stories of a woman who'd gone from house to house before they were destroyed, waving white sage that burned smoky with one hand and in the other carrying an open jar or bottle. He'd never seen her, but he'd gotten word from some of the last residents, before the razing had begun in earnest. The woman had performed this ceremony or madness in apartment houses and corners and the zigzag alleys that used to cross this place like stitches needled into flesh by a drunkard. The neighborhood had become haunted by itself and this woman had somehow precipitated it, pulling spirits out of brick and wood and despair and anchoring them here.

Some of the residents had called her broo-ha, or something like that. It wasn't a word that Clyfford had ever known, nor did he have any real interest in learning what it meant more than "witch". Evil concentrated could be made to burn. That was all he needed to know.

Mostly the witch had gone to places where people had died, drawn to murder. Molly Ragnelli under a streetlight on Moore, found between half-empty crates of vegetables on a wet Tuesday morning. Terry Bancroft in the storeroom of the Aero Club, strangled with her own nylons. Martella Ruiz ended in her dingy apartment with the shutters open so that anyone could have seen the murderer. But that murderer was never seen or witnessed. Not even when he killed Bailey Hutchence in an upstairs hallway of the Rookery. The house was no longer the home to that sugar family from Miami. The building been subdivided into apartments that got cheaper with every wall and door raised. All of these shabby cubicles inhabited by people who would not be missed, even as ghosts.

Then why had the woman spent so much time preserving them, sealing these last psychic breaths into bottles and jars? Why preserve this it all? Why indeed? Clyfford had thought about this a long time and he knew that the only conclusion that made any sense was so that these ghosts could be kept and then unleashed at the right time, opening up a floodgate of spectral evil. The ghosts remembered and were a wound left untended, flesh boiling and running, capable of transmitting that rot to anyone within reach.

Not to Clyfford, though. He'd been chosen. Not because he was a perfect vessel, but an imperfect one.

He hefted the valise and within it the jars of kerosene clinked together, their shifting weight reassuring. He strode to the house, ready for it to not let him in. This final blot would be stricken from the ledger, the page left blank.

Bobby Withers opened his eyes to the heat and the sunlight streaming in through the window of the upstairs room, relieved that the whispering hadn't returned. It felt hotter than it should have been, or maybe that was just the breeze coming in from the pass. Too early in the year for the devil winds, but maybe. He wiped across his forehead with the back of his hand and snuck a peek out the window. Still best not to be seen. The sunlight glared off the emptiness where Bunker Hill used to be. He couldn't cry at that. He couldn't even cry at it when he'd first made it back, after an odyssey of twenty and some years that had started with enlistment and went to Italy then Germany and the sights that had convinced him that it was best not to spend much more time amongst his fellow man.

The remnant curtains breezed listless and Bobby thought he heard his name whispered in it. Soft and quiet, not sharp as the sergeant calling names down the line back in Europe.

He'd done what he was told, no more and no less. But he hadn't found it fit to even write home, much less try to come back. Not until the stabbing sense of absence drove him. Not until that whisper came to him in the train yard in Petaluma unwanted and galvanic. The word sent him running and for the life of him he couldn't even remember what it had been, but it put him on the first southbound train he could jump.

But he'd been driven to what? His home didn't exist anymore. It had been erased, all but this place he was hiding out in. He'd laugh at how he ended up in the Rookery after staring at its peaked roofline so often as a kid, thinking it was scary and pretty, like a haunted house before it had gotten haunted. It was a beautiful thing. Maybe that's why people were bending over backwards to save it. Putting a house on a truck and driving it across the city? Nonsense. And where was all that heart when it came to saving the people that lived here, he wondered. But then he knew the answer to that and felt a heaviness constricting his heart.

Sometimes people don't want to be saved, can't be saved. A house doesn't have a will of its own, so maybe it wasn't so crazy to try and save it. The realization this was the last part of his childhood still standing picked at him and asked for a tear that he would not give.

Not even Moore street was left, where he shot marbles with Whitney Combs and Petey Gordon and Joey Chin or where Mr. McGregor used to let them sneak apples from his produce stand ("from the bottom, boys, leave the shiny ones on top"). They even took the street, he thought. Erased it. Couldn't even leave us that much. Now the street was just sunbaked clay, a plain that looked like God himself took a disliking to things as he'd made them, moved to start all over again.

The task of mourning for his old neighborhood was bigger than any mountain than any man could ever climb, so he stood at the face of it and drew a heavy breath.

"Wish it was that easy," he said to nobody, or maybe just the house. Bobby felt like he hadn't been alone since he stole into the Rookery a couple of nights ago. He didn't have a good reason for staying here, not that he could explain. He had a couple of bucks to find a flop or could find family down south of the city. Ruthie was in Long Beach if she was still alive.

But that wasn't gonna be home. Nothing was. This shell with its peeling wallpaper and wind-shimmy because it was up on a stand and not on its foundation any longer, this was the place that was closest to his memory. But even that wasn't what he remembered, just a wooden frame that he could try and hang those memories on. He'd wanted to come home so bad after twenty years of rejecting it. And all that was left for him had been crushed down to four walls and a roof.

Bobby craned his neck outside and looked around, pushing past the corner-ripped screen that felt like a sticking plaster on a bayonet wound. The workmen weren't here and neither was their truck. One of 'em was always singing, so it must be lunch break or something else. Bobby thought he'd heard that tonight was the big night. Maybe they were doing some last-minute errands or getting tight downtown. He knew he should go before they got everything rolling. No telling what it was going to be like not belted in when this show got underway.

Moving a whole house at once. Amazing. A chuckle slipped out of him. Better that than a tear, he figured.

Regret pangs stabbed at him as sure as hunger. This was it. Something was not letting him let this place go. He looked down out the window and imagined himself thirty years before looking up and waving in the street, wondering who could afford to live in such a wonderful castle. And now nobody did, nobody but him. Who alive even remembered what used to surround this place or was he the last to do that, too?

The echoing slam of a car door crashed and he tried to sneak a look. No view from here, so he tiptoed to the room catty-corner from where he'd slept. Out there in the faded-rusty plain of clay and soil was a shabby small car, stained white and with a shape dusted out on the hood in red like a bird caught in flight. A black-suited figure walked towards the house with a purpose, dusty and undeterred by the heat. His eyes were down at street level, hadn't heard Bobby or didn't care. Being overlooked was one of Bobby's specialties. The figure carried a suitcase with one hand, steadying himself against the weight as he marched.

He looked like an exterminator crossed with a priest, walking like a man who was sure enough that he was right, he'd bet everyone's life on it.

"Yeah, that's a lot of not good," Bobby said. He wondered what was inside the bag and didn't figure that the guy was going to take kindly to any questions, particularly from a man of the world such as he was. That dude looked uptight. Like he was here to lay down the law. Maybe he was the fire inspector, come around to check the buckets of sand the moving crew left behind or to make sure that cast-iron and enameled bathtub that must have weighed as much as a tank wasn't going to come loose.

Either way, it would be best if he wasn't seen taking advantage of a perfectly good house left open and fit for sleeping in. He stole back to the room and squared his kit away, stuffing it into the rucksack that had seen him go everywhere from Sardinia to Belsen without so much as popping a seam.

Clyfford marched up, onto the flatbed trailer, sweating determination. He dusted himself off and stood at the threshold of the house, the front door hanging open like a loose tooth. The paint on the exterior cracked and peeled like leprosy showing the rot beneath. If he looked carefully, he could see the air inside shivered with something like negative light, not merely a shadow, but the evacuation of radiance, its erasure, its consumption. Breathing in let in sweet rot, something that crept into bones and turned humans to something much lesser. This place was cancer that had been excised, but yet some fool thought it should be moved and planted in new ground, so that it might grow and spread.

Unthinkable.

This had to be ended today. Bunker Hill had been scourged but still allowed a single vector, an ark of escape.

"I should burn you," Clyfford said with a sneer. "They'd never be back in time. Even if they saw the smoke from City Hall." But he had to know first about the witch's work and her bottle-fed ghosts.

He hauled up the bag and kicked the door hard. Something in the house groaned in response, as if it knew what was coming and was powerless to even beg for release. Veils of dust and fabric folded over themselves like skirts rustled between teasing thighs, shuddering.

No. He cut the vision off, didn't even give it time to bleed before it was forgotten.

The stained glass to either side of the door let in reds and yellows, lurid and aflame. But it was all fake wasn't it? These were all traps of flesh, traps of blood he'd sought. Bailey Hutchence's blood.

No. That wasn't how it happened. That was upstairs. That's what the stories had said. She'd been killed upstairs. This bloody light was nothing more than an admission of guilt on the part of the house, itself as much an accessory to her death as the actual murderer. It knew what it had done and would it would do again, given the chance. The house ate people and their very spirits, not hungry but mindlessly chewing.

Clyfford pushed through the dry red mist of light towards the downstairs kitchen. All the plumbing ran through that west side, wooden shafts and beams behind the walls all interconnected. He'd studied the blueprints. And inside the kitchen, there were cupboards and a large pantry that could conceal fires started until they were far too hungry and powerful to be stopped.

Where were the bottles? He wasn't sure how to destroy them safely, but he could at least secure them so that whatever they contained couldn't harm him. Couldn't harm anyone. Maybe the fire would burn hot enough to unmake whatever enchantment had been used to lock those ghosts up. If anything else, they would be scattered and powerless.

The dining room smelled rank, of cheap food eaten in sullen silence around a table occupying people who couldn't fit in anywhere else. In the dim splash of red from the entryway, he could make out a number of red-enameled fire buckets filled with sand or water laid out in corners or crossways. Someone was prepared. If only there was someone around who wanted the fires stopped. He chuckled and kicked one of sand pails over, useless.

"Where's the harm?" he said to himself.

He slid the vanishing door into the wall between the dining room and kitchen then stepped through and felt a pang at what had been lost when this finery had been abandoned to creeping squalor. Echoes of past wealth and taste in the textured wallpaper and fine furnishings were reduced to a state of decay, mirroring the souls of everyone inside this house.

Not him, though. Not him.

Faint daylight reflected in from the window over the sink, just visible below the hems of the grimed curtains. Clyfford's eyes adjusted to the dank and dim. He took a step and smacked into a heavy wooden thing at about hip-height, almost as heavy as he was, not yielding at all to his weight. A sharp ache throbbed where he'd made contact. And then that clatter of glass.

He set the valise down and put his hands out to examine the table more closely, eyes still not yet caught up with the absence of light here at the center of the house. Opening the valise, he went for the ribbed silver aluminum shaft of the flashlight.

SCRAPE

The sound from upstairs stopped him in his tracks. Old houses creak and shift in the wind. Especially when lifted off their foundations. But this was something meatier and more compact. Something being hauled across a floorboard and a door being forced open. Someone not something.

Clyfford counted out breaths and waited. Who was there? The workers had driven down for their lunch minutes ago. He breathed through his open mouth and wished he had something like a nightstick or a gun. The flashlight was comforting, but not a proper club. All he'd brought was kerosene and road flares. That was supposed to be enough.

The house was protecting itself, that thought raked fingernails across his mind. But that was nerves. It was just a man. Someone else who didn't belong here, either. He'd still have time. Watery yellow light snapped on from the flashlight. He shook it a few times to squeeze a little more life out of the batteries. There was barely enough light to see, but enough to figure out what was on the table he'd smacked into.

It was an old wooden crate, made for carrying milk bottles. There was a name stamped or etched on the side, in a fanciful script that had been out of fashion well before he'd been born, all but unreadable due to complexity and faltering light.

Sticking above the lip of the crate was a collection of different bottles, all shapes and colors, thicknesses and clarities of glass. Nothing matched, all refuse, just like the denizens of this place. Every one of the bottles had been stoppered with what looked like sticks or stems, all wrapped up in fabric strips. Some were sealed with wax. One of them was topped with a barely-on bottle cap painted in bright red enamel. He froze and locked on that.

Bailey Hutchence had been found with a Coke bottle. It had been an odd detail that had made it into all the police reports but had been kept out of the press. Unopened and chipped on the bottom from the fall, but still whole. Clyfford reached out for that bottle, gently and tenderly, stopping only when he noticed the circle of white powder that had been drawn on the tabletop around the antique crate. It was marked off with strange symbols, drawn in some kind of powder, maybe fine ash, not like cigarette remnant, but something else.

And salt. An old recipe for trapping spirits, that much he'd heard from ghost stories of magic circles. He brought his finger down to break the line, between two symbols that looked like they had more to do with madness than any church he'd ever known.

But was the ring to keep things in or out? He couldn't decipher it. It seemed fresh, maybe not even a day old. Surely the crew would have erased it if they'd seen it. Was this tied to the sound upstairs? Clyfford had to stop himself from dragging his finger through and tasting the substance. Not until he knew more. He knew enough. That the charm wouldn't keep the house from burning.

He swung the light around the room, looking for the best place to set the kerosene. The bottles were nothing. He'd been distracted long enough. It was the house more than anything else that kept this evil bound.

Bobby jumped as his jacket caught on the doorknob and rattled the door against the frame behind him. Given away by the sound, he crept down the stairs. He weighed less than a mouse as he moved, silent as his steps through the Bois Jacques in that distant dark. Whoever was down below must have known by now that they weren't alone. Or they were thick. Or they didn't care because they were here for something more important. But who on earth breaks into a house that's about to be moved? Then he thought about who he was and laughed at that.

Aside from himself that is. And he had good reason.

Sound clawed up from the kitchen. There was still nobody singing like the workers had, so it must have been the man in black, joyless as he'd looked. He wished for the workers in their semi-cab to get back. At least they could be talked to, if nothing more than to chase him out.

Bobby saw a weak flash of light coming from the kitchen on the other side of the dining room. But not a sign of whoever it was. They were silent still, just rustling and the creak of leather like old shoes. Then the high, clear clink of glass jars against one another like weird birds. Then humming? Low and focused, but meandering. Not a tune that he recognized, just notes strung into one another, without melody. Something about it was unsettling, crawling down his spine. Bobby eased from the second stair step, remembering the first one creaked like it was auditioning for television. He landed soundless on the dingy low carpet. It looked half-melted in the red light from the stained glass.

The humming stopped and so did Bobby, caught in mid-step. He strained to set his weight down soundlessly, knowing he couldn't hold this position long. He held his legs tense, remembering tiptoeing past Nazis and railroad cops. The memory and instinct was so strong, he felt a snap of cold and half-expected the footfall to be mushy with icy mud and slush.

There was another sound, an indefinite pop and then a hiss. He'd heard it before, but where? Weirdly pink light flew out of the kitchen, guttering and intense. A fuse. He'd seen enough of them used to signal at night or mark off a roadway or even jammed into a man's—

His hands tensed and shook. No. That's done. That's over.

Only it wasn't over. It never would be. Bunker Hill was supposed to be a refuge, a safe place to hide from all that, everything that had chased him from one part of the world to another. And he couldn't even have that. Just the hot sick glow of guttering light and the memory of what it once took to extinguish one of those.

The humming started again by the time Bobby could put his weight on both his feet. He looked at the door and how whoever had just come in had left it a little ajar. He could be through it in a second and gone. Then just an open dirt run and disappear into the city. Across fields that gave no cover. Yeah that was a dream.

Something glass broke wetly, musicality drowned in a splash of liquid.

"This is it," someone said from inside the kitchen. There was a weakness to the voice, as if convincing himself.

Bobby saw a gloved hand linger on the edge of the doorway, fingers very black against the pink-red light that spilled. What was that smell? Oily. There was the sulfur of the fuse and the hot-hair scent, but beneath that was something else.

He froze though his body screamed at him to run, something else, something distinctly apart from him made him stay.

A hungry woosh chuffed through the air, greedy flame sucking the oxygen as it came to life and yellow light flickered and grew, increasing in intensity. This was not the flare but something else. Light, angry and dooming made shadows like skeleton hands, fingers dancing.

This was arson. He's here to burn this house down and that thought exploded in Bobby's mind. The rucksack hit the floor before he realized what was going on and he was stepping towards the kitchen as the man lingered at the doorway. The man who was taking away Bobby's house, Bobby's neighborhood and Bobby's memory of it all.

"Hey! What're you doing?!" he demanded. His voice barked out, harsh and unfamiliar. He didn't have a lot of call to speak and even then, it was always low. White folk always scared of the sound of a black man's voice raised above polite whispers. But he wanted fear to happen this time.

The figure stiffened then the shape broke as it tried to dart past. Fingers of smoke were unfurled out of the kitchen around the arsonist, like he was born by it as much as anything else.

"No!" came a shriek of protest. "You can't!"

Bobby marched towards the kitchen and the figure darted towards him. He knew there was the chance to stop the guy or to grab a fire bucket and pray. No choice at all. He scooped up the bucket of sand, wire handle digging in as the figure scrabbled past him and out the door. Billy spat at him.

"Save that for the fire, friend," the guy said.

Bobby burst into the kitchen and tossed the sand bucket at the pool of fire on the floor, at the tongues that had started working up the wall. Grit and dirt scattered onto the burning oil, dimming the flames on the floor some. Dirt clattering on coffin lid sound as Bobby stomped on the remaining fire as best he could. Heat seeped in through the holes and cracks in his shoes but did not stop him.

He looked around for another fire bucket, thinking he'd seen one in the entryway. Dashing out and back, he hefted the second bucket and let fly. The sand flew out against the vertical wall and bounced off, acting as little more than an inconvenience to the greedy flames.

Greed. It was always that. Burn the place down, drive the families out, scrape it clean. He'd heard it even in his days here. The city always wanted the place gone. Make it clean, make some money on it. He stomped harder.

"Well goddammit," he hissed. He slammed the last of the fire on the floor but couldn't do the same for the wall. Then he remembered his rucksack and everything in it. The blanket might do it or the fabric of the sack itself, if it were emptied.

Tears streamed out of his eyes, more from smoke than fear he told himself. He stumbled breathless out to the bottom of the stairs and unclipped the bag as he snatched it up then overturned it and shook violently. His last possessions bounced out on the dirty floor, worth nothing. He coughed with exertion, furnace breath in his lungs. At least it was only wood smoke, he told himself, not powder and bone and flesh and fat.

"No!" he shouted. "No more." The images of those human skeletons painted grim and bloodless over his eyesight. He scratched past them to that fire.

He grabbed the blanket in one hand and the empty sack in the other, wadding them up like oversized mittens to smother the flames with. He hoped.

The flames climbing the wall danced to head height. Bobby went to work, boxing with the flames, imagining that they were the guards of that camp, the kings of the barbed wire and charnel. What he couldn't do to those men, he did to the fire. He worked until it was just light on wood and not anything else. Just light on wood. Not memories.

He heard a voice thank him, but maybe he was just letting himself off the hook for once as he slumped down in the smoky kitchen, wrung empty by exhaustion. He eyed that wooden crate and the sealed bottles on that butcher block table. Those and the weird writing in salt that looked like something final.

The sun dug itself down and the house was still there. Clyfford was lurched over his steering wheel parked on Third Street at a point where he could still see the skewed roof of the Rookery and not stand out. He leaned on the hood of the Falcon seeing a few scrawling clouds of smoke rose uselessly into the sky. He cursed himself and spat at himself and hated himself for not seeing it through. He'd depended on dry wood to finish a job that he should have seen through already.

They would know.

There was the bottles and the salt and the fact that the house even had a guardian at all. None of those things were supposed to happen. He was simply supposed to have scratched that thing off the face of the earth, destroyed any evidence so that nobody would remember the place. So that the evil would spread no further.

No further than him. But he could hold it in. He'd done it for years, feeling it claw at him at night and alone. He could be stronger. He could.

His fingers tightened around the wheel as he watched the red semi cab backed up and hooked up to the trailer. There was still time. Time to make that negro pay. Time to erase all of those tracks and traces.

His knuckles boiled and went numb and he released his hold. The scraped remnant of Bunker Hill was almost perfect. He hoped they never built anything more on top of it, just absence, absolute obliteration so that nobody would remember any of it. Having it buried under more buildings, tombstone skyscrapers, that would be acceptable. This aberration, the remnant scar that sat on the truck was enough reminder that the evil would still be remembered.

Clyfford wondered if the negro was still there or if he'd run. Either way, the place and its ghosts would be banished. No more half-measures. He hadn't gone halfway as a young man and he'd have to be twice that to see the job through.

The sun went down like blood cooling and not long after the truck's lights went on. Twin spouts of black smoke snorted out of pipes. The house shuddered atop the truck and the whole works slowly inched forward. The last house to leave Bunker Hill was on its way. Clyfford already knew what the route and destination was going to be. There had been news stories about it, though no interest in real life. Just on the television. The rest of the city wanted it gone as much as he did but not for the same reason.

It would be an easy enough matter to get ahead of the truck and slow it down. Easy enough. Slow it down and climb on and then he'd have all night to take care of the ghosts and burn the place down, hot enough to burn even memories, all but his.

He watched the truck crawl at walking pace for a moment and then gunned his car through the darkening streets. His fingers curled around the imagined Coke bottle he'd held. He wanted that one. That one would be his forever.

Bobby's hands still throbbed, but it was all surface-level pain. Though he would've traded everything he owned for a bucket of ice water and some butter to put on them after that. Not that he owned much of anything any longer. Just what he had on his back and what was scattered across the entry room of the house, those trinkets and bits. Everything else was burned or halfway to it. Maybe some little mementoes had survived. Maybe even his medal had. He couldn't go down to check it out just yet. Maybe after the house had been moving for a little while and he could be sure there weren't going to be any other visitors. And maybe it wasn't even worth that much, not even the medals.

Fat chance. That guy was gonna be back. If he was dead set on burning the house down, he wouldn't give up. Bobby slowly flexed his singed hands, every joint stinging. That guy would be back and Bobby would just have to wait him out. Something outside him agreed with that and it sounded like his name being whispered in another floor of the house. Or maybe it was just the pain and tired making him think things up.

The whole place shook like it was afraid of where it was going, but determined not to show it. Slow and methodical as a glacier carving out a valley. The house was fleeing destruction at a snail's pace. Watching the cast of the streetlights creep across the upstairs room threw him. Nothing this big was supposed to move. The whole house creaked and shuddered, slow turns becoming an agonizing and discordant chorus of wooden settling sounds, a hundred ghosts playing in the timbers and shaking cupboards. The big iron tub clattered on its claw feet over tile upstairs.

That one worried him. The fire had been underneath it, but as with his hands, only the surface of things seemed to have been harmed. Tough to tell in a house this old, though. The ceiling would hold. Maybe. Bobby had listened to the two movers cursing about things when they'd gotten back from their three hour lunch. But both of them had agreed that there hadn't been enough damage to call anyone or to throw off the schedule. Just some lousy 'bos, one of them had griped.

Yeah, I was a pretty lousy 'bo, Bobby thought and then laughed at that. Even after more than twenty years of practice. What about the crate and bottles, the other had asked. Clean that shit up? The first one had said not to touch it, that it was voodoo and you leave that like you found. Bobby didn't think it was voodoo, but that didn't mean he knew the first damn thing about it. Other than it shouldn't have been there, other than most of the furniture had been stripped out of the place, other than the things that were too big to move. Someone had left it here and the house and men moving it were okay with that. Good enough for him.

And then that thing outside him that was inside told him not to worry, but not exactly to relax either. That his thoughts needed to be placed elsewhere. Every time it touched him or spoke to him, it was a different voice, like a chorus where the lead voice always changed, but something of the character retained. Voices in his head, but they weren't.

Maybe it was time to give up wandering on foot, Bobby thought. Just get a house that moves around with him. Just have it take him from place to place, get take-out and otherwise live a life of leisure. But he knew that more than a night in any one place and memory was going to catch up. Right now, it was the good memories, before learning what people looked like on the inside and seeing it was ripped and wet. He didn't want to have brought all this home with him. Those twenty years and more of walking? So he could have found a way to leave those thoughts behind and not have them infect the only place that really mattered. And here he was too late to come back to more than the merest sliver of it. Still those floodwaters choked with bodies and despair ran beneath his conscious thought, not erased with alcohol or anything he tried to scratch them out.

But there'd been murder here. Not just the neighborhood, out in plain sight. People there in their ones and twos. And Bobby had murdered, only he'd done it under orders or to preserve his own life. It was no less murder. It was--

Something whispered reassurance as he came up for air inside himself, pushing out of the icy black where the only thing that he could touch besides the water were the bodies that choked it, bodies flayed and starved and their tormentors. Something whispered for him to climb out of that to--

He slapped his hands together so that the red welt of pain would snap him out of it. Pain would have to do.

Blue trapezoids of light jittered across the darkened room, making dust and smog dance within them. He watched the trapezoids along with the uneven black silhouettes of downtown rolling past. Once in a while, he'd see a flash of neon or burnt orange from the sky. All just color and shape and light, not even a city anymore.

The house crept through the not-city and Bobby wondered if people were out watching the sight of this giant wooden ghost tiptoeing its way out of life and to whatever zoo they were making up for it. That's what you did with old things past their time, right? Put them on display? Or you parade them one last time, all in uniforms then leave 'em to their own devices all that dirty work having been done.

Maybe burning it was a better fate. But if he'd believed that, his hands wouldn't sting. He'd leave this place tomorrow and after that, whatever happened was gonna happen. If there was magic in those bottles in the kitchen, they were going to have to bless or curse someone else.

"Just stop talking to me," he said to the nobody.

The house slowed and creaked to a juddering stop over what felt like minutes. Bobby got up and watched as best he could from the upstairs window without being seen. They were on a boulevard at the edge of downtown, just raggedy low buildings with Japanese and Chinese signs and flickering neon or lightbulbs all lit out like Christmas in August. In that multicolored light, Bobby could see a car parked sideways across the street, blocking it, not completely, but enough so that the truck couldn't nose around it.

"Get that thing out of here," one of the drivers growled. He was talking to something outside the cab.

"Ain't nobody in it, man."

The driver laid on the horn long enough for it to echo off buildings and concrete, coming back like a sigh of resignation.

"I said nobody was in it."

"Figured they were hiding. Just kids messing with us."

"Nobody messing with us."

"Well how about you go check."

Bobby's eyes narrowed on the car askew on the road and he was sure he'd seen it before, white with the stains. And that big one on the hood, that bird-mark. Sure, there might be a thousand cars like it in LA, but not parked there. Whoever had set the fire had left that car there. Which meant they were probably climbing on the trailer if not inside the house already. Bobby didn't have it in himself to put out another fire like the last one. He was wrung-out and probably couldn't make his hands into fists unless his life depended on it. And even then, it would be a fight between him and fatigue. A fight he could barely see standing through two rounds of much less fifteen.

Something else told him he had more, but he shook it off.

The engines chattered back to life and the rig started up with a lurch that jarred Bobby to his feet as sure as Ma rustling him out of bed on a Sunday.

"I can take the hint," he said to the house. "You get my back, I'll get yours. That's a deal."

A low peal of bending timbers rang through the upstairs, the hallway a giant sounding chamber. It was a sad and helpless noise, lost as a sunshine kid dying on a snowy field, surrounded with the supplicant figures of winter-naked trees. All those clutching limbs just holding blank chill spaces.

"You don't have to make me remember," he said. "I'm going."

He couldn't tell when he'd decided that the house was talking to him, if it was even that. Maybe it was Bobby just remembering what the place, the street that the house and he both remembered, had lived in and through, maybe it was just that and maybe it was just Bobby trying to make it up for being away all that time and the house was the only thing that was there to listen.

But it was listening, sure as it had spoken.

A muddy purplish oblong of streetlight through red stained glass crept along the stairs and floor of the entry, light and shape shifting geometries that angled and distorted as the whole world revolved around some fixed point. Bobby felt like that, like everything he'd been was still there, just pressed through and bent by circumstance into something almost unrecognizable. But those little fleur-de-lis carved into the windows, they showed up no matter how much the whole bent or twisted. The leading between the panes, the skeleton of the thing, it was still recognizable, still holding everything together.

As the light climbed the opposite wall like cold and slow flame, Bobby's eyes tracked back to the door. It bobbled open and ajar, closed improperly. And Bobby had heard the movers click it back on that sticky latch when they made their last pass.

Bottles clinked in place like someone had run a hand past them, fingertips rattling on that cold glass. What he'd seen in that room before was an act of devotin, was something that someone dearly believed in, even if he didn't. That was Ma again, talking in his head surely as if she'd been standing right there. But that couldn't be. Ma had passed before he'd even left the neighborhood, before the Japs had blown up Pearl and before half the boys in the town had enlisted in a fervor that none of them could have imagined. Bobby remembered how, just for a minute, everyone in that line was treated the same, white or black or yellow or red. All of 'em just so eager to line up and serve. Who was the army to judge? Willing is willing.

Bobby flexed his fingers and each of them shrieked at him in turn as harsh as frostbite that last winter, just a different tone. He sighed and tested the door. It swung loose on old and ungreased hinges. The last bits of Chinatown rolled past as they made the slow climb up Hill Street and away. A child standing at a lighted window pointed at Bobby then smiled and waved excitedly. Bobby returned the wave but not the smile then closed and fixed the door again.

Clyfford panted slowly as he caught his breath in the closet down at the end of the entryway. He watched the man at the front door and tried to hold down his excitement. His blood burned freedom within him, close enough to grab. The past that had chained him? Bleeding out. That was the truth that he'd hidden from himself after the years of piety and abstention. His knife or club or hands would be free to do what he wanted them to do. Once this ragamuffin man was out of the way, then everything would be free to start over again. The why of his presence was unimportant, only the removal was.

Clyfford trembled as he held the knife unsheathed at his side. Sweat trickled down the flesh of his face, flesh that was the root of all sin, flesh to flense. He rode the lurching glee that was coming. No, that was the wrong word. It was more than that, more primal, less emotional. It was triumph and satisfaction and awe in the face of the struggle that so very few allowed themselves to even accept much less embrace.

He opened the door just a crack more to get a better look. The light danced slowly around the skinny figure, weight on his shoulders like time itself turned to gravity. The shabby clothes and hair. This man was beaten. He lived on the streets. Nobody would mourn him. He could be erased just as easily as an entire neighborhood had. Welcome to the present.

The knife's blade slid across his slacks, making a noise like a snake on sand. Only he was the serpent. Throat or kidneys? One took longer, but there was the noise to worry about. There were two men in the truck cab not twenty feet away. Even with the badly tuned engine, a scream would be heard.

The throat then.

Clyfford slid through the open door and crept as quiet as smoke down the length of the entry hall. The constant sirrush of house creaks and groans would cover him until it was too late.

Bobby checked the knob out of habit then began to turn down the hallway.

"Bobby," something said, but it could have been a board coming loose or the thunk and echo of something falling from a shelf.

"Yeah?" he asked without thought, as normal as anything. It was then he saw the moving empty coming at him from the hallway. It looked like an un-man, just a purple-limned shadow robbed of depth but something he could fall into. There was a flash of something cold and bright down at hip level and Bobby knew.

He heard a grunt of surprise with a questioning rise at the end. Silver slashed and carved something like an elongated Z in his vision. It caught more air than skin. He lashed out to a space behind the brightness of the blade and tried to knock it away or get a hold on the arm that held it. Was all a matter of keeping the knife to the outside. Hand-to-hand taught you that. Out of the center mass, disarm, reverse.

It was cold and slushy and Bobby was fighting some other poor son of a bitch who believed it was him or them and there was no use talking. So Bobby didn't talk, but the wound at his wrist did, hot and hurting.

Bobby took a knee to his midsection and lost his breath but not his grip. He held onto the shadow and tried to bend the arm back. No dice, and worse, he'd have to let that arm go sooner or later. Instead of finesse, he went for a bull-rush, trying to take the guy's full weight down into the space under the stairs. All Bobby could see in the filtered streetlight was someone white, someone angry, young enough to have something better to do but not old enough to know that.

"How?" was all the guy said.

"Skinny but heart," Bobby growled, ignoring the seeping pain that was locking up his left forearm.

The shadow's arm snaked free and he brought it back for another thrust. Bobby felt the weight shift with his good hand and pushed against that, putting his center of gravity too far back and forcing a drop.

Clatter of the knife slipping into the gloom of that grubby carpet and then a thud and pattering of fingers and hands trying to recover.

The thought of chasing down the knife fleeted through Bobby's skull but there was no way to even see it much less grab it before the guy got back up. There was time for a kick, one that jarred bone through his cracked shoes. He hoped it hurt the other guy more than him.

"Kitchen," someone said. Or maybe it was the rasp of a window sliding shut, harsh and sibilant with a bang of finality at the end. Bobby didn't question it, just did it. Between the crawl of the moving streetlights outside and pain and dizziness, Bobby more swam than ran, bouncing off the wall like a tumbleweed trapped by a wooden fence.

There was cursing behind him, feral and biting. He pushed through to the kitchen and drew the hideaway door. It slammed with a sound that Bobby heard as "Good!" He fumbled for any kind of lock, finding only an eye but no hook to thread through it.

Outside the house, the truck downshifted violently and the whole works lurched like they'd hit a patch of slick. On the table in the middle of the kitchen, the bottles rattled with a strange yet confident musicality. It almost sounded like roll call down the line, each voice a little different, but all of them signaling their readiness.

Clyfford pulled himself up to his feet and cursed. Intolerable. He'd have won if the house hadn't cheated, hadn't told the negro that the knife was coming. He shook stars out of his eyes and tried to find the blade once his sight was clear.

The truck and the house were straining against gravity and incline. As weight shifted, the frame and every joint and the stacked railroad ties beneath all grunted from exertion. Much more and the house would shake itself off the stands. Something upstairs clattered and rang like a half-muted bell with another, more sustained sound of protest following that.

Enough of this, Bobby thought. He set his jaw and worked it, making sure nothing was broken after catching some boot leather. As the light traversed the hallway, revealing the dirty and mottled carpet that looked like a half-haired tumor, he watched for the glint of steel, but could not see any.

There wasn't time to look for it further, either. The colored could go for help or get a cop or something. The thought that the house was talking to the man came to him, those rattling bottles with whatever knowing they contained. Clyfford had to end this foolishness and if there was pleasure to be gained from that, then so be it. He anticipated that as he limped on a game ankle through the dining room to the closed door.

Clyfford ripped at it with both hands, expecting it to be locked and resisting. Instead, it slid and landed like a hammer hitting an anvil, bouncing on its track before jamming to a halt at a quarter open. He tried to see into the kitchen but could only make out the barest shapes against the streetlights trying to push through the grimed curtains like dirty sheets of translucent agate. He growled as he went for the lighter in his pocket. He fumbled once with it and then it caught, throwing guttering yellow light in a radius around him. The shadow of his hand blotted out the fire momentarily as his eyes adjusted.

Two wide eyes watched him from a sweat and blood-marred brow of black skin. The man gulped air silently. How could he be so quiet like that? He was standing by the table and its crate of bottles, all the tops made weird in the firelight, a strange bouquet of flowers made only to scratch and grab, all of thorns. They were all there but for the one the man held in his hand, the Coke bottle of sea-green glass with a chip out of the bottom that glittered like a broken headlamp.

The blood that had been so hot and resurgent in his veins cooled and pooled, going sticky as a new scab.

"What you got there, friend?" he asked with a dry voice that he could barely recognize.

"I ain't your friend, am I?" the colored asked with a scowl that was begging to be slapped right off his face. "Name's Bobby. Bobby Withers. Live right here on Moore Street."

"I'm so pleased to meet you, Bobby Withers."

The truck downshifted and it sounded like hell readying to claw its way up to the surface.

"You didn't ask me about my friend, here," Bobby said. He turned his wrist so the bottle spun like a mirrorball over a dance floor, catching more light than the lighter itself was giving off. "Her name's Bailey. Hutchence. But she tells me that she knows you already."

"No," Clyfford mouthed.

"I'm only repeating what the dead here are telling me. They've all got a story, don't they? That's all a ghost is, right? Something trying tell a story where it ought not to be."

"You're a ghost."

"Nah." A brief smile flashed, but it was a smile from living past a sad thing or series of them. "I used to be, though. Ghost in my own life, such as it was."

Clyfford became aware of the pain in his hand, held too close to the flame for too long. It wasn't just that, though, but a phantom pain, remembering the tension of the scarf he'd used on her as he dragged her up the stairs bump bump bump. He was sure there was a welt, so sure he'd never look at it again.

"That's a sad story, Billy," he said, forcing out each word as normal and even as he could.

"Not as sad as hers." He brought the bottle down and the shadow of it fell across his face like moonrise through leafless trees. "Wonder what would happen if more people than me heard her story. You know it already."

"Friend. This doesn't have to end like this. I've got a lot of money, maybe more than you've seen before."

"What would I do with that?" He shifted his grip on the bottle, letting it drop past his hand until he held it by the neck. "I got no place to spend it. My home's all but gone. Every street, every rock, every house, almost. Came all the way around the world, and that's no easy trip. Only to find it all gone."

"Not all gone."

"Oh, this ain't my house, my home."

"But it wants you to stay."

Clyfford got ready to hurl the lighter at him then use the distraction to grab him and crush his skull if need be. The ghosts were still bottled and would stay that way. He could take them home if he had to, just hide them from everyone, drop them in the foundation cement of the new buildings going up in Bunker Hill, toss them in the river in winter or throw them in the sea. Nobody would hear their stories. Not ever. He'd be free.

"You're trespassing, friend," Clyfford said, if nothing more than to rattle.

"I was invited." A snarling grin flashed and he smashed the bottle against the table, leaving the neck and its end of now razor-sharp green glass in his fist.

Clyfford swore that the bottle breaking sounded like brittle laughter, unhinged. He couldn't say where it had come from. Maybe inside. Something echoed in his ear.

He tossed the lighter more in panic than calculation and tried to make a dash for the door. An arc of flaming wick and flint tracked a reckless and shallow apogee into Bobby's chest. But Clyfford didn't stick around to see anything past that.

Chuy's eyes were heavy. This was supposed to be done an hour ago. Then there was the fire when they were at lunch and the stupid car in the road. He just wanted to get home.

"Tell me another one," he said. He had his feet propped up out the window, short legs stretched and boots into the hazy night.

Raphael thought for a moment. The truck strained against the uphill but kept steady. He patted the dash "Poquito mas, tortuga," he said to the truck. "Okay, I got one." His eyes flicked over to Chuy and off the road for a moment. "You ever hear the one about the priest and the prostitute?"

"No, ain't never heard that one. Is it a good one?" He was all but asleep, rumbling of the truck lulling him into a deepening snooze.

Raphael's eyes flicked back to the road, thinking he'd seen something move. There was a woman there, crossing the street at a dash. She was pale white and moved deerlike in flight. Overcoat and heavy clothes but only one shoe. Dead run towards the truck's path. Red scarf unfurled behind her like a lengthening wound.

"Holy hell!" he shouted as he jammed the wheel into the oncoming lane, hoping that she'd cross cleanly in front of the rig in time. He crossed himself and prayed there was no thud of meat on metal.

Screaming, the truck jumped and shimmied as it jackknifed across the asphalt, taking up all the road. The brakes screeched and as far as Raphael was concerned, it was the song of saving angels. The truck hit the opposing curb and hopped up on it with a jarring crash.

Behind the cab, the house groaned in protest but seemed to stay in place.

"That's a really short joke," Chuy said after taking a couple panicked breaths. "Maybe air it out some."

"Shut up and let's look at the load." Raphael killed the engine and unfastened the seatbelt, glad that he wasn't needing a change of pants.

"The hell happened?"

"Just do what I said, okay?" He looked around, even swiping a flashlight over the front end and bumper, seeing nothing but dirt-smudged paint and clean chrome. There was nobody on the street or anywhere nearby. He thanked Jesus for that.

Stupid woman running in traffic. He thought about it some more, how she was pale and blurred and he could pick out details like her clothes being really old and maybe something wrapped around her neck like a scarf but too thin for that, but he'd only seen her for an instant before jamming the wheel. How she looked like she wasn't even scared but instead happy or not even that. Like it was a triumph.

Chuy stood by the trailer and looked at where one of the railroad ties had cracked unevenly down the center. "No way I'm going in there."

"We don't gotta go in there."

"'Cause I'm not going."

The lighter smacked into Bobby's chest in a nothing. Only the second it fell to the floor, all hell broke loose. A giant hand grabbed the house and thrust it across the road, a careless child thing to do. He was tossed into the counter and only barely caught himself as he went to his knees, ribs into the edge. He saw stars as the breath got yanked out of him.

Clyfford had it worse, spinning to turn after throwing the lighter, off-balance and panicked as he tried to flee the kitchen a second time that day. He shouldered into it so hard that he bit his tongue and yelped, mouth splashed full of his own blood. He slid to the floor, back against the doorway and staring into the kitchen. His eyes had adjusted to the gloom or someone had opened the curtains. Somehow he could see everything clearly as if by moonlight. Things were flat but distinct, etched out in bluish cast. But what frightened him most was something he didn't see so much as heard, not heard so much as felt.

Something above the room was rumbling and pushing towards being born. Clyfford could see clearly where the fire earlier had burned and blackened. Much of the wall and ceiling was still pale and white-blue. The burnt area yawned open like an unexplored cave mouth, quivering faintly as the sound deepened and tightened. Then there was a cracking. Like a neck breaking. Clyfford knew the sound though he'd only heard it once, but that was enough. He'd heard it here, but upstairs. Not in the kitchen at all.

Bobby turned, clawing at breath. He'd heard the sound too. To him, the source was known and unmistakable. That big iron tub that had been too heavy to move? It was going to move.

There was a sliver of blue from upstairs let into the kitchen and it hung there for a moment, hesitating, anticipating the drop and the crash and the consequence that was brought about by time and gravity, slow and inescapable.

Clyfford's eyes flashed to the crate of bottles on the table, unmoved and fixed as the North Star. He didn't want to contemplate what hands had held it place. But then he thought about the broken Coke bottle and how it had laughed at him and then he couldn't not think about her.

The ceiling roared as the fire-strained beams gave way and the gigantic iron and porcelain tub crashed through. It slammed onto the table and all the fragile glass bottles waiting atop it.

"No!" Clyfford shrieked. "No!" He watched it drop like a wrecking ball or the fist of an angry god, smashing the crate and bottles alike.

The worst of it was the laughter. Some of the voices he even knew, but only some.

Flinders of wood and glass lashed out in a lacerating cloud, peppering clothes and skin, uncounted needles that wrote out a poem of vindictiveness and revenge all across him. He would be marked forever, as long or short as that was.

Bobby came to his feet and watched the guy scream as he scrabbled out of the room. The house was filled with singing, voices raised in greeting. It sounded like the old neighborhood for a moment, when people all shared a space and claimed a bit of it for themselves. In turn the place had claimed them too.

Bobby walked out the kitchen with care and told the house goodbye, thanked it for waiting for him to see this much of home.

But he couldn't tell if they'd heard him at all.

Clyfford ran down the street, even though there were men behind him who yelled to stop. The August night was hot but he was cold inside. Everywhere he looked, just at the edge of his vision, he could see them. He couldn't bring himself to say the word "victim" but he knew it all the same.

Blood wept from his tattered skin and tears from his eyes and over and over he just kept saying please. Maybe if he said it one more time, that would be enough, maybe once more after that and then again.

He kept saying it as the steel arcs of the bridge on 6th street came into view, big black knuckles against the light of the railroad yards and the industrial shops on the other side of the river.

If he ran fast enough, he might make it. The trains were still running.

They were loud, but not enough to quell the haranguing shouts of the victims turned victor.

Not yet.

He ran and ran some more.

He might even catch that rumbling train and the silence that those wheels promised.

CUT/PASTE

The guy was dead and alive.

I was stuck on that thought and how I was gonna die alone as his dry hand pressed at my windpipe and I thought about Rosa's collage art and how I'd seen it in that nondescript but very clean hallway in that new building downtown. Mostly I thought about Rosa if we're going to be honest with ourselves. And honesty was about all I had at the moment. It's easy to drop the lies and trickery, the verbal sleight of hand that's stock in trade to a cheapjack detective.

Or maybe it isn't easy at all to drop those habits. Dishonesty never came hard and the more you do it, the easier it gets. You're a process server. You're a delivery boy. You're an honest guy whose car broke down and you just need to make a phone call. Little disguises like for stick-up jobs. Be someone new for a bit. Live a half-life for an hour. All those little lies lubricate one another and over time they come easy as breathing. Fine unless you spend any amount of time with someone who wants the opposite. Like Rosa finally decided on.

The dead hand found a grip it liked and bore down. Stars tore at the sides of my vision, clawing their way in more insistently with every half-breath. Color streaked across my sight, mismatched and ripped out in little strips and glued back into something that looked like nothing. Not until I lost yourself in it and then the picture made itself clear. The owner of the dead hand wasn't breathing at all. Sure, his chest rose and fell and his cheeks sucked in over that starched Arrow collar that had never known a sweat stain or lipstick, as clean as the day it had been broken out of the cellophane or taken off the rack or wherever it was that dead guys got their clothes. His life was fake as the one I'd been living since Rosa.

He was dead. He didn't laugh or joke or say anything other than "How's it going?" or "You too, have a good day." His eyes were bright but empty, filled with not hate or curiosity, but instead a yawning emptiness that a hundred lifetimes couldn't fill. Still he wore his hat a little crooked, top jacket button unbuttoned, pants a little low, all these little details that suggested a real life, but a fake personality, weightless as a blown egg on Easter. He only looked alive, pretended to have a life. I had a little more at stake, or should have.

The fraying at the edge of my vision went deeper and blood seeped into it.

"How's it going?" he asked.

That was a good question.

Back in those days, I maintained an office over 6th Street, but I didn't sleep there. Never sleep where you work, else you never stop working. Credit me with at least that much self-respect. So I had that, sure, but not enough smarts to follow my own advice. Little personal rules like "You have clients and you have friends, but never both at the same time."

My office was just a couple blocks up from Broadway in one of the oldest parts of the city. Back when the men with the money practiced civic planning instead of brushfire management. They swept the streets regularly, with a kick when a gentle suggestion didn't do. The street looked about the same as when everything had gone up, excepting the roll-up steel shutters and bars that were clustering like cobwebs in untended windows. The neon marquees still lit up at sundown, though the gaps in the letters got bigger every year.

But when they lit up, it was a beautiful colored haze that swept over everything like a dream. It was enough to forget the ugly realities for a few magic moments every night as I strolled down to the Criss Cross Bar. The smoke and chatter was going to be pure comfort after a day of no phone calls, no jobs and no cash.

I knew when I saw Ronaldo there with his face in his beer I was in for a sob story. He was being kicked out of his place due to the fact that his old lady held some resentment at his not being paid for his last mud-up job. Some place not far from here, used to be a factory, used to make something. Now it was just being used to make money.

"Asshole is good for it. Look at his clothes and you know he's good for it." He finished growling and inhaled the last of his beer, looking like there was a more drool or tears than Modelo in the bottom of the half-pint glass.

"So," I said "just go to the Better Business Bureau. You had a deal and he's stiffing you on it. Make him pay."

His sigh hit like a dropped hamburger in a puddle. "Look at me, man. They're gonna say I'm a wetback and unreliable and this fine upstanding citizen couldn't have done what I said. Besides, I haven't been bonded since Watergate."

"And your back fees are way more than this. I get it."

"Dude knows it. He knows who he can screw and get away with. Shit, I knew that job was too good to be true."

I finished my Johnny and 7-up and then made a huge mistake.

"I can talk to the guy, Ronny. Maybe lean on him. For say fifty."

Leaning was not my regular business. Not directly. Usually it was enough to say that you'd been hired by whoever was paying the bills and mooks either gave up or ran. Leaning was something I was more on the receiving end of. But that meant I knew how to dish it out, too. And pushing an asshole around sounded like not the worst way to spend an afternoon. Especially if it kept Ronaldo off the streets and in good with missus Ronaldo.

"He owes me two large. You get it by Wednesday night and you can have a hundred." There was a tiny light pooled in his eyes. Maybe that was just the TV rolling more news about the upcoming Olympics, still years out. It was all anyone wanted to talk about. LA was back on the map.

"Just the C," I said. "I don't want to steal from my friends."

"Then maybe you can spot me this round," he said without skipping.

That's me. Riley Sullivan. Maker of mistakes.

I wondered if those fingers left prints, if they'd be able to pick up the guy once he broke my windpipe. Something told me no and I fought for another breath.

I sat at the back window of the van and watched the place through the one-way Mylar film. The eggs and hash steamed in the tinfoil take-out container on my lap while I chewed down the oncoming heart attack. My back told me that it was about time to start living in a place that I could put a real bed in and not schlep around town like a tortoise with his home on his shoulders. Maybe someday. Let's just pay some bills.

Used to be a lot cheaper down here. Used to be that I could make rent in a week or two at the transmission shop and be set up pretty nice. Just me and Rosa in the loft and her nonsense art. Just a few blocks from here. So close. Used to be close.

"Shut up," I told myself and took another bite while I waited for the kind of car the building's owner would drive.

As it was, memory wouldn't stop yapping at me. What's more memory got its back up and me trying to dismiss it. Just those long days of her working, me assisting when I wasn't up to my elbows in grease, watching TV or walking up to a Dodger game after. It's easy to remember the breezes, those goddamn zephyrs of perfection. Harder to remember why we drifted apart or why we even said what we said to one another. But it was all said and that was that. Perfect can get knotted and twisted into broken shapes so easily.

"I should track her down," I told myself and then laughed at what I was hearing. Rosa didn't want or need that. I was in the book if she did.

I chewed hard enough to hear my teeth grind together like a fault going seismic.

That was when the white Cadillac drove up, hood long enough to lay out on after a weekend bender were one so inclined. The driver got out, uniform freshly-pressed in the morning sunshine, creases so tight that he looked like he should have been in a Nordstrom's window. There was something stiff and off about him, but I couldn't figure out what it was. Maybe it was everything.

He opened the back door and the fat man wiggled himself out of it. His clothes were expensive but weird. Rumpled and too-tight at the same time, like he was carrying weight where the suit wasn't cut to hide it any longer. He had wavy and sandy-blonde hair that was slicked and wetted, more from sweat than from styling.

Another dude as fresh-pressed as the driver got out of the other back door. He was dry as a Santa Ana wind. Looking at him made me thirsty, all lips cracked and asphalt throat.

The fat man wiped his brow, animated and shouting. Both the other men could have been peeled out of an antiperspirant ad. Not a hair out of place, clothes perfect. I'd almost thought they were made up.

I shoveled the last of the hash down and chased it with coffee that had too much unstirred sugar at the bottom. Then I popped open the back door and let the morning heat crawl all over me. I rattled off different identities that I could use. Inspector? Delivery? Potential tenant.

Every landlord loved potential.

My hands went for his face, struggling to close. He had no breath. Not sweet or sour, just not there at all. About like I was getting to.

The lobby was clean glass and chrome and something that might have been leather stretched and suspended over tubular frames. It was supposed to be furniture but it looked more like an art installation. Yeah, I know the term. I spent more than a few nights helping Rosa get her art set up, first at student shows at UC Irvine, then at a string of seedy galleries downtown, usually next door to all-night clubs or bail offices and the crowds of spill-over clientele. Once I had the luxury of doing assembly and placement at a place in Santa Monica. They brought us mineral water and little slices of the tiniest orange I'd ever seen. I was thinking she'd made it then.

We might've kept talking after that, but not for long. Maybe I was never going to be the installation guy, just like the whole happy mechanic act was wearing out. I'd let that one play a good long time.

I considered how to hold myself so as to sell the role. Scott Douglas, movie producer, sleazy but a known quantity of sleazy, so you could think that you'd be ready for it but never quite see the deceit coming. The story wrote itself.

"Good morning, can I help you?" The man behind the desk was neither wary nor welcoming but tried to be both.

"Yeah. Scott Douglas. Looking for a change of scene. Tired of all those fake shits up in the hills, you know? Always looking for you to turn your back just for a second." I tried to inject a little coke comedown into my voice, just to sell it.

"I wouldn't." His eyes narrowed. "Movies or records?"

"I've done both. I'll do anything."

His lips moved as if to say "I'd bet" but remained silent.

"But really, I just want to talk to Gordon Barr. This is his setup, right? We've got some mutual friends. They said he could set me up with a new pad."

"Let me see if he's in." He made a face like he'd just given up a shred of self-respect then punched a button on his phone. "Go ahead and take a look around."

"Maybe I'll do that."

The lobby was void and airy as an aquarium without fish or water in it. Money laid out in furniture and art like bait. I glanced down the hallway to the elevators and caught a flash of color amidst the polished granite tiles and flat grey walls that shone. Sealed against graffiti, bet on it. Couldn't mark that with acid.

The elevators seemed very active, but nobody got off on the lobby floor. Must have been pedestrian access on another floor or on the 4th street side.

A little weird. I rounded the corner and took in the sight, that detail that had dragged me back here.

There was a huge collage behind glass, museum quality and probably even bulletproof. Thousands of scraps of magazines and newspaper, ads and news stories, little fragments of moments and bits of text over those. There was a weird symmetry in it, radiating out from the center. It was an early piece of hers, before she went strictly three dimensional art. I'd wondered if I was ever going to see it again after leaving our apartment. Guess I was. Took a couple years.

This was one of Rosa's. There was her signature down in the bottom right corner, the R turned backwards like Russian so it was back-to-back with the L. She'd never parted with this one. Wonder what drove her to sell it? Maybe everyone gets hungry enough finally. Maybe she'd made it big enough to want to move on.

The elevators chugged and churned, still moving but nobody got off. It was like the building itself was pretending to be busy.

I stared at the collection of flecked color, the thousands of triangular tatters of everyday junk pieced together in a way that suggested a pattern or order where there had never been one, where we only *thought* there was one. She had never appreciated my read of this work, of collage in general. I wasn't supposed to be in on the joke. I was supposed to be the joke. That whole regular life thing.

Yeah, maybe I can see why we were meant to fall apart. Acting like I really regretted it because I was supposed to. Then it wrapped around to the real thing eventually.

I climbed up the stairs to the second floor and wondered what the hell any of this had to do with Ronny's missing money or my outsized sense of obligation towards my friend who was not my client. Nothing at all, but there wasn't much else to do at least until I could talk to the man.

The door was marked TEMPORARILY OUT OF ORDER but I tried it anyways. I was just looking for the bathroom, right? A lie that usually worked.

The sun was hitting the windows on this side with a wash of light that stung hard as bleach fumes. Nothing could have been that clean. Humans are messy creatures, disorderly. Yeah, disorder. That was what Rosa's work was really about but she insisted it wasn't. Things are always about what they refuse to talk about. Read that somewhere.

The elevator door opened and out walked a family straight from the pages of the Sears catalog. Husband in a suit, charcoal gray and fresh-pressed. His little woman in a sunny yellow dress with frills that read more like '74 than '78. Two kids: stripes and dungarees, a dress like mom's. They were so clean and wholesome I felt dirty just standing there, but then I'd been sleeping in my van since forever so maybe there was good reason for that.

Then I watched them go from one elevator opening to the next one, all smiles, dad pressing the button without a comment and the whole crew just waiting for it to come down from whatever floor and open up.

They hadn't forgotten anything. There was no embarrassment or chagrin, no sense of any presence at all. They were just out riding the elevators. I wondered if they'd come back down and continue the cycle if I waited. The thought of that sent a chill through me for some unspoken reason.

The fourth elevator, the furthest one down the floor, opened up and two figures came out and then walked lazily to the door, some dude in a Travolta's leftovers white suit with collars and lapels that could support his weight in a stiff wind, his lady in something tight and glittered, fringe catching the morning sun like all the gold in Fort Knox. Maybe they'd just left the party from last night. That's it.

Maybe I was just tired and edgy from seeing Rosa's artwork here and remembering it all. Maybe I should stop sleeping in my goddamn van. Maybe I should grow up and get with the program. Money moving in everywhere, reshaping things.

The elevator that the family had gone up in came down again and dinged. I wanted to see them come out. Instead I got a hand on my shoulder.

"Mister Douglas, there you are." I turned and while the voice had come from the desk man and his sharp European suit cut to make him look like a space alien, the guy who grabbed me was the driver from the Caddy earlier. His hand came in real close on my shoulder, brushing the open t-shirt collar, making me realize exactly how vulnerable my neck was with all that blood and breath running through it and to the rest of my body. A finger pressed down and I thought about that flow being interrupted.

I've touched dead men before. Sometimes an alimony case becomes a murder case and you have to know before you call the cops and blow everything up. Can still remember Mr. Simpson very likely dead with that ragged rose of blood under his Brooks Brothers saffron button-down, but yeah maybe he breathed in just a little. He was warm and yielding, but he was gone. That was just the memory of life hanging around until the stiffness set in.

The guy touching my neck wasn't even warm. There was a rough feeling of torn fingernails or fine-grit sandpaper or a cat's tongue if it had been dead for a week. My skin crawled under that and I'd lived in this moment way too long already.

The desk clerk smiled, warmed by watching me squirm. "Mister Barr is ready to see you, and I'm sure he'll be quite irritated to learn that I had to go track you down."

"Was looking for the bathroom--" and I forgot the rest of that well-practiced line. I tried to crane my head back to see if that family was still running their circuit from elevator to elevator, but I felt those fingers scrape a little and thought better of the attempt. I didn't really want the confirmation anyways. I probably would have started screaming.

The chauffeur said nothing as he whipped me around to follow the clerk back down the stairs. I caught a flash of the sun on his cheek, under his wraparound shades. I could have sworn that I saw the faintest ghosts of writing on it, just in places where the light hit differently, like that part had been clipped out of a newspaper and pasted on.

I tried not to think too hard on it as I got marched down the stairs and past Rosa's collage. In my side vision it looked like art for a dentist's office, indistinct fish sprinkled over a field of swirling blue.

Barr was wedged behind his desk and he laughed when I told him that I was looking for a place. One bedroom, not a studio. If I wanted that, I'd have asked for a loft, you know where I could have enough space to partition out my life neatly and have a space to work, a space to sleep and a place to entertain.

I didn't break once.

"You a process server? Brenda send you or Yvonne?" He was sweating still. Maybe he always sweat.

"Okay, look. If you can't offer me a deal, just at least let me take a look around. I can pay a full rate."

He leaned forward like a Malibu cliff face ready to wipe out a million dollars of house and drew in an exaggerated breath then smiled to himself. "You smell like couldn't afford any place where you have to pay by the month. That's a terrible disguise. Scumbags from the hills smell like swimming pools or sex. Not like the street."

"I got thrown out." I glanced around the office and found nothing to bargain with. Usually I can pull out something to throw them off their game. Picture of kids or some other little clue that connected thing. "Slept in the mission."

There was a stack of invoices on the desk, twin horseshoe-shaped impressions of sweat on them, like he'd been pressing on them with his hamhock hands. METHOD MOVE or something on the top. It was tricky to read all upside down.

"Not the first time, right? Come on, give it up. I'll take the goddamn paper. Maybe I'll even give you a ten spot to get the fuck out of here." He held out a fleshy hand that you could have bathed a terrier in.

The chauffeur stood behind me and to my right. I'd have bet everything in the van that he hadn't breathed once this whole time.

"No blue envelope," I admitted. "I'm here to collect on a debt. These walls didn't go up themselves, much less get plastered and painted. Fella I know just wants what's coming to him."

His smile retained. "That goddamn Mexican. Cut a corner, save some money and it still bites you on the ass."

"Maybe just pay up?"

The frown on his face pulled so hard I could hear it. "Or what? You want to beat it out of me?"

"You said that, not me. Besides, do I look like the type to try and muscle someone like you?"

"Buddy, you don't look like you could muscle a Girl Scout out of her cookies."

"Right. So let's just settle the two large my friend is owed and call it a day?"

He at least thought about it, or maybe he was considering lunch and how I was interrupting it. "What the hell. I'm feeling generous." He radiated magnanimity as he slid open the desk drawer. "You can take a check, right? I mean, what's to say that you won't just run off with the cash and then your friend gets nothing?"

"I'm good for it. Better than you were."

"Fair point," he said, sighing. "I don't want to hear shit about this again. You and he are lucky to be getting even this." There was a click of a key in a lock and creak of a metal box protesting at being opened. He came up with a fist wrapped around a folded stack of bills that must have been moist to the touch.

"Sure thing. And while I've got your attention."

"Oh, this is sure to be good. Listen up, Clarence," he said, apparently to the chauffeur. "I don't want you to miss the pearls of wisdom that are to no doubt come."

"Where'd you get the collage art?"

"'Collage.'" Barr snorted. "A scholar. An unwashed but educated scholar." His gaze narrowed on me, sharpened and malicious. "What the fuck are you on about?"

"That big piece on the way to the stairs to the real first floor. The collage by Rosa Layton."

Barr had started pale and oily but went as dry as sharkskin in a heartbeat, flushing red beneath it. The hand holding the money shook like a baby earthquake. "You know her?"

I leaned back and got ready to rake in my winnings. I didn't understand what the connection was, but I'd cut right down to the quick on this guy. "Buddy, you can take that to the bank."

"Clarence. Lose this piece of trash." Barr yanked his hand back and shoved the wad into a pocket with the speed of a coyote dashing across the boulevard.

I felt the dead hand pick me up by the shoulder and got whipped around like I was on a broken tilt-a-whirl. The ceiling lights zipped past me in a iridescent blur and I was sprawling in the hallway on the other side of the office door before I knew it. My knee got barked on the landing and pain jabbed all the way to my hip. I tried to get up out of it and heard Clarence speak finally.

"How's it going, buddy?" he asked as if we'd just bumped into each other on the street. Something about the utter disconnect between his tone and the moment clawed at my brain.

"And don't you fucking come back, loser scumbag!" Barr yelled seemingly from another county. "I run a good place here! Families want to move in! Real people! Not trash like you!" His voice harangued me as hard as August heat.

I tried to get myself collected but someone did the job for me, lifting me as easily as a dead possum.

"How's it going, buddy?" the voice asked, a stone repeat of his last line, like a record stuck on a groove.

"Fine, pal. Just put me down and I'll get out of your hair."

He carried me through the hallway back to the stairs. Guess he didn't want to march me in front of any potential clients at the rental desk.

Then he half-dragged me up the stairs, just low enough that I could count them with my shins. By the time he got to the top, my legs were screaming red welts below the knees. I couldn't have stood on a bet.

He pushed through the door with a mechanical smoothness and we came out on the elevators again. Damned if the happy family weren't getting off and making their circuit.

"Don't mind me, citizens. Just out for a walk with Clarence here."

They wouldn't have noticed me if I were on fire.

"How's it going, buddy?"

The repetition started getting to be funny, funny in a way that made me want to check into the cheapest looney bin I could find. I caught our reflection in the glass windows that opened up onto San Pedro road. He marched without effort or wasted motion. He looked like he could have walked me right to Santa Monica without so much as a glow on his brow.

"Hey, you wanna put me down? You've made your point."

Clarence said nothing as he opened the front door with his right, pinning me with his left. This had to be my opening, not that it was a good one, but with just one hand on me, I might be able to grab an opportunity.

I reached back with both hands to grab his left and went dead weight with my body, hoping that the shift in gravity would force his stride off, maybe get him to balance where I could help it all the way to the stairway down to the street. Clarence shifted all right, but didn't go down. I could only get my right around his wrist by reaching all the way back, no leverage, no nothing.

He didn't say a word, not even a breath as he righted himself and shook me like a big dog would a dead rat. He tried for a throw, but my right was strong enough to keep on. That put him off-balance enough to force him to loosen up.

I turned to face him and scrabbled to stand upright. There in the sunlight, I got a real good look at him. There was a texture to his skin, something irregular but repeating. Where I thought I'd seen the shadows of words before on his cheek, I saw it was all over. Subtle, but unmistakable once I'd locked onto it. Were they scars or tattoos? Whatever it was, it was just in fragments. Chunks of type cut and paste over other chunks. Which made me think of Rosa's work for a split second.

His right snaked at me and got a hold of my neck before I could begin to move back. The dead fingers rubbed against my skin and I wanted to shit my pants then and there. Breakfast boiled up at the back of my throat. This wasn't a living man, but a thing being ordered around by Barr.

"How's it going, buddy?" There was no effort behind the breath. We could have been sharing a drink. Instead, he was looking for purchase so he could choke me out. He bore down on the hollow of my collarbones and pushed in hard enough for me to feel his fingerprints. They felt like headlines, big as you could print.

He pulled me closer and there wasn't a goddamned thing to do about it. There was no light behind his shades, though I could see the contours of his cheeks and eye sockets behind. It was a dead space.

On his forehead, I could clearly see the ghost of a word, a whole word, standing out amongst a swarm of half-words, a somnambulist language babbled out of the deepest sleep. Then his fingers found my throat.

The word was ALIVE.

"Don't you fucking say it," I warned.

He dragged me close enough so that all I could see was blurry letters embedded in his flesh. Breath came harder to come by.

The thing that really ate at me was the absence. Dudes beat you up and assure you that it's nothing personal, but damn if they aren't getting a kick out of kicking you around. That's a thing I understand. But Clarence had none of that. He was following an order that maybe he himself didn't even comprehend. Just obeyed. Just like that family was going to run in circles all day simply to make the building look occupied.

My vision was beginning to cut out. Curtain time or there were going to be two dead guys on the street, just one of them still moving.

I lost it. It was undignified and unmanly, sure. I screamed and then clawed at his face. If nothing else, I'd give him a scar to remember me by. Assuming he could integrate something new into his programming.

His dead skin was underneath my fingertips and I dug down as hard as I could as my vision clouded over, purple then blue then black.

I swore I could feel the ridges of letters and characters under my skin, nails catching on their edges and finally hooking on one big enough to hold onto. It ripped my fingers to hell, or felt like it, but I held on and shoved hard enough to feel it in my shoulders and my triceps as tight as a high-tension line.

"How's it going?" he asked once more, but his voice edged in to something else. Maybe he was asking himself for the first time ever.

Something cracked, brittle as bird bones and there was a low sigh like a whole body deflating. The grip on my neck went slack and I didn't have words to describe that feeling, of a dead man going frozen with his hands on my throat.

I kicked back and fell in a heap, coughing and spluttering, my throat and vision bloody raw. I spat but didn't look to see if blood came out with it. Every breath brought me closer back to myself, pushing back the ragged vision. Sure. I hurt just breathing, but I was alive.

I was lucky.

Clarence, whatever he was, his luck had run out. He stood there frozen as a stuck film frame. His clothes were still perfect, none the worse for the struggle. His glasses lay at his feet and I picked them up. Ray Bans. They looked expensive.

"How's it going, buddy?" I asked him.

There wasn't an answer, just a dusty seethe, barely audible. It issued from the hole in his skull, black and empty. I resisted the urge to stick my hand all the way down, simply to see what I'd find. A still-beating heart? A little munchkin driving wheels and pulleys? Worse yet, I knew I'd find nothing. A hollow with a skin of papier-mâché, emptiness all the way down.

I opened my right hand and looked at the scrap there. There was only the ALIVE printed on what clearly was nothing more than painted newsprint. Like the rest of him. A crisp suit on a hollow doll the size of a man. But a moment ago it had been walking and talking and pretty set on killing me to death.

I wanted to laugh at the nonsense until I passed out. Instead I made my way back to the van and tried to think about what I was going to do next. Pieces of thoughts ran together, but nothing complete, so many of them that they just came at me as a scattered jumble, dislodged syllables. A chorus of idiots screamed at me, the biggest idiot of all.

I had to make the pieces mean something. Just like Rosa had. Make a collage, make a thousand bucks.

The Caddy was still parked out front, so I made a note of the plates. Wondered how long Clarence's absence would go unnoticed. Wondered why Barr was so upset that I knew who Rosa was. Wondered how the hell I was going to get Ronny's money or if that was gone forever. Going back in to lean on the fact that I'd just been attacked by a goon who was made of arts and crafts wasn't going to work. Hell, the place was stocked with them, all pretending to be alive. I got lucky with the one, but I bet the fake seven-year-old could take me apart if he was told to.

I cranked up the engine and headed back to the office. Then I placed some calls with my friend Sleepy down at the DMV. Was gonna be a bit to run down the caddy. Went for a drive. Did my best thinking when I wasn't thinking.

Midday clamor oozed all over Broadway and I dragged my way down the boulevard between lights like a pulse of slow blood. The sun was up at highest and raining down hard, shadows on the roads like shy inkblots barely edging the outlines of whatever cast them. No place to hide from the light or heat, ripples so thick on the road that you could drown in them. But the place was alive at least.

Folks clustered around the fronts of restaurants or whoever else had the AC up and blowing out. Dudes selling ice cream or paletas out of bicycle stands or pushcarts were making money as fast as they could reach down into the cold. Yeah, the place was still alive even if it was feeling more abandoned every day. These were all real people, not clockwork or origami-perfect. They were sloppy and made mistakes and I loved that for the moment, after the morning of robotic paperwork that wanted to push my face in or just ride the elevators.

I turned up the radio, fumbling the knob. Soaring guitar, fully-glittered out and shimmering poured from the van's speakers and mixed with the murmuring of the crowds and the heat and I stopped thinking about mechanical things and instead started feeling my way through them as easily as picking up on the ebb and flow of traffic. Yeah, things still happened in a traffic jam, you could still get home, just slower. If you got mad about it, well that was just making it worse for yourself. So that was the approach I took to thinking about things. Since that I was out of Clarence's grip, I could not-think my way through this.

"And that was Tommy Fade with 'Diamonds in the Sidewalk,' a dude we haven't heard much from lately." The DJ sounded a little sad about it, like there weren't a hundred other guys with guitars ready to step into the mangler in hopes of getting the brass ring before they got chewed all the way up. "But a little bird tells me he's working on something big, maybe this year, maybe next. So don't give up hope. Now here's 'Turn to Stone' from E-L-O on K-M-E-T."

Don't give up hope. Yeah, easy to say.

I coulda had that money and been done with all this. But no, I had to open my mouth about Rosa's collage. Wow did that ever change his mind on the double. What was that all about? Maybe it was about him having wind-up paper men as bodyguards. And as residents. Sure, okay. But why and how? And Method Movers were who exactly?

Mostly how was I going to get the money without being pounded into pizza sauce.

And how I should be looking Rosa up.

I drove circles around downtown just letting the same pieces orbit around my head. Every time I tried to put real thought into it, grab it, the idea would just laugh and flip me off, slippery as a snake dipped in motor oil.

She always told me that the trick with collage was to let the pieces make sense out of themselves. I always thought that was academic garbage and she was just pushing a meaning onto them. Life makes itself. Art isn't that.

But here I was doing exactly what she said and damn if she wasn't right.

I tried not to think about how Clarence had been made out of layers of words and scraps of paper just like her collage work had. Or that she'd gone primarily into sculpture before even we'd broken up. It was one thing to fashion something out of paper pulp and clippings. It was another to make it move around and follow orders and beat dudes up. Wasn't it?

Signs going up everywhere. New apartment development, urban renewal, luxury living downtown. That was a laugh. There hadn't been upscale living here for a long time, unless you counted the Eastern Columbia maybe. But that was definitely for a particular class of upscale. All these new signs were another thing entirely. Factory buildings had been closing out for awhile. Fashion district still did what it said on the sign, but that was becoming more the exception than the rule. Hell, that place I'd been thrown out of, that was all industrial floors not a few years ago.

The new residents were colonizing the place slowly. Only some of 'em were not residents so much as furnishings to make the place feel lived-in. Yeah, that was a first for me.

But hey, Olympics coming in a few short years. Nothing like a good excuse to burn out the old and make a neighborhood safe for money. Hell, it worked on Bunker Hill, right? Who said it couldn't work anywhere else. Got us a bunch of unaffordable apartment towers and office buildings all made up like fortresses to keep folks from this side out. Got a sludged-up freeway the splitting town in two.

Was Barr a symptom or a disease, though?

I started making lefts to work my way back towards the heart of the city and the library. Maybe I'd done all the thinking I needed to do and it was time for a little research.

Coughed up a dime and dialed my message service. Sleepy had come up with registration on the Caddy. Address way out in the Valley towards

Van Nuys. Barr's name wasn't on it. Instead it was a business. Prime Realty Innovations. That was a start. But it wasn't the name that I'd seen in Barr's office.

Went through the business listings at the reference desk, breathing in the bureaucracy and the folks who spent their whole days there, poring over the same newspapers over and over or the almanacs or anything that just put something to read in front of their eyes so they could burn hours until the sun went down.

Didn't have time to track down Method Movers, but I had time to look through issues of *Artforum* and *American Artist* and some of the weeklies from around the time that Rosa and I had been an item. Sure. I had time for that. Maybe her name would pop up or an artist's rep or something I could track her down with. Could always call Tracy. That would cost me some pride, but I'd already been giving it away. I only found references to a couple solo shows and the name of that gallery in Santa Monica saying that her work was being carried there, but it was pretty thin soup.

Thin soup is still better than water.

Santa Monica was only a few miles away from downtown, but whiplash different. Instead of August heat, there were cool Pacific breezes and the lulling pulse of the surf off in the distance. The Vista Visions gallery was just off of Third street, heart of town. I dusted off the coke-addled producer character and gave him another run. That was the nice thing about running into different people every day. You weren't around long enough for the stink of your bullshit to catch up. At least if things worked well.

Maybe Rosa just caught a whiff of it one too many times. And maybe we just shouldn't have been together anyways. All I did was give her a break on that ramshackle Karman Ghia she drove into the place in Long Beach when I was all but quit. God she was gorgeous. And I hated that skinflint manager, so I did the job for nothing and made the mistake about asking her what was going on with the weird art project she had in the passenger seat.

"Can I be of assistance?"

I snapped back to the moment. Today was catching up with me. I'd walked into the place and stood there like a space cadet.

"Oh, yeah. Sorry." I continued to stare in awe. "I was just taking it all in, you know."

"We pride ourselves on curation." He tugged at the points of his bowtie then steeped his fingers. "Anything in particular mister…?"

"Douglas, Scott Douglas. I produce things."

"Delightful."

They still had one of Rosa's pieces, a pair of shiny military-style boots. They were streamlined and spotless, sterling silver on the tips, just looking for a helpless orphan to kick. Maybe a jaw to grind down. Next to them, tossed off casually, were two papier-mâché feet with laces as if boots, expertly crafted, scarily lifelike. It was one of her early dimensional pieces.

I peered at the feet, oversize, large enough to conceal the fascist bootheels, looking for the texture, the shadows of words, like Clarence had been made of. I couldn't see it.

It was titled "You Never See the Disguise."

I stared at it long enough to make the curator think that I was hooked. He was impressed with my taste, deferential. This was LA. I could have been made of money, just looked like a dirtbag because I wanted to.

Rosa wasn't making more pieces like this anymore. He knew her agent and she'd just fallen off the map.

"It happens sometimes. This world isn't for everyone."

"Which one is, my man?"

But I was able to get the agent's name and number from him.

Another dime and I reached out to touch the agent. Probably better use my real name. Felt like the lies were beginning to load up and slip around. Better play it straight. I remembered meeting her before and she might recall me.

She did, her voice lifting a bit at that. Right. Red wine and stinky cheese and sweet black grapes at that reception at that upscale shithole in Venice. Part of me loved it and part of me hated it. Loved it because it was in the shabby part of town that was never going to get rebuilt no matter how much money poured in. Hated it because the folks here got a thrill out of slumming, when it was just like any of the half dozen places up and down the coast where I'd grown up, from Chula Vista to Long Beach to Ventura. My dad never had money but he always loved the ocean.

"She's gone, Riley. I mean real gone."

"Like…?"

"Like I have money for her. Not a small amount. But she left her apartment months ago, time still on the lease. There's a huge demand for her work."

"I saw that boot one, with the feet. It was catching flies in Santa Monica."

"Yeah, Vista's run by a moron. There's demand, but not at the prices they charge."

I watched the swollen orange sun heading towards late afternoon in a yellowing sky. Same color as that dress the fake wife and fake daughter robots had been wearing. I just realized I'd seen their eyes and they were as empty as Clarence's insides. Maybe they really were the window to the soul and there just wasn't anything there.

"Are you still there, Riley?"

I startled and gripped the hand piece tighter. "Yeah, sorry. Been a day. You said she could still be selling her work then?"

"Easily. The right people liked her. You were with her. You know how it is. Critical consensus hits critical mass in a world as small as ours and the gravity of everything shifts."

"But if you disappear, nobody cares, right?"

"That's not fair. I care."

"Then where is she?"

"Don't think I haven't looked. You're still a PI, right? Or were you a mechanic? Sorry, it's tough to remember it all."

"I'm both."

"My guess, and it's just a guess."

"Go ahead. You won't bother me." I picked at a curlicue smear of grime on the booth's inside glass.

"She doesn't want to be found. Or she doesn't want to come back to everything she's made for herself."

I thought about that and it didn't seem likely. She'd worked so hard building up her name and body of work and voice within that. Yeah, her words, not mine, but I wanted her to be happy. She just never quite was.

"Maybe she found something better."

"Well, if you find out, will you please have her call me? I'm worried, but I'm not going to burn that on someone who isn't interested in coming back."

For what it was worth, I actually believed her. She didn't have anything to gain by lying to me, not money-wise. I was still nobody. The receiver went down hard and the coin clinked into the phone's guts, property of Ma Bell.

I grabbed a burrito from a shop nearby and wolfed it down on the way back to the van. The burn would have to be a problem later. Not a lot of time left to try this today. Made my way back to the office, showered and cleaned up as best I could, yanked my old repair shop togs from the closet. They looked like a delivery guy's uniform if you squinted some, or had dead empty eyes.

--

Prime Realty Innovations office was anything but, being out on the dumpy end of San Fernando Road, seemingly a hundred miles from Studio City and Burbank, just driving further and further out to places that used to be busy and thriving industrial parks and were languishing through the end of the seventies like everything else was.

It was a terrifically lonely place, not even busy in rush hour, though I-5 was bumper to bumper with the Valley's working population fleeing to the suburbs in the north. Anywhere but LA itself. I turned off on Cobalt and parked the van out of sight of the door. Sure, I might look like I was delivering for a large, national chain delivery company, but my van looked like rolling trouble. Or a good time.

And appearances mattered.

There were no cars parked out front. But it didn't look like the kind of place that depended on drive-up clientele either. Just a big concrete box front with PRI in lettering that was supposed to look futuristic but just looked like a cheap sci-fi title that had run off from the drive-in marquee. I marched in, all business. It was nearly the end of the day, all the more surprising. And if you can get them off their guard, things usually went a lot smoother.

The woman behind the desk was staring at the door like it was the only thing in the world. Her gaze caught me as I came in and every plan I'd come up with just disappeared as I caught a boot in the gut. Silver tips, even.

I'd seen her before but wasn't quite sure where. She was thin and pretty, far too pretty to be here. She could have been modeling upscale dresses, lingerie or just bare skin. Lots of that in the Valley. But her gaze was empty, so much so that it weighed on me.

"Can I help you?" she asked. Her voice was sweet and scratchy as an old record. The first touch was nice but after the first note, it rasped to bone.

"I, uh." I tugged at my collar, just to remind myself that I was dressed for the part, I had a role to play. "I've got a delivery for Mr. Barr. From Philadelphia. Overnight. Urgent. Important." I spat words until they stopped meaning anything.

She smiled and her nose crinkled a little, but all I could see was the empty. I've met people who weren't all there and people who just pretended like it. Take Marilyn Monroe. She wasn't empty, but you could be easily tricked into believing it. You'd also be the dummy.

Not this time. There was only absence behind this woman's eyes, heavy as an engine block. Like Clarence. Like that family. I began to wonder how many real people I had run into today.

"Well I'll take that, then. Come on over."

I crossed the office, all contemporary austerity, chrome and curves and glass, more to look at than sit in. The dropping sun gave it some warmth, oranges and reds, but inside I was only feeling a chill in August.

"You, ah, need to sign for it."

"Of course." She held a hand out for the clipboard and the dummy form I'd printed up by the gross to run this gag. Looked very official, very real, authentic delivery company. She scratched out a signature that looked like thorns on the page when I reviewed it.

"Thanks, Ms… I can't read this."

"Mrs. McGillicudy. Millicent." She smiled but I only saw a pantomime of cheer, nothing real about it.

There wasn't a ring on her finger so far as I could tell. But then that wasn't a surprise to me. She hadn't worn a ring when I'd seen her last, and I had before. She'd been in Rosa's studio, modeled after a composite of some twenty different *Playboy* playmate models, all leggy and tall and elegant, yet earthy and I bit my cheek to keep from screaming.

"Are you all right?"

"Oh. I'm fine," I whispered so I wouldn't yell. "I just had this funny feeling that we'd met before."

"I get that a lot," she said with a shrug.

I looked at her in the final rays of the setting sun and I swore that I could see a multitude of seams and corners where the scraps had all been stuck together, so many of them that there weren't individual pieces any more, but a reformed whole.

"You should be in pictures, you know," I said finally. "You're a looker."

"They don't call them that anymore. Movies." She ignored the rest and took the plain envelope that was as empty as the rest of her and read over my block printing. "I'll be sure to see that Mr. Barr gets this."

"That'd… That'd be great." I took the clipboard back and grimaced. "Hey, is there, uh, a restroom or something I can use? I had a bad burrito for lunch and it's killing me." It was only half a lie.

She half-grimaced and I swear I could hear pages crinkling. "Well, I'm not supposed to."

"I don't want to be crude, but it's that or I'm afraid I make an awful mess before I make it back to the truck."

"Ugh, okay. You look like an honest guy." She pointed to a door on the other side of the desk that said NO ADMITTANCE. "Through that, on the right. Can't miss it. Don't be long."

"Sure thing, thanks a million."

I could feel the sweat rolling down my temples, in my pits and crotch as I got out of sight and let out a breath that made my toes flex. The cold water hit my face and I drank some of it in to wash the bile out of my mouth. I'd just had a conversation with one of Rosa's art pieces. I was cracking up. Or I was misremembering it all. Maybe Millicent was just a stone fox and sure that happens in LA. It happens everywhere. But I remembered clearly watching Rosa shape her face and lips, the rest of her, asking me if the model was *Playboy* perfect yet and let me tell you that's not a thing I was comfortable talking about. On multiple levels.

I took a few more gulps of water and waited for my pulse to pick up again. Then I wondered how long it would take Millicent to notice that I hadn't come back. Then I remembered how easily Clarence almost made me part of the pavement in front of that building this morning, a thousand years ago. Millicent would probably break me in half and smile sweetly.

And I would've gone back out had I not heard the music filtering down the interior hallway from somewhere deep inside the building. The sound felt like it crawled out of an airplane hangar, all echoed and hit me like years of isolation, of utter loneliness all in the space of a heartbeat. I recognized the song, all sparse and mournfully dancing guitar, with a broken and lilting woman's voice laid over that. Karen something. Not someone most people would know and I only did because Rosa did. But there was no mistaking it, that smoky and kinda shattered voice echoing down the hallway.

What was the harm in looking? Maybe Millicent wasn't programmed to break intruders into little pieces. Maybe I had it coming.

I considered the thought as the song faded out and I nosed my way through the bright and dingy hallway ending in a solid metal-framed door with locks on my side. The door was ajar, held open with a sculpted human foot, double size easily. Not one of Rosa's but unsettling all the same.

Through the door, I came into a passageway piled with tidy stacks of boxes that opened up onto a larger space, one I couldn't quite make out. I stopped when I thought I heard a voice say "That one," but it was so quiet in comparison to the music that maybe I just imagined it. After a moment I continued on and there was the POP of a needle hitting vinyl and surface noise before the song kicked in, kinda country kinda rock but with Stevie Nicks' unmistakable whiskey-warmed tones. Yeah, I listen to pop radio. It was that one from last year, one-word title, wasn't coming to me right then.

The passage opened up to a large workspace, well-lit concrete floor and flat white walls. The spaces blended into one another, suggesting a wide and empty horizon, but for a few pictures and magazine covers tacked up here and there like postage stamps affixed to the side of a glacier. The bits of repeated pictures gave the whole place an unsettling scale, of limitlessness, shored-up by the echoing music.

I came up on the first ranks of lifeless mannequins stacked in ranks on the walls, five deep or more. They were incomplete or maybe just abandoned. Or were they just shells to be built upon? Men, women, some children, all mostly within a certain height and weight range. Probably someone's idea of ideal, or at least average enough to pass without notice. An army just waiting to be awakened.

Further into the room, there was big metal tank with a crusty spigot or pour spout at about hip height. It was sheened over with something semi-opaque and amber and the whole place had the dull tang of craft glue. On a work table, there was a row of instruments, shaping knives and spatulas, wooden blades and a nest of scissors.

She still worked messy. She may as well have signed it.

My heart raced stupidly. She didn't want to see me, probably didn't want to see anybody distracting her away from the work. The song came to an end and then I heard her voice, clear this time.

"Okay, what's your name?" she asked, her voice coming from the other side of the metal tank.

There was a rustling of paper as if in reply and I drank that in then choked over it.

Rosa continued. "Trudy, I think. Right. You're Trudy. You used to be a bohemian but then you settled for a square job. You hate yourself more every day you work for the Man."

A long pause while the mournful and accusatory guitar line of the song picked up, recrimination just boiling up to the surface. I sneaked in closer so I could hear her over the stereo, only part-way seeing her through gaps in the shelving.

"Ugh, who writes this copy?" Rosa asked. She set down a sheet of printed paper she'd been looking at.

There was a muffled reply, as if made by unfinished or glued-together lips.

"Yes, I really should make up a better story for you, Trudy. Barr needs to stop leaning on clichés. You're saving up to start a dressmaking shop. You have a few clients and your reputation is getting around. You can see your goal. It's in reach. You want to make beautiful clothes for musicians and other, ah, weirdos. How's that?"

There was a sound in the affirmative that chilled me down to the hollow spaces in my bones. She was… talking to them? Were they talking back or was she just pantomiming the reply. She'd never done that before. But then none of her creations had walked around under their own volition before either.

I sneaked around the corner and saw her in the bright overhead lights. She was wearing her favorite paint and glue splattered overalls, unmapped islets and continents showing in stains accrued over the years, an incomplete world, one in disintegration. The figure before her was slight, woman in silhouette, thin features. Her skin was half blue, half mottled in a collection of dressmakers patterns and fashion advertisements rearranged into something new, pieces granted new meaning and new life by Rosa's hands.

I only was disgusted a little by finding the curves of that body as erotic and welcoming as any woman's shape I'd ever seen. I was cracking up, or she was a master.

On the figure's forehead was a single word in bright yellow capitals, ALIVE. Just like Clarence this morning.

I watched as Rosa took a scalpel and finished the incision between the top and bottom lip. I'd seen her do it before, but never, never when the work was moving. Subtly, impatiently, moving.

"Sit still," she admonished. I don't want to reconstruct this. Her tongue stuck out from between her teeth like she always did on some tricky bit.

"There." The speakers seemed very far away as the world collapsed to what was happening here. I absorbed it all.

"Thank you," the mannequin said.

"Fuck me," I whispered or maybe even screamed.

Rosa froze in place.

"Oh Jesus. Sully. You shouldn't have come here," she said without looking at me.

Trudy did, swiveling her head in my direction. I thanked God that she had eyes, and not simply empty spaces between sculpted eyelids to take me in. She didn't say anything, only trying out a crooked smile, maybe for the first time. There was something friendly in it, despite the alien nature of her being.

"Rosa. What the hell is going on?"

"He's cute," Trudy said, her voice all breathy as if it had come from nothing.

"Not now, Trudy. Ssh."

The mannequin nodded but the crooked grin remained.

"How did you get in here? Clarence guards the door in the evening." Her brows furrowed as she looked me up and down. "Why are you dressed like that?"

"Delivery gag. Got me past the secretary out front." I didn't bring up that I knew her from before. Or that I was insane.

"You have to get out of here, Sully. These people will-"

"You mean Barr? Or someone else?"

"So cute," Trudy whispered like I wasn't even there.

"Go sit please if you're not going to behave."

Trudy did, walking casually over to a nearby plastic shell chair and sitting, legs crossed. There was an effortlessness to the steps and hip swing that terrified me only half as much as she drew me in.

"Barr isn't dangerous. The men who he works for are." She spoke without looking at me. "You better go before they find out."

I took a couple steps to her and gently picked up her chin with the fingers on my right hand. She just about glowed, her skin made even richer by the contrast of the white walls and overhead lights.

"Tell me what's going on. You can tell me."

"I would if I could. I just. I make people. Just like before, only I've learned some, uh, techniques that make them real."

"Only sort of real. If you don't look too close. Come on, Rosa. This is crazy."

"Crazy or not, I can't get out of it. Clarence, he…"

"Clarence is gone."

"What? He's dead?" Her expression was more horrified than I wanted to see.

"Was he ever alive? Or was it just written on his forehead?"

Rosa shrugged in her coveralls. "Sorta. He was early."

I took both her shoulders between my hands and squeezed a little, trying to remind her what was real even for just a moment. "Well he was trying to beat me to death this morning outside of Barr's office. I tripped him up and got real lucky, took the word off him, didn't even really know it was there. You did a good job with him."

"Practice makes perfect," she said.

"So you're making paper robots. You were already doing great before. Hell, your agent still has money for you. Why this?"

"Because I couldn't believe it, not when they first approached me and said there was a way for my art to live. Really live." Her eyes gleamed with wonder that went cold quickly. "And by the time that I did, I couldn't get out."

"Sure you can. Clarence won't be coming around again. Let's just get out of here."

"Can't go," Trudy said with a voice crinkled up in something like disappointment. "Not finished."

"Don't worry, Trudy," Rosa said with insistence. "I won't abandon you." She turned back. "But Sully, you gotta do that for me. I don't want you—"

She stopped when the song started to slur and drag before stumbling to a stop. It hadn't faded out between tracks. Someone had shut the stereo down.

"Scott Douglas!" Barr shouted from somewhere and it echoed all around the both of them. "Is that even your name?"

"Run! Get out!" she hissed at me, pushing me away.

"It's Sullivan, Barr. Riley Sullivan." I wasn't sure where to aim the voice and felt like an idiot for talking to nothing.

"Never heard of you." He stepped out from around an opposite corner, gun in hand. Millicent the secretary was carrying Clarence's form, frozen stiff. "Who're you? And don't fuck around. You got too little time for that."

I kept my hands out at my sides, making it clear that I wasn't reaching for the gun that I didn't have. I didn't need him getting anxious and dropping me. "You already know. I've got a friend named Ronaldo who you owe two large to. Which you were ready to pay until I brought her up." I indicated Rosa who was standing behind me, frozen stiff as Clarence was.

"And then you flipped out. Quietly, but you flipped out."

"This is dangerously close to you fucking around," he warned.

"I'm not anybody," I said. "Just her ex and I got curious."

"You're not from Method?" He jabbed the gun a little, like he was going to poke the truth out of me from fifty feet away.

I glanced back at Rosa to see if there was anything to be read from her. Her lips tightened and one corner dropped and her head shook very slowly.

"You shoot me and Method's going to be very very pissed off at you." I threw some gravity on it. "You think you're on thin ice now. You'd drop right through."

"Bullshit," he said. "You're just a dog sniffing around and you got lucky."

"Lucky enough to deactivate Clarence right there. Didn't even break a sweat." I pointed right at my own head. "You think I didn't know how to do that? Come on. Put the gun down and we can talk like grownups."

"And if I say 'fuck you' for the second time today?"

I didn't get an answer before I felt a red rose of pain slam into and open up at the base of my skull and I crumpled to the floor like someone had just flipped my off switch.

--

I woke, dragging my head back on my neck so I wasn't just looking into my own lap. On the work table in front of me, I saw Rosa carefully laying sheets of paper on Clarence's forehead, trying to fill in the gap that I'd left there this morning. My head felt almost as good as his, only I couldn't be patched up so easily. My hands were bound with something, cloth it felt like, but nothing I could break easily.

I groaned loud enough for her to hear.

"I told you to run," she said. "You could have made it."

"And miss all the fun? Like being koshed on the head?"

"Well it was either that or watch you get shot after you lost the dick-measuring contest with Barr. Stupid macho bullshit." She set down the thin and curved blade of wood that she'd been using to re-shape Clarence's skull then walked over.

"Yeah, you should have listened," Barr said. "I didn't know you from Adam. LA's a big place. You and I never crossed paths again and it'd have been square."

He was sitting on another chair with the secretary on his lap, his hand around her hip, gun balanced in his grip like a cigar. Millicent neither liked nor disliked the situation.

"Then you shoulda blown me off. Preferably with my friend's money."

"Too late for that. Too late for a lot of things." He pecked the copper-red haired woman on the cheek and she endured it. "How long until you finish up that work on Clarence?"

"Almost done," Rosa replied. "It needs to dry then I can paste the word on and get him going again."

"Good. Then you can finish this order and maybe we have to wrap up the operation for awhile." Barr's other hand worked the secretary's thigh, ruffling her dress as he did so.

"You two ought to get a room," I snapped. My own voice sounded like crushed eggshells between pulses of my throbbing temples.

"Envious?" he asked with a leer. Though he moved his hand back, aware that he'd been overdoing it. "She is a looker, ain't she?"

"Stop," Millicent whispered with a grimace.

"Sure, doll," he sighed. "Go on and wait in the car for me." She got up stiffly and he smacked her on the backside as she did. I don't want to tell you what that sounded like. I'll never forget it.

He stood up with the gun in his hand and half-pointed it at Rosa. "Finish the job. Just get him going. We'll make him pretty later."

"What you gonna do with all these people?" I asked. I didn't even hesitate on the last word, to my own credit. "You gonna colonize more buildings with 'em? Use 'em to break in entire new neighborhoods? Hell, you could trick people into thinking that Pacoima's livable!"

"Hey, pal. I just make 'em for Method. What they do with 'em, I don't know and don't care."

"Not all of them. You got that building downtown. Or does Method own that, too?"

He scratched his sweaty moustache with one hand. "Nah. That's my little sideline. Nobody likes an empty building, right? Gotta convince folks that it's a place where good people wanna be."

"So just manufacture good people, right? Speed up that process."

"You're not all stupid, are you? Too bad. I could use someone with a decent head on his shoulders. Clarence is good for protection, but I can't even teach him twenty-one much less gin." He tapped the barrel of his gun impatiently on his own thigh and I hoped that the safety was off.

There was a groan of frustration from the worktable. "It's not setting, Barr. I'm going to need to start over."

Barr sighed out through his teeth. "Fuck it, forget it. There isn't going to be time. Bummer." He turned back to me. "Would have been much cleaner to have him finish the job from this morning. Then you go up when this place does and you just look like another petty crook caught in a tragic workplace fire."

"You're… burning the place?" Rosa asked. "Are we done?"

"Oh you," he said with a laugh. "Your work will never be done. You'll be doing this until arthritis makes it impossible for you. Way too valuable to stop. Method has told me that much."

I tried to get my screaming brain to work. The floor had just opened up into a pit of flaming shit and I was about to be pushed into it unless I came up with something and fast.

"I'm not going," Rosa snapped. I knew that tone. My jaw clenched by reflex.

"Not for discussion. Sorry." He jabbed a fat finger at me. "But him? The dogshit dude? Yeah, he stays. We start a new workshop, you and me, get Method off our backs and everything's cool." The sweat popping out on his forehead told me that even he didn't believe it.

But I was still going to be removed from the equation without an assist.

"Hey, Trudy!" I said real loud. "You hear that? He doesn't want you to get finished!"

There was a rustle off behind me, like papers shuffling against each other, like snake skin on itself.

"Who doesn't?" Trudy's voice was sweet and breathy but colder than the ocean in February.

"The fuck?" Barr asked as he saw the unfinished Trudy stand up from her chair. "The fuck is this?"

"That's the guy, Trudy. He says you stay unfinished forever!"

"What are you doing, Sully?" Rosa whispered. "You don't know what you're playing-"

"Is this true?" Trudy demanded. "I have to be finished! I can't… I can't make dresses like this!" She held up her hands, swathed in thin shrouds of layered paper and blue dress pattern ink on onionskin. "I'm going to make dresses!"

"That's not what he said, Trudy. He wants to burn the place down and take Rosa away!"

"Shut up!" Barr all but shrieked. The nose end of the revolver jittered, flashing in the shop lights.

"He doesn't want you to make dresses, Trudy. He doesn't think you're beautiful!" And if I'd known where that last line came from, I'd never have said it.

Trudy's mouth opened partway as if to scream, only showing emptiness within. "Who says I can't!" She turned towards Barr and took a step. "Why?!" It was the cry of a child who realized that they couldn't stay young and innocent forever, that experience was arbitrary and unfair.

"Call it off!" The gun barrel went right to Trudy but kept swaying, like he couldn't bear to look at her.

"Get me out of these ropes!" I hissed at Rosa. "Right now!"

Trudy marched on unfinished legs, more under-shell than skin and muscle, more cut-and-paste than real. "It's not fair! You can't tell me what I can do!"

I felt the circulation come back into my hands and got to my feet just as the first shot went off. I could see light all the way through her, bullet having gone in right under the ribs, exiting just over her hip. Two little ragged holes.

Trudy didn't slow down for even a second, not a gasp or hiccup of pain. She knew what she wanted. She wanted to make dresses. And Barr had the unenviable position of standing in her way.

"Oh god oh god oh god" he stuttered, firing a shot between each repetition.

He might as well have been shooting at shadows on an alley wall.

"Come on, we gotta get out of here," I said, moving to usher Rosa out.

"Ohhhhhh god!" Barr cried. Trudy had her arms wrapped around him, lifting him clean off the ground, something I wasn't sure I could do as easily as she did. His arms were pinned to his sides, flashy gun empty.

"Trudy, it's okay," Rosa said. "Put him down."

"But he won't-"

"I think he might change his mind," I said, eyeballing him as he tried to wiggle out.

The bullet-hole-ridden Trudy turned to him with her blank face, awful yet soaked through with sympathy. "Is this true?"

"Anything you want. Just let go of me."

"I'm going to make dresses, right?" she demanded. There was no asking. "And you're going to get rid of these… holes!"

"Sure. Anything you want. Just put me down."

"And you're going to treat Millicent nicer! She's got feelings too!"

Rosa stared for a moment, lips faintly moving in a sleepwalking kind of singsong. "Okay, this is getting weird," she finally whispered, watching the life her art had taken really and truly breathe past any motive she might've considered.

Barr hit the floor like a sack full of pork chops, sheathed in sweat from head to toe, clothes beyond rumpled.

"Well go on!" Trudy shouted, fists balled up on her hips. "And don't let me catch you here again!"

Barr's eyes shot between Rosa and Trudy and Millicent and me like ricocheting pinballs, unable to choose a single target. He scrabbled back and up to his feet, running from the building.

"We gotta go," I said. "He won't be gone long."

"He won't be coming back," Trudy said. "I told him not to."

I stayed there the rest of the night, along with Rosa and Trudy, carefully patching up where she'd been shot as well as layering paper and paint where she was yet to be completed. It was the very least that I could do for her, really. I only just wish that I hadn't caught her looking at me out of the corner of her smooth and unpainted eyes.

But a debt's a debt. Maybe I wasn't gonna be able to help Ronaldo much more, but I could help someone else who needed it.

We stacked the unfinished mannequins in the back of my van as best we could and Trudy took the passenger seat. I turned the engine over and didn't know what else to say. She hummed along with the radio like she'd heard all the songs before and Rosa watched her in a way that I imagined my mother might've when I was a child.

THIRD SATURDAYS

All roads converged on 6ᵗʰ Street. At least that's how it was on Third Saturdays. Everyone who was anyone, anyone with a pulse and if you wanted to dance with a boy or a girl from somewhere else, well that was the night. Glorietta Leon was definitely someone with a pulse, hard and fast, too big for here anymore. Too big for her neighborhood and even too big for a town as big as LA was, endless streets and blocks all the way to Orange County, all the way to the beach, all the way to the ends of the Valley, all electric lights and dirty concrete.

She waited on her order, leaning her hips in denim on the steel coolers full of soda cans cold as you could imagine, pure relief on a summer day. Her pearlescent fingernails tapped out a rhythm on the faintly greasy enamel top, impatient and edgy.

"Just a little longer, Glori," Marta called, leaning out the pickup window. "Where the hell you gonna put twenty chili burgers anyways? Gonna get pig-fat."

"Third Saturday. Got hungry mouths to feed and they all like Tommy's. No matter how fast it'll kill them."

"Girl, don't you know nothing about nothing?" It's Friday night." Marta shook her head, black hair straining in the net under her paper cap.

"It's just a name that stuck. Happens when it happens."

A couple Impalas with loud pipes and candyflake paint like a broken rainbow rolled into the grimy parking lot. Arms hung out windows, drivers in gangster lean with good-times tunes pouring out for everyone to hear now that the engines were off.

"You goin' look for Tomás there?" Marta's grin was salty and mischievous. "You're dressed for the hunt."

At least someone had noticed, Glorietta thought to herself. Even if it was only Marta. Her best jeans, lovingly worn and shaped to second skin, satin top flowing, bound by a leather belt worn loose and high above her waist. Her blouse went from bunched and shining folds of light that you could get lost in all the way to a revealing tension. But it was something she could guide, not there for just anyone. Certainly not for Marta.

For Pecas. She could say that much to herself.

"Tomás is yesterday. I'm more interested in tomorrow."

"Girl, you interested in tonight and nothing else. Now get your burgers." She shoved the stack of two cardboard boxes out the window onto the counter.

Marta had that much right. It was all about tonight and if there was a tomorrow, well, that might be okay too. Just so long as it was in a place bigger than here.

Glori sidestepped the wolf-whistles from the boys in the Chevys and their low chrome. She wasn't after their attention, either. Not even worth flipping them the bird. Better to show them that you didn't even hear 'em, that they weren't worth noticing. She fired up the Camaro and let them hear her disinterest. Eight cylinders and three-fifty cubic inches of fuck-off loud. Like gold, they could look but never possibly afford her. Not that Glori was about money, just they didn't have what she was after.

She slid out the parking lot and onto Beverly towards downtown. The sun going down glittered hard on that long hood like it was the only clean thing in this grubby town and she nosed her way into the city. Towards Third Saturday. Towards Pecas.

Nobody remembers the first Third Saturday, not anyone that Glorietta had ever talked to. They'd always just been, though sometimes there were years that there was just one or two of 'em. Sometimes twice in a month. Kinda like rain in LA. It happened, but maybe not all that often. That's what kept it special. If it was a thing you could just drive to anytime, order up on demand, then the magic would disappear. At least that's what people said.

Was it so bad to want the magic all the time? Wasn't that what life was supposed to be about? Glorietta saw it in people's eyes. They were all walking around wanting something else, anything more than what they had. It was what they were after whenever they came through the doors of the dress store she worked at with the weird and sometimes-crazy kind-hearted owner. People wanted something that made them feel like they were glowy soft focus in front of the cameras, like they were made of stars.

That was Third Saturday. Everyone out, dressed fine, cars all polished up as bright and shiny as the girls' lips and nails. Or the boys. They could be fine, too. Most were too tied up in whatever they were brought up to be to even try anything else. Third Saturday you could be whoever you wanted. It was okay. You were given permission to bring it out.

This time it was out under the Sixth Street bridge. Starting at sundown, going until the cops chased everyone out or people just got tired, crashing in their cars or propped up against someone new or someone old that maybe they'd forgotten or would see a new way.

There you go again, girl. Daydreaming. Easy to do at sundown when everything went hazy and chased with color, shadows deepening to oceans of black and sparkling streetlight. Words glowed in the sky all haloed in what just looked like dirty smog during the day but at night went stardust. Anything could happen. Even something like a girl loving another girl. And not just any other girl, but her. Glori herself.

She gripped the wheel tighter and pressed the gas, following Santa Fe past the railyards, all the steel laid out and shining with the last sun. During the day it was just dirt and metal and concrete with mud running down it. Right now it was a beautiful other place. And that was before the crew got together, wherever it was they came from.

The engine thrummed and she felt it all the way through her thighs and body, alive and dreaming. Dreaming of hands and bodies and more than that, hearts pressed close together and beating as close as she was to this big V-8 that ran her through the streets, made her weightless. She felt dirty, beautiful as the city at dusk, that time that was neither night nor day but the best of both.

She hurried because nobody but nobody was going to want cold Tommy's. Not even if that was the only way to get it. She'd heard a rumor that whoever started Third Saturdays came from somewhere that wasn't here, but was like it. Mostly the same. They didn't have Tommy's over there. It sounded like a bigger place, like twilight all the time.

She hurried, throb of the machine filling her and that pushing her to lay down the gas, go faster, fast enough to catch that future that was waiting for her if she was brave enough to grab it. Hoping that it would grab her back.

There barely any river this time of year, just a slack line of water in the concrete expanse of the riverbed. It was a tiny line of silver and bronze with flecks of color as it made its way down to the ocean, miles away and unimaginable with a forest of skyscrapers and buildings between here and there.

Under the length of the bridge they'd set up big steel barrels filled up with anything that would catch fire, flames licking up, light pulsing on its own time. Just up the river there were a couple of bales set up to burn, that same sweet stuff that they burned at all Third Saturdays. It wasn't dope from anywhere that Glori had ever heard of. This smelled like spices or flowers, not drugs at all.

Really it smelled like Pecas, which is why Glori liked it so much. Pecas' real name was Mary and she lived up in Baldwin Hills somewhere. Her dad worked at a factory in Van Nuys, but Glori couldn't figure out quite where. There was just that Ford plant, but that was going to go away sooner, not later. Layoffs killed the job her cousins had there. Then the older one went bad and bounced in and out of jail for a couple years. The younger one always found a way to slide, some weird luck. Just as dumb as the luck that bumped Glori into Pecas that first time.

Pecas and Third Saturdays couldn't be pulled apart in Glori's memory. They'd met a little over a year ago. She was small and had red hair and was all curves top to bottom. And her freckles where she got her name, they were dotted over her face and neck like dark stars in a pale sky. Pecas had been over to the side by herself and Glori was still trying to decide if she wanted to ditch Tomás who she'd driven over there 'cause his ride was still in impound and he'd never have the money to pull it out. Tomás had been wanting something that she just wasn't interested in. But it was tough to tell the cutest guy on the block that you didn't want him any more. People were gonna talk if that happened. "You don't want to be a spinster at eighteen," tía (not really but lived next door forever) Jeni had said. She'd clucked her tongue when Glori had brought up that she was bored with him, like having a man was everything, but tía had been unhappy in her own house.

Glori couldn't say what it was, but that she didn't want him and maybe not any boy. Glori had heard her father talking about her mom's real sister Elena, the one who never took a husband but had lived with another woman in the same house. He talked about her like she was a bug and how he didn't want to see her around family events, mostly around his daughter like she'd make Glori sick somehow.

Trouble was, that she already knew what she wanted, just hadn't had the heart to go and ask for it. Maybe she didn't even tonight with the moon up over the jagged dark of the skyscrapers and the sky turning purple, chased with sparks from the barrels and the bales of the stuff the kids called el cielo. Some called it estrella or azul. Nobody ever had it or knew where to get it. Only on nights like tonight.

There was a snap and hum of electricity as the speakers came up and that echoed in the space under the bridge, everyone going from chattering to whooping. Third Saturday was underway.

Glori looked around from the fender of her Camaro, eyes hungry. She scanned over the fire-lit bodies all coming together in orange and amber, black shapes familiar and strange. Boys stood different, shoulders back, arms relaxed and almost dead, putting their weight in their hips and the birdies swinging there. Like that was all that was worth anything.

Birdies weren't nothing without a woman, and Glori knew she wanted what boys wanted. Not just their swagger and their confidence but the opposite, who they pursued. Glori wanted that too. Only she just wanted one.

Disco thump and waves of strings with shuffle guitar out in front and all the bodies started moving to it like a command or hypnosis. A couple beats and everyone was on the same groove.

She began to fear that Pecas wasn't going to be there with all the heart flutter and drop that caused in her. But Pecas never missed a Third. Not since that first one where Glori had seen her all by herself, sad and slumped like someone had taken all the passion and breath out of her.

"What's the matter, girl? You okay?" Glori had asked.

"I don't want to go home tonight," Pecas had said then. Only then she was just Mary Daly. Just a cute girl from Baldwin Hills. Not that far away, but she had seemed so different. Her clothes were different, skirt cut a little longer, slit on the side a little higher. Enough to see a darting of freckles on her thigh in the triangle framed by the fabric's cut. Her tank top with the wide straps said CAROUSEL in glittering neon-style lettering, catching just enough of the light to be readable as she shifted her body around. Glori had stirred at that even then, shocked at the sudden heat in her breast and blazing up her throat.

"Sounds deep."

"It ain't. Just that there's nothing there for me anymore."

"I'm Glorietta. I've seen you at a couple of these." She had to catch her breath, push herself to come over. It'd never been like that for one of the boys, not even Tomás. They were just… around.

"Mary."

"That's a heavy name where I come from."

"Me, too."

"Gonna call you Pecas. You know, freckles."

She smiled at that then wiped her eyes. "Sorry, I don't want to be a bummer. This is a party, gotta have fun."

"It's okay. Sometimes fun isn't having fun." Glori sat beside her. "Sometimes you just wanna be."

"Yeah."

The WHOOSH of bales going up in flames and murmurs from the crowd snapped Glori out of her thoughts. Purple-blue smoke roiled off the bonfires and everyone pulled back like they were making a runway or processional path.

It was always a thrill to see what came next. It was like real magic, not a top hat and card tricks, but something deeper than that, flesh deep, blood deep down to bone beneath.

There was a distant sound of engines echoing off the concrete but more than that, echoing from a place that you couldn't see but was nonetheless real. The ripples hit before the first of the cars blasted through the drifting wall of smoke flowing off the bales of cielo.

None of the headlights ever looked quite right. Glori could read them, 'specially cop cars. Good to know what was going to creep up on you if you were on the boulevard. Her brain tried to guess what kind of car was coming next but never quite could. Some of them echoed old designs, some were rectangular and too bright. Beams poked through the smoke and then drew down something like strange eyes in that space under the bridge. Glori wondered why there and why you couldn't hear them coming until they were right there.

Ten. Twenty. More. The shapes were familiar but just a little off, even the Falcons and Mustangs that showed. Shaved or thickened just a little, just enough to feel off-model but not pure custom iron. But there were those that were totally other. Mercer, Clay, Ruth. They were cars just the same, shining and decked out tight only from factories that nobody had heard of. Some were glittering sleds that rode low and slow and others were channeled for speed, left dull because all that mattered was squeezing out another bit of horsepower. Didn't matter. All were welcome.

Glori hoped they brought some Little Coyotl tacos. Those were the best. She had looked all over LA for the stand but couldn't ever find a stand with that name. But the guys who brought them always wanted Tommy's, which was why Glori was set up for the easy trade. She marched the boxes over to the tangerine-rainbow sparkle Impala-looking ride that always showed. If she couldn't find Pecas, she'd at least get some tacos out of the deal.

Boys and girls all slid out of the cars and greeted the crowd tender and loud as cousins at a family gathering. Different music poured out of open windows, sometimes familiar, sometimes just weird at least at first. It all ended up being about the same things, just wrapped up differently.

"¡Oye, Glori!" Chuco called over from the car. "What's real, sister?" He had dark hair slid back and a face strong as an eagle, chunky turquoise in silver hanging around his whipcord neck. "You got chili on those, right?"

"They look at you funny if you order 'em without, Chuco. Ten in a box. Maybe you got some tacos in there?" She tapped her foot.

"Maybe you can spot me this time?" His smile might've worked where he came from. "How about some records? Got some Carousel, the Cremation. New one from Electric Friends." He held out an album with four dudes in tuxedos and identical makeup, blue eyeshadow and black lips. They looked like they belonged on another planet, one run by machines where humans were slaves.

"You know what I want."

"Claro, sis." He reached on the bench seat beside him and pulled out the white bag with the red coyote silhouette stamped on it. "Mixed batch."

"No lengua, right?"

"You don't like the tongue?" he asked and flashed his for a second.

Glori jutted out the knuckle of her middle finger and punched him in the upper arm. Enough to hit, not enough to hurt.

"Just the tacos, hermano."

"Okay, okay."

The exchange went. Chuco and his crew dug into the burgers that made Glori wonder what the big deal was. But then what was the big deal about Little Coyotl? What made it special? Was it just that she couldn't have it whenever she wanted?

She watched other kids trading stuff back and forth, stacks of comic books and records mostly, little flashes of things she only half-recognized. It was always electric watching both sides getting crazy excited over the commonplace. She could get those comics in a record store or newsstand yet the other kids always treated them like stacks of treasure. It wasn't a thing Glori got.

Maybe everyone had their own Little Coyotl. Or Pecas.

A figure in jeans and tube top with translucent and open blouse came running at her. With the light behind, she looked like she was wore burning wings.

"Glori! Hey, girl!" It was Louise, not quite from the block but close by. "Have you seen…" She stopped and took a panting breath, rocking on her heels. "Have you seen Tomás? He's looking for you."

Glori ignored the chill. "I'm not looking for *him*."

"He is pissed. What'd you do to him?"

"More like what I didn't do and he's saying he did."

"So, you…?" Louise's dark eyes went wide.

"He's stupid and dull."

"But all lean and tall. That face and that ass? He doesn't have to be a good talker." She grinned with something like hunger then smacked Glori on the arm. "I'd chase him down if I wasn't already with Barry."

Glori shifted in her shoes, uneasy. "Hey, have you seen Pecas?"

"Yeah? Mary? I think I seen her back there. Hanging out by that big black tank." She pointed blindly behind herself towards a big black car parked some distance off. "Hey, are those from Coyotl?"

"Yeah, I got a few. But they're for--"

"Can I have one, just one?"

Glori sighed. "You know it." She hoped it was lengua as she handed one foil-wrapped taco over. "You owe me. And if you see Tomás, you didn't see me."

"Sure, sure," Louise muffled around a bite, disappearing back into the crowd. "Hey, thanks!"

Glori nodded uselessly then made her way back to that shiny black sled that Louise had gestured to. She edged through the bodies, watching girls hugging and exclaiming, pointing at each other's clothes and exchanging jackets or shirts on the spot, utterly in love for that moment.

The PA started blasting "Rock Creek Park" and bodies moved to that like seas in motion, all sway and dip in time. Sure it was a little old, but those memories got shared in that group motion. Firelight glowed over sweat on skin and polished steel all the same. The big old car stood there like a shadow cast by nothing, just hits of shine and reflective chrome.

People came to the car, to the back window, rolled down like it was a confessional booth and they had to clear their names before time was up. Glori was never sure if this car was from here or wherever the other kids came from. She only ever saw it on Thirds, but there was a lot of LA to hide in the rest of the time. A skinny kid with an oddly-cut zoot-length jacket and feathered headband stood deferentially at the open window and passed over a bouquet of dark flowers that sparkled just as hard as chrome. Glori rubbed her eyes, thinking that they were going out.

They were just wet, she said to herself as she looked for Pecas.

The feathered kid moved off with a wrapped package under his arm, bigger than a magazine. Could have been anything, an anything box. Whatever it was, he looked as if he'd just peered through Heaven's gate, open to him and he was saved.

There, in the line. There was Mary's red hair falling like waves of sunlit copper. Glori just wanted to run her hands through it and feel the softness and the energy there.

She waited instead.

Until the hand went down on her shoulder. It wasn't strong or heavy, just there. That itself was enough weight to drag her back to the small world, the one she wanted to run away from. Just cross a bridge to nowhere and disappear. To go wherever these kids came from.

"Hey, Glori," Tomás said. "Hey, girl."

Glori bit at the assertion. She already knew who she was. She didn't need him saying so with the unspoken rest of it a hanging reminder of everything she fought with.

"Tomás." She turned around finally.

He stood there, not angry and tall. If anything, there was a bite taken out of him. Like realizing he'd been shot and was walking around with the bullet still inside him. He was pretty, even when he wasn't wounded. He was pretty even when he was fluffing out his feathers around all the other boys. Gotta pretend if that's all you've got.

"I been looking for you. We gotta talk."

"Sounds a lot like *you* gotta talk. So say it."

That set him back, another bite taken out. Glori glanced around and saw that there weren't any of his crew around, nobody noticing their talk, nobody taking notes to use it later.

"I need to know why you got a problem with me. Why I ain't good enough."

She waited a long time, counting the backsides of her teeth before answering. He simmered to boil watching her.

"That you even think this? That's why you have a problem. Maybe it's not you at all."

"That leaves one other person." He shifted his weight and stiffened his hips and shoulders but wasn't pointing yet, afraid to. The firelight made his eyes dark and glittering points, bottomless and hungry.

"I'm not the one with troubles. That's you, Tomás." Glori pointed first, but didn't jab the nail in his chest like she'd wanted. "You chased and can't catch me."

He took a step closer and smelled like blood but there wasn't a cut on him. "'Cause you don't want to be caught."

"Not. By. You."

His hand shot out and took her by the upper arm, firm but not crazy. "Well I got you now. What are you gonna do about it? Maybe I take what I want?"

Glori pushed forward on the balls of her feet, right in his face. "If that's what you really wanted, you'd have done it. You'd have done it last time we went cruising.

"Like you told everyone we did. Better a lie than you lose your rep, right?"

"Why are you being such a bitch about this?"

"Because I don't want you, Tomás Himenez! I thought I did and I was wrong. If that kicks you where it hurts, that's too bad and nobody's sorry like I am about it." She gutted it out in harsh whispers and still hoped that no one else would hear. It was all she needed for her words to be use to cut him up later. Things were bad enough as it was.

He stared at her, refusing to understand what she'd said to him plainly. The light played on his face and every flicker turned over another emotion: disbelief, anger, shock or deep sorrow. He was being eaten by it.

"Do you even…?" He stopped and stared, unwilling or unable to finish the question.

Glori knew it before he said it and wondered when that was coming. Her heart raced because she'd never thought of it meaning anything to her, whether it was lesbian or dyke or chancla or whore. She didn't want the word. She just wanted to be.

But he couldn't even bring himself to say it, not even the slur that covered up the actual truth of it. She'd almost wanted him to say it just so she could hit him.

Instead he swallowed that unspoken truth and kept it between them.

"Don't… Don't think of me like that, T. Go find a different girl. Someone who wants all of you. Not just a lay."

"But you're—"

"I'm not anything. I was your cielita for a little while, but that was when we were both kids." She was surprised at her own tears at this, crying for the both of them. He wasn't allowed, no more than he was allowed to want a woman who didn't want men.

She hugged him like a brother and nothing more than that. "You go," she said. "Go chase someone who wants to be caught. Tell all your friends that you had me and I was done. I don't care. I know what's real."

He stood there like stone and drew a torn breath and nothing more than that.

"Go," she said. And that was the moment she knew she really had to leave here, that she'd seen the ends of this world and had to go find something in another one if she was going to be happy.

Tomás walked tall into the crowd, and Glori could still see the bites taken out of him, the places where the blood flowed like from Valentine's arrows. She turned to track Pecas down, only to see her walking from the car, pocketing something in an oversize coat, shrugging out of the range of the firelight. Glori pushed through the line of supplicants to catch up. As she passed the window she heard someone asking for attention and the reply came back with gentle patience, saying that the queen would listen. She wanted to turn and look but only had eyes to track Pecas down as she walked towards the concrete angle of the riverbank.

Light filtered through the crowd and their shadows spread out and danced on the walls, slanted like they were falling over. Somewhere behind Glori an engine roared, sound splattering off the concrete loud enough to chop into the flowing music. Another engine blasted out, lower-tuned to a dirty flood. The races were starting. Tempest versus Firebird, Mercer and Clay going up against MOPAR and Chevy. No hate in it, just competition. Which side was faster this time. When the only challenge is another kid you can only see here. You'll never find them on the boulevard or rolling through the neighborhood. Only here.

Glori wanted to race and run, but there was something else first. Something that was going to be ten times harder than talking to Tomás. But Tomás hadn't been important in the way that Pecas was. Glori had already taken that hurt, understanding what he was to her and what that really meant.

Ahead of her, Pecas ripped open a package of cigarettes and lit one, drawing hard as two hot rods going head on. The lighter flared on the curves of her face, the soft slope of her chin and neck and she sighed in exhale. Smoke encircled, a halo of it that clung to her and then rose up.

Glori's heart raced harder than any engine and she felt empty, thirsty, wrung out. Tomás was the past and he hadn't known it, but Glori had. This moment broke into the future, building it from blood and stones.

"Oh, Glori." Pecas' voice was stilted in surprise. "Where you been?" She turned from the wall painted in shadows and took a couple steps.

"Hey, I…I got some tacos for you. Coyotl." Glori held out the bag and tried to keep her hands from shaking. She tried to think of a thousand different things to say, anything to pave the way to the truth that she loved Pecas like she wasn't ever going to love anyone else. With her heart, her body, her soul not that she thought of that like they taught her at church. Because the church taught her about all the things that she could not do and could not be. She was tired of *not*.

"Thanks, sis. Come here." Pecas took the cigarette out after a fleeting half-drag then blew the smoke out as they hugged.

Glori hugged her like she had Tomás. She couldn't go further, filled with not what really fueled her, but with the fear that it wouldn't be returned. She didn't even know how Pecas felt about girls, much less her.

Pecas pushed back and dug into the bag. "Chuco brought these, huh?"

"Yeah, I traded them for some Tommy's. Don't really know why they don't just get it themselves."

"Oh, you know. It's sweeter when it's part of a deal, when it's given or traded, right?" She unwrapped the foil and it flashed like an ember in her hand then took a big bite. After a second she looked towards Glori, eyes big in the light. "Aren't you hungry?"

"Oh, yeah. Sorry. Just." She sighed out a heavy breath. "Just a weird night. Feels like I gotta do something big. And I just told Tomás that I didn't want to date him any more."

"You mean screw him, right?" Pecas grinned. "That's what he really wanted. It's what all the boys want, at least all they'd admit."

"Yeah, maybe." Glori grabbed a taco from the bottom of the bag and then unwrapped it, fidgeting. She took a bite to give herself an excuse not to talk. "Oh, dammit. Tongue. I hate that."

Pecas' hand shot out. "I only had a bite. Take this one. I'm fine with whatever."

Static charge of thrill went through Glori's fingers when they made the exchange. "Thanks."

"Boys will slip you the tongue whenever." She laughed at her own joke. "Come on, Glori. That was funny!"

Glori managed a smile and took a bite. "You smoke?"

She looked at the cigarette like she'd forgotten it. "Oh, yeah. Still a habit, just not an all the time one."

Glori shrugged. "That's what my dad says about drinking, only he still gets wrecked every Saturday. My mom is okay with it because on Sunday morning he can't fight back when she says it's time to go to church."

"Hah! Moms know who got the power in the house." She finished her taco in a gulp and shook her hand clean then took another hit off the smoke.

"You wanna let me have some of that?"

"Oh, yeah, no. Not just yet."

Glori went chill and just whispered. "Oh, sorry."

She moved in closer, softer. "Hey, no. It's not like that. Just that this is. Well, it's complicated." Her breath was sweet with the smell, like cielo, like the bales and the smoke. Glori wondered if it was a drug or something else. The association had always been there with Pecas, like oranges on Christmas. Something special, something rare. Even if you could get oranges all the time in LA. On Christmas it was something else.

"Come on. Let's go dance. I did my business. Time for some fun."

Glori was being dragged along before she knew it, buoyed by the scent and Pecas as she'd all but tackled her to get her moving. The signs were confusing to Gloria. She couldn't figure out whether to just tell her or if she herself was saying something. And what business?

Tired and a little dizzy from the dust-devil dancing and sweat under her blouse, Glori half-leaned on Pecas as they watched the cars screaming down the river bed. Their headlights and taillights seemed to drag out forever behind them, bright and purple burns in her eyes even when she closed them and shook her head.

The crowd whooped and yelled as the Tempest with its chunky front end and sloped fastback blew past, leaving El Viejo's flashy Chevelle two lengths back.

"Wooooooooaaaaaaoooo!" Pecas screamed. "That's right! Nothing faster than that Smoketown steel!" She jabbed at the air in front of her as Viejo crossed the line too far back.

The roar of combustion and adrenalin faded down and Glori asked. "You mean Detroit, right?"

"Oh, yeah. Sure."

Glori had heard the word before, but only here and only very rarely. It was like Neverland, she guessed. Or an afterlife, but not Heaven or Hell. Some other thing. Or maybe it was right here, just in this moment, just in the breath of the cielo and being with your own. She tried to reach for the strength she had driving here, that strength from desire, knowing what she wanted and that she was right next to it, only feeling hesitation and resistance. She knew it was in her and nowhere else, if only she could call it up.

The next set of racers lined up, way down the river. In the distance, their headlights jittered as they gassed-out in neutral, playing for the crowd. The echoes of their engines rolled down like spring flood and the starter girl waved that green and off they went. Glori thought about being that engine, that car, screaming as fast as she could right at what she wanted. Car don't care. Car wants to go fast.

Dual V-8 screams and fire out the pipes coming towards them like earthbound comets. The racers kept edging each other out, barely the space between the two cars to fit a newspaper, rough-kissing and paint-trading. Then the nearer one juddered and spun, headlights going wild and the silhouette of the car nosing down then flipping. The front corner caught and the headlights spilled onto the concrete in a blaze then the whole mess went ass over tits, up in the air. But not for long. The crowd cried out all as one, no triumph, just shock and fear.

Only then, seeing the shape of the car and catching a flash of the tangerine paint in its own reflected headlights, did Glori realize who it was in the airborne car.

"Chuco! That's Chuco!"

"Oh shit, come on!"

By the time the car had come to a stop in a rising cloud of dust and smoke, the crowd was running to the scene of the crash. The other racer crossed the finish line unnoticed. Glori only barely registered the green Nova as the other car, knowing full well who drove it.

A semicircle of onlookers formed around the flipped car as flames started to lick out of the upended hood and undercarriage. Glori didn't think, she just ran right to it. She'd always been fast and she'd never been afraid of a wreck. Her uncle Gilbert raced over in Riverside and Orange

County sometimes and she knew that you could survive a crash, but not blowing up after.

Someone, bloodied and scraped, hung halfway out the driver's side window all roadkill-graceful. Glori grabbed his hand without hesitation and pulled, muscles tensed all through her body. Everything she had been holding back tonight came out and Chuco dragged across the concrete.

"Ow! Fuck!" he half-yelled. "Fucking cheater." The last came out as a mumble at best.

"Gotta get you away," Glori grated.

A couple others ran up and took Chuco's other hand and they pulled him clear. Glori was so focused on it that she ended up tripping over her own feet then on her ass. The crowd of kids and onlookers all chattered at one another, anger sneaking as easily as a riptide on a sunny day.

Chuco was talking still. He was beat up pretty good but alive. The Redtail that he'd driven to its end was smoking aggressively, flames licking out the wheel wells and interior cabin. Wouldn't take long to get to the gas tank.

"Back the hell off!" someone yelled. "That thing's gonna go!"

The green Nova idled back up towards the wreckage, tentatively. Glori watched it after getting to her feet.

"Tomás, you idiot. The fuck were you doing?" she said to herself. Then she was stabbed by hurt and what it could make you do and she pushed the thought away.

The dancing light from Chuco's car grew, crackling and hissing of the fire's consumption growing. When it went with a series of thumps growing to a single huge BANG of explosion, the Nova peeled out hard, laying down what must have been a hundred feet of scratch behind it.

"That's right, you motherfucker! Mess with Chuco like that! Mess with all of us!"

Glori didn't know whose voice it was, whether he was from LA or was one of the other kids. The sound of it was ugly and wounded. As were the murmurs from other voices in the crowd.

"Hey!" El Viejo yelled. "If there's a beef, it's between Chuco's and Tomás' crews! This isn't one side or the other." He was standing tall but out of breath from running. "We ain't gonna let that wreck this! It's too good!"

"Hey man, Chuco needs a doctor. We gotta get him back home," a skinny kid in a tooled leather vest said after stepping out of the crowd.

"Oh this is fucked sideways," Pecas whispered. "Kids are gonna pick sides. Nobody needs this."

"Hey, Leather, you gonna get Chuco taken care of?" Glori asked. "You need a ride? My wheels are just down there."

Leather vest looked her up and down briefly. Glori could see Pecas shake her head 'No' in her side vision, but she didn't know if it was for her or for the other guy. He agreed with it and said "No, we're good. Lefty and I will get him back home. But we're gonna remember that green car. Whoever he was, he ain't welcome at Thirds no more."

"And he better count himself lucky that's all we can do," someone, presumably Lefty, said. He was a strapping dude in a black tee that said THE CREMATORS in skinny letters that looked like burning matches. He then spat like a warning.

The column of smoke from Chuco's ride rose up into the night sky like an awful stringy fungus, thick with plastic and vinyl and gas fumes. It smeared the stars right out of the sky, leaving only murky dark.

Off in the distance, the sounds of sirens rose, fingering their way through the air, audible over the now-distant tunes of the party.

"Goddamn cops," someone spat.

"That's all we need," Glori added.

"Guess the show's over, sis. Feels like the last Third for a long time. Nobody wrecks here. That's not how it works." Pecas stood right next to her as people shuffled or ran back to their cars, loading gear up and shoveling belongings into trunks or the backs of vans.

"Come with me," Glori said, grabbing her by the hand. "I gotta talk to you." Her heart pegged 7000 RPM in her chest, fitting to burst.

"Yeah, okay," Pecas answered, on her heels.

Glori tried to figure out if it was the need to talk or the wreck or the tension between groups that was behind that. If she was right and it was the last Third, then maybe this was the only time. Tomás could have been blown off whenever. It should have happened weeks ago, only tonight because that's how they crossed.

There wasn't any more time. No more than Chuco's car was going to cruise down the boulevard any more, candyflake in the paint shifting and glittering as it passed under streetlights or neon signs, spelling out suggestions of words in color and light. It wouldn't have anything else to say, 'cept being a black scorch and shrugging bent metal, a monument to losing and loss. Hell of a gravestone for Thirds. It'd last until the next big rains at least, sudden wall of water scouring that concrete clean to the graffiti and spraypaint.

They walked through the scuffle of trash, food wrappers and oddly-shaped beer and liquor bottles, cigarette wrappers with brands that Glori didn't recognize. All this stuff was from somewhere else, somewhere a lot like here, just not exactly the same. A couple dudes were kicking the last of the bales of cielo down to the slow tug of the river, throwing up sparks with every step. You couldn't even hardly smell it anymore. Except when standing next to Pecas.

The big car that the crowd of supplicants had hung around inched up to the two girls as they walked to Glori's Camaro. The rear window was down and an elegantly-dressed woman's hand hung out it, resting like it was on the thigh of a lover. As they passed, the woman's fingers waved out in slow sequence and then collapsed into a half-closed fist. Glori waved back, unable to think of anything else.

"You know her?" Pecas asked, astonished.

"Nah. Just saying goodbye."

Glori stopped a couple steps short of the bronze Camaro, its shape picked out in the last of the firelight up the river.

"I gotta tell you something, girl. Something that's been on my mind for a long time and well, after seeing Chuco go out like that, it's now."

Pecas rocked back on her heels and smacked her lips all sly. "What you got to say?"

The fires guttered and popped weaker and weaker, fading down to stacks of coals that glowed in their barrels.

"I'm leaving tonight. I can't stay here any more." Her face flushed and she wondered if it would show in the eerie firelight. She hoped it didn't. That moment of resolution had gone out just like the fires had.

"Where… Where are you going?" Pecas leaned against the side door of the Camaro and watched with wide eyes.

"I don't know. I thought I was going to go wherever the kids from Thirds are. Figured it was just another part of LA. At least at first." Glori came around the car and hopped up on the hood, on the same side Pecas leaned on.

"You don't think it's LA?" Pecas asked. "Where do you… Where do you think they're from?"

"I think it's a lot like LA. Maybe even the same place from a distance. Just different. Just… better, you know? It'd be like moving to a new town but the same town. It's just tough here."

"Maybe it's tough wherever they come from, too." She sidled a little closer to Glori. "Maybe it's not any better where they're from. Maybe you, we're, just imagining that it's all that different."

"I've seen their cars and their clothes. I've looked all over LA for Little Coyotl and I've never found the stand. They walk different, stand a little taller."

Pecas snorted. "What if they're the exact same? What if Neverland is just like here?" She pushed off the car and shook her head so that the copper curls radiated around her in the orange light like slow fire. "I've been with a boy from there. He felt and tasted nice, but no better or worse than anyone I've been with here."

Glori didn't like the stab that she felt at that. Not that the other kids were just the same, but about Pecas and boys. But then she'd been with Tomás like that and that didn't change what she felt. Besides, she was still dancing around the real point.

"But they got a shine."

"Girl, that's just Thirds. Or it was Thirds. Maybe that's all done. It's the party and the estrella azul. This place is special. But they're just people."

A heavy breath welled up in Glori and she didn't want to let it go, else she'd start crying. It hissed out slowly like breathing out a mountain a pebble at a time.

"So they got parents who hate their kids too?" Glori felt something stinging but was afraid to reach up and wipe the tears away, unwilling to even acknowledge them.

Pecas put her arm around Glori and squeezed hard. "That's everywhere. You can't escape that no matter where you go. So you and your folks fight?"

"My dad. I can see it coming."

"See what?"

"I can't say. I just know it's like, a fire that's gonna destroy everything. I won't have a home to go back to if I tell the truth. But I can't lie anymore."

"This about you and Tomás?"

Glori froze tight. "No."

"Don't lie." Pecas squeezed again. "You just said you couldn't do that anymore."

Lights from the sirens flashed on the other side of the riverbank and a spotlight stabbed at Chuco's crashed car.

"Dammit!" Glori hissed. "Come on, we don't want to get caught here."

"Where are you going?"

"We, girl. Come on."

The Camaro woke and growled them back to the downtown side of the river and they drove past street-lit industrial buildings and brick walls, past chain link and razorwire on top. All the metal shone in the silver cast but there wasn't any magic to it.

Pecas turned on the radio and punched the first button. Norteñas poured out of the speakers and Glori turned it down a little so she could talk.

"I like girls," she said. "Like everyone says you're supposed to like boys. That's what is gonna make my dad flip out. You told me to not lie, so there it is. The biggest not lie for me."

Pecas didn't say anything and Glori couldn't figure out if that was good or bad.

"I broke it off with Tomás not just because he wanted sex, but it was gonna be harder if we did. Or maybe it'd be easier 'cause he'd just lay me and then move on. But I didn't think he's that kind of man. After tonight, though, I don't know that I was right."

"Turn on Mesquit street," Pecas said. She pulled out the pack of cigarettes and shook one out.

"Back towards the river? Cops are gonna see us."

"They won't. Promise."

"Okay."

Glori made the turn slow, hand over hand and ate at herself. It was going bad. But she hadn't demanded to be let out of the car, hadn't called Glori anything. Just took it in, lighting her cigarette.

"Stop so you can see the bridge good."

"Yeah, okay."

"You wanted to know where they came from?" she asked Glori. "It's easier to show you than to tell you. But you gotta take it slow. Gotta take everything slow." The lighter came on and flame at the end of the cigarette pulsed like a slow and heavy heartbeat as she breathed in.

"I don't wanna get high."

"It's not like that. But you might get a little dizzy. I've seen that happen. You get used to it, though." She let out a smile.

The concrete structure of the bridge base rose up to the right and the engine idling was enough to drown out all but the percussive beat of the music, like it was coming from a distant party. Like Third Saturday was still happening somewhere and it hadn't all ended up with a burning wreck as an exclamation mark. The bridge itself wasn't lit except from the lights of the city and what moonlight was left. The twin steel arches led off from Sixth street before the long span of elevated road that turned into Whittier boulevard on the Los Feliz side. The stars looked like they were trapped in the criss-cross ironwork.

The heavy scent of the cigarettes, not spice, not flowers but something as sweet as both, began to fill Glori's head. She wasn't dizzy but her head felt gauzy or was that just the inside of the windows fogging up? She couldn't decide.

"Do you see it yet?" Pecas asked.

"What am I looking for?"

"It's what you won't see that's important. What's missing?"

Glori looked ahead and saw an open field of black with stars scattered over it and moon up high, just a sickle-thin slice in the middle of the sky.

"Why is the moon out? And it was full hours ago."

"Yeah. Okay. What's missing?" Pecas squeezed her hand and Glori just soaked that in.

The sheer wall of the bridge foundation remained, scratched all over with unfamiliar tags and paintwork. Coyotes and ravens sketched out in black spray, a pachuco in feathered cap with a feathered serpent behind him coiled and ready, staring down a cop with hand on his gun, a sky filled with stars and they were shaped like a woman looking down on it all.

"The mural. That wasn't."

"Look over the river. What's not there?"

Glori whispered "The stars. Where's the bridge?"

The quality of the light from the city was different, shades and colors off. Not better or worse, just not what she remembered from a moment ago.

Glori fumbled with the latch on the door and Pecas squeezed her hand harder in response.

"Don't do that. Not yet. Not until you know what you're in for."

"I don't… I don't get it. Where's the goddamn bridge? How can it disappear?"

"It was demolished in 1978 after a tanker crash on it a couple years before. Illegal gas shipment."

Glori looked at Pecas and she was just watching out the windshield, sorrow welling up and pulling her down. "That's crazy. That never happened."

"It didn't happen where you're from."

The car radio went to static, a bubbling hiss where there had been song before.

Glori realized and her heart jumped up into her throat, nearly choking her words out. "You're from here, aren't you?"

Pecas nodded, tears bright and slick with starlight.

"That first night, you said—"

"I wasn't going home. Yeah. That's here."

"But why?"

"Because I thought the place I went to on Thirds, I thought that place was better than here. Total neverland. I could get Tommy's every night I wanted. I could get *Love and Rockets* comics. No more Carousel albums, but I could always get someone to bring a new one to me."

"Neverland is wherever you are, Glori."

Glori tried to breathe slowly and keep her heart from racing right out of her body, keep her brain from melting. She was there. It was right outside. LA but not. She could jump out and start over.

"If I open the door and go out? Am I stuck here?"

Pecas drew a ragged breath. "That's complicated. But you stepping out here shows intent. And intent is the first step towards a thing."

"You don't want to go home?"

"Home is where your hat hangs. I don't want *you* to go here. I don't want you to leave." She swiped at the tears with her jacket sleeve and only spread them out so they reflected bigger for a moment before drying. "Oh give me a second. This is hard, harder than I thought."

Glori stared out over the river, realizing that Chuco's car wouldn't be there. It was stuck over on the other side, where everything Glori had ever known remained. She'd thought that all so plain and in this moment it was as impossible to reach as Neverland. A helicopter swooped down and shot a beam of white sun-bright light onto the riverbed. It looked like the sail of a phantom ship passing, a flat white triangle easing down the course of the river.

"It's not just the bridge, right? There's other differences?"

"Lots, but they don't matter. Everything else is the same as what you already know. Kids fighting with their folks, cops picking on kids, boys fall for girls and girls fall for girls."

"Not for boys?" Glori turned from the view of not-LA, the LA made out of smoke. She ran her left hand through Pecas' hair, down the side of her face, gentle and firm, shaking not at all.

Pecas leaned into it and Glori's hand stopped on her neck.

"All the same heartbeats," she said. "No difference, huh?"

"Not where it's important. And it's important that I be with you, Glori. I'd hoped and wished, but never knew and I was scared, too."

Glori brought her closer, as close as she could. "We can go back home."

After a moment, the Camaro turned around on the narrow street. By the time Glori reached Santa Fe street, the artwork was gone and the bridge restored. The stars still glowed above it.

IN WHAT FURNACE

The video playback was gray and blown-out, not silvery and gauzy as old movies but something more austere and stripped-down. On the screen a kid slid down the rain-swollen drainage channel, gripping a makeshift raft as the water bucked and bulged. Eddies swirled around him and the engorged river rushed without interruption all the way out to the Pacific Ocean. His head and eyes were down in a child's fearful prayer.

"KTLA footage, right?" Watkiss lit another cigarette and promised that it would be the last one of the day. "They're not gonna mind?"

"They can only mind if they know, J." Fabian sat at the console, finger-nails clean and almost bright dancing over the buttons lit beneath them. "You wanna spin some copy for this?" he asked over his shoulder. His keen dark eyes fixed on Kenneth wedged into the corner of the edit bay.

Ken looked up and sighed a little, drudgery weighing it down. He shrugged his shoulders, bone-skinny underneath an outfit that was fashionable six months ago. His black leather tie printed up like piano keys faintly shone in the monitor's light as he sucked on an imaginary cigarette then exhaled. "Timmy Robbins, age ten, had been told by his mother to stay away from the channel, especially after the rains."

The kid was dragged by the river, bits of landscape whipping by and showing the real speed of things as the camera stayed loosely trained on the boy's raft.

Watkiss exhaled, tense and looking for something more. "The river really doesn't look that fast. Can we make it, you know, scarier?"

"Sure, J. And they can zoom it in," Ken said.

"And get it in color." Fabian snickered and it came out angry.

"It's just that it doesn't look like that much." Watkiss pointed in at the screen.

"And I thought you liked… ambiguity," Kenneth said with some bite.

"There's ambiguous and there's lifeless. How much before he hits the bridge?"

"About a minute."

"Okay, we only need about thirty seconds of this unless there's something that jumps out." Watkiss took another drag of the cigarette counting that it was half-done already and knowing that he was going to need another before lunch. "Ken, keep whatever you get down to about half a page as lead-in on this."

"I *know* what thirty seconds reads like, John." He fingered the wall where the plaster was peeling away. "About as long as this place will keep standing the next earthquake we get."

"When we can afford a higher rent we'll get a better place. We've gone over this." Watkiss looked over his own hands in the flickering light of the big monitor. He hated being in here. Every wrinkle and crease stood out in the video light, making him feel seventy though he was only fifty. Last year. Or two years ago. He could still get away with the lower number.

"Here it comes," Fabian snapped. "Watch the magic trick. Don't blink."

The border of the viaduct came up fast in the lower part of the image.

"Is that Riverside?" Watkiss jabbed a cigarette at the screen.

"Yeah and…"

One second the kid, whose name may or may not have been Robbins, was riding down the river, holding on for dear life. The helicopter kept tracking at the same speed, following the flow of the river. Then it swept past the down-current edge of the bridge and the kid was nowhere to be found. Just the inflatable raft that he'd been riding on, only now it was capsized, wrapped around a tree limb that had lodged in the river. Air leaked out of the raft and it began to look like a flag in a dead wind before it sank beneath the churn of the surface.

"Presto!" Fabian's voice rang out in the edit bay.

"Nothing up my sleeve," Kenneth added.

The video whipped back to the bridge scanning around hungrily for the boy, finding nothing but the river, moving frightfully fast once seen in a fixed perspective. A long gray blur in the video.

After a moment a figure staggered out on the sloped bank, several feet away from the rushing water. It was the boy.

And something else behind him, only for a brief moment. Maybe it was just an artifact of the video, maybe it was something else. An arm or hand, distorted in the video.

"Freeze it," Watkiss said.

"We've done-"

"Do it, Fabian."

He grumbled and the video mostly froze, edges still juddering, fields crushed into one another. At the edge of the shadow cast by the viaduct, there was something dark, maybe a giant's arm.

"That just could be a branch, J."

"Branches don't grab. Things crash into them." He finished the cigarette and stubbed it into the aluminum tray stamped into a flying saucer shape. In the light of the console, it glowed like the *UNS Intrepid* had in *Starlanes*, the show that had made Watkiss a minor star. Once it looked like it could fly. Today it just held smears of ash and cinders.

"They do when they're being carried by a river," Kenneth added, more than a little bored. "Come on, John, we've done this ten times."

"Let it run," Watkiss said.

The boy staggered back and stared behind him at the bridge and then looked out where his raft had wrecked in the river. His body bent with the weight of whatever had happened, but what exactly had wasn't clear. The arm or limb or whatever it was drew back under the bridge as if it never was. Then the camera pulled back to reveal squad cars and a fire engine rolling up to the fence closing off the riverbed. It looked like another regular emergency, just like any thousand that happened every day in Los Angeles.

"We can't blow this up, can we?"

"If it was film, maybe. It would still look like crap."

"Sorry, I'm still getting used to the production side." Watkiss drew a heavy breath. "Can we maybe shoot something there, do a re-creation?"

"If I wasn't editing and answering phones and doing the books, I could give you the answer." His lips pulled back for a second in a muted disgust. "You know, Charlie could do any or all of those things, too, yeah?"

"Leave her out of this. Just can we do it?"

"We've run out of credit for soundstage time. *Quest4* isn't bankrupt yet, but until we get paid, we're on fumes. And I won't put on the monster suit again."

"But you looked so good in it," Watkiss said warmly.

"We don't even know what you'd want to re-create, John," Kenneth said. "What did we just see?" He picked at the wall just to watch pieces fall.

"Knock it off unless you want to plaster up that hole." Watkiss sighed and drew another cigarette out of the pack. Not even to lunch. "We just saw the Bigfoot of the Southland save that kid from the river. That's what we saw. That's what the kid told the cops. We're still on for that interview with the family, right?"

"Yes. This afternoon," Fabian sighed.

"Okay, great." Watkiss tapped the console facing and it rang dully. "Let's open with this. It's still the only eyewitness stuff we've got."

"It's the only stuff we've got, J. Gonna be tough to sell this."

"We have to sell it, or *Quest4* doesn't deliver and that means not even a sliver of nothing from the distributors."

Fabian rested his hands on his head. "I shoulda taken that job at KABC. I could've been a camera op instead of a gofer."

Watkiss rested a heavy hand on Fabian's houndstooth-clad shoulder. "But here, your possibilities are limitless. Why you're already a producer."

"On a show that nobody has seen or heard of, J."

"Not yet, they haven't."

The edit bay door opened and light from the hallway spilled around the woman in the doorway, tall and practiced imperiousness. "Why are my ears burning?" she asked.

"Because they always are," Kenneth grouched. "Nice to see you, Charlie."

"How novel. You're working and not staring at the intern. Little weirdo." Charlie's expression of disgust radiated in the ghostly light of the video.

Kenneth pursed his lips halfway then went dead. "I'm going to go work up that copy, John. I'll have the open and close before you take off."

"How do you know how it's going to end, Ken?" she asked.

He drew a breath without hissing and counted to a number he'd chosen in his head. "It's gonna end the same way it always does. With the mystery never being solved because we can't." Kenneth stood before her in the doorway. "That's what keeps the viewers coming back, right?"

Watkiss nodded, contemplating another surrender drag on the cigarette. "At least *someone* gets it."

Charlie's head shook, grimace as sharp as a knife across the throat. "It's because you refuse to close the deal, college boy. You don't tell it in black and white. Facts."

"Facts aren't the business. Now if you'll excuse me?"

She finally moved aside partway, making him shimmy hard to get past her. "I don't know why you keep him around," she said without waiting for him to get out of earshot.

"Because he's got a very good ear for the narrative, no matter how much you do or do not like him." Watkiss moved aside so she could take the second chair at the console. "And he was here before you."

"And he meshes well," Fabian added.

Charlie snorted faintly. "He's lazy and you could get twice the work out of him you do." She turned over to the screen and grimaced after a moment, realizing what the image was.

"What's wrong?" Watkiss asked.

She stared at the monitor. "This is the riverbed." Her gaze locked on Watkiss. "We're doing the bigfoot shit?" She tapped the screen with a fingernail and that made an itching sort of sound in the room.

Fabian gently took her hand from the screen. "I'm tired of telling you not to touch this." He grabbed a nearby soft cloth and wiped the smudges out.

"John, I thought we were going to do the Skullface Killer for the last episode? We talked about this last night."

Fabian snickered and leaned back.

"Quiet, Fabe," she warned without looking at him.

He pantomimed cat claws raking just out of her vision.

"John," she added.

"We did talk about it, Charlie. And it was clear to me that we were going to do the Bigfoot of the Southland. We've got most of the material assembled and don't have the resources to start something new out from scratch." He wanted to reach for the room lights, afraid that the monitor lights made him look a skeleton covered in wrinkled flesh.

Even though that's not what she thought. At least not last night and over the last several months. He still couldn't believe that she was with him in every way, at work and at play. Sure it happened with couples in TV back in the sixties and even the fifties when he started, but to be so open and unabashed about it.

"This Bigfoot bullshit is not going to get people to tune in on Saturday at 7:30 much less a prime-time slot ever. Skullface has legs. It's real and people are goddamn afraid of him. No monster suit needed."

"Charlie, do you ever think that people might want to tune in and watch about something that could be but isn't really real? That space between what we know and what we believe. That's what Ken gets that you don't. That's what we're doing here."

She leaned away from the monitor, tossing her bangs back out of her face. "Every time there's a story about Skullface, people pay attention."

"We're not selling the nightly news at *Quest4*. It's about something different."

"Well maybe we ought to be if you want to dig out of the hole, John." She pushed the chair back with a screech. "Because from here, I'm not sure you do want to."

"Charlie."

Her eyeroll was visible even in the half-light. "I'm gonna go get the suit. It's the only way we're getting footage of this goddamn thing and you goddamn know it. Stop being such a witless romantic!" Her heels clicked hard on the linoleum as she stalked out of the room.

"I'm not wearing the suit again," Fabian warned as he rewound to mark the cut-in time on the tape.

"You're not tall enough," Watkiss said with a heavy sigh. "We'll have to get Shrug to do it."

"He won't fit. He barely fits inside the city limits."

"Be nice. He's exactly as God made him."

"Yeah. Nobody else could've."

The boy's name wasn't Robinson, but Dupree. Mark Dupree of the Dupree family in Burbank. He'd taken his fateful ride a couple months ago in December. Mark Dupree wasn't the only kid to try and ride the rain-swollen river, but he was the only one who was fished out of the water by the Bigfoot of the Southland. Not that anyone actually believed in the Bigfoot, even the burnouts who lived in vans down at the beach. The important thing wasn't that you believed or didn't believe, but that you were open enough to it to sit down and watch it for half an hour.

That was what Watkiss had chosen to work with *Quest4*. It was what people wanted today, in post-Age of Aquarius California. Part science, part history, part occult, part paranormal. Anything on the outside, but not so much to make parents freak out that you were trying to sell their kids on Satan. Okay, there were those folks and there always were. All this stuff was already floating around out there between the Eastern philosophy that the hippies and their Alan Watts reading had brought in, and the Zodiac fad. When Watkiss saw those little rolled-up predictions for sale in bars and in hotel rooms, he knew that they were onto something. It just took a little while to get it going.

And now the thing was halfway in the grave. Thirteen shows. Not twelve and an outline. That's what he had to deliver. Lucky thirteen. He'd gone for the Bigfoot of the Southland story on the hope that he could land something new, a footprint or even a sighting. There were those odd tracks that had been seen down in the riverbed and through some back-yards around Griffith Park, not too far from where Mark Dupree had been snatched out of the river.

B-roll, texture and background footage, but nothing substantial. Lots of muddy marks that, amongst all the other runnels and tracks in the riverbed were barely even interesting noise.

Maybe he should have taken on the Skullface Killer. Seven deaths in the last year. But it was so common, so tawdry, so… real. Yes, it sold news-papers, but that's not what he'd done so far. He couldn't compete with the *Times* and the *Examiner*.

"Right, right, right!" Charlie snapped at him.

"Where?" He looked at the signs but they were all too far away to read in motion and he didn't have his cheaters on. Everything was a blur of housing tracts, block after block of them. The magma of the postwar sub-urban boom congealing into block after block of sameness.

"Right here. Baldwin!" Charlie jerked the wheel and the Volvo wagon shuddered into a turn. Shrug and Fabian both yelled as they were thrown around the back of the car, Fabian pressed right into the door by the much larger of the two.

"Ow! Dammit, Shrug!"

"Sorry, the belt barely fits. It's uncomfortable." Shrug's shaggy red hair and beard caught the afternoon light and behind the lenses of his glasses, his eyes were huge, bright blue.

"You don't have to yell," Watkiss said.

"I wouldn't if you weren't daydreaming."

"I'm not. It's tough to read." He straightened out the car. "Look for the house number."

"Someone has to," Charlie replied.

"If you don't want to work on this one, you don't have to. You're angry that we're not doing Skullface. Fair. We can open up with it next season."

"Next season," she said like he was talking about getting a suntan on the moon. "If there is one, I bet he's caught. And then it's over. There's no more mystique."

"People still talk about Jack the Ripper."

"That was a hundred years ago and never solved."

The Volvo came to rest in front of a yellow stucco house with white crisscross latticework covering the walkway to the front door, perfectly squared-off hedges and a lawn so tightly mowed that a tank couldn't leave tracks in it. Perfect quiet neighborhood.

"Still." He took her hand after she reached across herself to undo the safety belt. "We can do the story."

She squeezed his hand in return. "Look, I'm sorry, okay. We disagree about the direction of the show and I'll commit to this episode, one hundred percent. I don't want to fight about it."

"Good."

"Can you get me in front of the camera for this segment? Just the segment?" Her hand held steady until Watkiss looked her in the eyes. They were green and fierce and there was never a time that they were not.

Watkiss heard nothing from the backseat. It wasn't the first time that she'd brought up the possibility, but the first time that nobody had objected.

"Just this segment, John. I need something for my reel, something that's going to go live."

Her fingers moved slowly beneath his, skin over skin.

"And how do we explain you haven't been in all of them?"

"Just label me as a special correspondent or something. Come on. This way you know for sure that I'll give one hundred ten percent… to get the show done."

He asked himself why she couldn't have waited for the others to at least have left the car. He knew why and didn't really like the answer. But he didn't have a good reason to say no, either.

"What the hell. I'd always planned on having multiple teams cover the stories once we got rolling. May as well get the audience used to you. I know that I am."

He pressed his fingers into hers but didn't feel much of a reply.

It was too bad that Ronette Dupree, the lady of the house was of no mind to let anyone interview her son or anyone else. Even though this had been set up for more than a week. Shrug stood there with the camera and his ELO t-shirt like a mountain who'd fallen through a Gap store and managed to get clothed, just barely. Fabian watched from the car, suit gleaming sharkskin.

Charlie held the microphone so hard that it shook, just outside the camera's view. John knew that if she had been in the shot, you could have asked her to hold a snow-cone in her palm and it would not melt.

"Why don't you just leave that poor thing alone?" Mrs. Dupree asked. She stood in the half-opened door in jeans and a jersey that said "BEARS MOM," evidently one of her kids' baseball team. Or swimming maybe.

"Mrs. Dupree, we're just trying to tell the story of the Bigfoot and people who've seen him."

"He's not a Bigfoot." She took a draw off the cigarette in her lips then exhaled. "He's a man. And he saved my Marky from drowning. That's all I need to know."

"And people want to see that," Charlie said imploringly. "They want to hear about how it… he's not a monster. Your son told the police he was big and tall and strange-looking, but still, the thi…, the *man* pulled Marky from the river then put his finger to his lips like a librarian shushing someone. We have that in the reports."

Mrs. Dupree thought about it a moment, multiple emotions playing it out over her face, skirmishing. "You put him on television and you may as well just shoot him."

"But we're just talking to you and your son."

Dupree blew smoke and shook her head, hair swathed in a bright pink nylon scarf like a bundle of cotton candy. "If you don't mind, I have to get cupcakes ready for after practice." And whether anyone actually minded or not, the door snapped shut, hand-painted sign saying "Home is where the heart is," clattering in the impact.

Charlie stared back at John for a moment before saying "What's plan B?"

Watkiss shook his head and laughed. "What plan B?"

"How about that Layman guy? The one up in the Angeles National Forest?"

"Flake." Fabian shook his head. "A nice guy, but a flake. Nothing checked out."

She tapped the microphone on her palm like a nightstick. "What about that deputy and the liquor store? The one in Van Nuys? At least it would be a talking head. We could dramatize the rest."

"Vince something, yeah." Watkiss snapped his fingers trying to recall the conversation he'd had. "What'd he call that guy? It was something weird."

"'The Scarman'," Shrug said, scratching at his beard with his free hand.

"It's not great, but still better than 'The Bigfoot of Los Angeles," Charlie said. "Can we still get him?"

"Sheriff's department isn't returning my calls," Fabian said. "Something about us not being a real show."

"There's always…" Watkiss started to say.

"Don't," Charlie warned.

"Yucaipa."

Charlie's eyes half-closed and she made a face in disgust. "That's a nothing. And it's all the hell way out there."

"Fabian, how much time do we have to fill out in the Bigfoot episode?"

"Seven, maybe eight minutes depending how we cut things. We could pad your intro. Maybe even cut some time to introduce Charlie to viewers. Still, thin."

"I didn't know you cared, Fabian," she said drily, disgust filtered from her face to her voice.

"I'm just thinking about the show."

"We all are," Watkiss said. "Shrug, how much film do you have?"

Without delay, he answered "Two reels of 35mm, five of 16mm. That's back at the shop. And we owe on those."

"How much can we get processed?"

"Artie said and I quote 'Stay the fuck out of my lab until you get me my money.' I can get Stan to let me in and I can run some reels on the sly. But after that, I got no more favors. And…"

Watkiss held up a hand and hid behind it. "I know. Payday's coming up."

Shrug sighed softly. "Just wanted to remind you. I like you guys and all, but I have rent to pay."

The apology was unsaid but hit like a paint can dropped on a toe.

"Well then, we best hurry." Watkiss glanced around to register potential objections. "We can make Yucaipa tonight after traffic dies down."

"Van Nuys is a lot closer."

"Intern says that Pizza Chalet there is a must-stop," Shrug offered. "She grew up close by."

"You just ate, man," Fabian snapped.

"But you gotta plan ahead."

"Okay, we'll go back then pack up for an overnight trip. Get some great footage and put this thing to bed." Watkiss clapped his hands together and rubbed them in anticipation of getting to work.

"And if we don't?" Charlie asked, bitter. "What then?"

"Plan C."

***

Yucaipa was one of a string of several small towns growing into small cities that filtered eastward from Los Angeles all the way out to the mountains with Palm Springs on the other side. Watkiss saw them as mostly embracing a kind of tired boosterism that had marked a lot of California, particularly in the south, that he'd noted since moving here in search of work. Small places that were grudgingly becoming larger as they became bedroom communities for long-distance commuters or filling up with people who wanted a different flavor of suburbia. Yucaipa was far enough out that you could even be tricked into thinking that you weren't part of the yawning sprawl that crept anywhere there was an interstate or a stretch of arterial road.

At night, it was a somewhat tacky yet charming collection of illuminated signage and gas stations and mom and pop restaurants along with a string of businesses that passed as a downtown. Lots of low stucco, lots of cheap construction, lots like Los Angeles without the sense of consumed history. It was the kind of place that a lot of people were from but never came back to.

At least the pizza was good. Mostly.

"Cashews?" Fabian asked. "What the hell?"

"If you don't like them, pick them off," Watkiss said quietly.

"Or give them to me." Shrug took a healthy gulp of beer from a glass mug thick enough to cave in a skull, were he so inclined.

Pizza Chalet was small and loud and crowded, tables laid out with red and white plaid vinyl-coated cloths, red and pebble-flecked glass lampshades and a jukebox weakly pumping out "Best of My Love" over the sound of mostly kids and a couple late-night family pizza dinners.

"You called those kids already?" Charlie asked before tearing into a slice.

"Ollie Mendoza and Jodi Barnes, yes. They'll go on camera."

"Beats v-o. What was their story again?"

"Driving on a road not far, overlooking a creek bed. Slid off and their car went in."

"Exciting," Charlie sighed.

"Excitement starts after they hit the riverbed. A fuel line ruptured and fire started. Both the kids are stuck in the car, door's stuck. Then someone really tall and strong shows up, wrenches the door off the frame and gently pulls them free."

"'Gently.' So like the kid in the river?"

Watkiss took a swallow of beer and nodded. "That's the detail that made me want to look at this one. That's the link."

"And did they see their mysterious savior?"

"Tall, on the skinny side, bumpy and wrinkled skin, not hairy. It's far from LA, but a lot of the other facts fit."

"No tracks, of course," Charlie said, knowing the answer.

"No physical evidence. Rescue crew after made sure of it. But there've been other sightings since then. Some weird stuff, too. Glowing eyes, missing pets and people."

Charlie's eyes grew wide. "Missing people? That's a little creepy."

"It's not a detail I want to linger on."

"Oh, so you're only interested in *friendly* bigfoots."

"Well, I was hoping that if we see one ourselves that it is friendly, that it is… kind. The sort of thing that pulls a child from a river and saves two kids from a crashed car."

"And if it isn't?" Her fingernails rapped on the pizza pan.

"Then hopefully we only see it from a distance."

"Or we can throw Shrug at it," she suggested.

"Please don't," he answered. "I wouldn't hurt a fly, much less something that could think and feel."

"Besides," Watkiss said. "You and Fabian will be getting b-roll in town. "Charlie and I will take the 16 and do the field shots."

"You're going to run the camera?" Shrug asked her. "I didn't think you could."

"I can, Shrug. Besides, I made a promise to get Charlie on-camera for a segment this season and this will be a good way to do it. We'll all group up for the interview with the kids tomorrow and then go get the other footage and pull something together after. Let's relax a little."

"Eat drink and be merry," Fabian said.

"Don't finish that sentence, Fabe."

"I wouldn't dream of it."

The kids meant well, but they didn't have much to offer. Watkiss watched as Charlie handled them well, better than he could've. Age was still a barrier. And she'd started in local news and he couldn't imagine how brightly she'd burned the bridge behind her once she figured out that there wasn't anything more to learn in her first couple of jobs. Still, the weather cooperated and Watkiss refreshed his memory of the camera controls as he worked the 16mm Kodak and burned a roll out of their dwindling pile of film stock. He'd worry about processing it somehow later.

Ollie had a broad smile and good skin and the two kids radiated good-natured charm as they recounted the story of being pulled from their wrecked Olds by a man who didn't say a word and didn't much look like a man the more they thought of it. But both agreed that he was "gentle" and "careful." It was a good story, and things were unclear enough that it could have just been a helpful vagabond in scabby clothing or maybe it was a big, hulking brute with a heart of gold. There was plenty of space for the viewer to write their own story on the narrative and that was impossible to fake, actual TV gold.

That was the real secret to *Quest4*. That all these things were things that could happen to you, the viewer, if you were lucky or inspired enough. A touch of something that you could not even imagine, beyond words, beyond experience. Something beyond explanation, like seeing a unicorn. Or being the unicorn and finding a maiden, resting your head in her lap. Something equally rare for both. It had to be special for the unicorn, too, yes?

Watkiss tried not to think about last night, her drawing his head down from her neck, between her breasts then pulling him down further even than that. Which one of them was the unicorn? He knew, and it wasn't him. But he was no maiden. Experience weighed on him, more every day it seemed.

"What do you think?" someone asked.

Watkiss' mind snapped back to the now, here on the dry creek bed just outside downtown, sandy floor strewn with the marks of long-gone water's passing.

"I'm sorry, what? I was just trying to remember how to, ah, work this." He indicated the camera perched on his shoulder. "Easy to get tunnel vision looking through the viewfinder."

"I asked," Charlie repeated "if we want to get some more coverage of the landscape here."

The sun was up high, everything overexposed, no place for anything to hide, even with the irregular thickets of foliage that grew weedily from the sloped hillside, bounding the creek bed.

"Wrong atmosphere," he said after a moment of consideration. "Too bright. Maybe we can double back if we get time in the afternoon. Get some slanting light, set a mood."

"See? A romantic," Charlie said.

"So, are we, uh, done?" Ollie asked. He stood there in his Dodgers shirt and jean jacket, unsure what to do other than to stand on his mark with his arm around Jodi.

"Do you guys need some more?" she asked. Her long black hair tumbled around her shoulders.

"Was I okay?"

"You were both just great," Charlie told them with reassurance. "You're naturals."

"Is there anything else that might fit into all this?" Watkiss asked. "Like some more sightings? We've heard about the events near the junkyard, but anything else?" His shoulder ached from the weight of the camera, but it was easier to hold it up high than just drag it.

"Hey, lemme get that," Shrug said, lifting the camera as if it weighed no more than a football.

"What do you think, Jode?"

"There's that old factory. Weird stuff there."

"But they're not interested in that. That's not the bigfoot."

"What factory?" Charlie asked.

Ollie scratched behind his ear. "Well, not that so much as a kind of industrial park. Mostly abandoned. There was a crew there for I dunno, maybe a year. Then there was a fire I think."

"And?" Watkiss asked. "Need something more than that."

"Well, it's only mostly abandoned. Kids have been out there and seen weird lights and maybe someone walking around. Cops go check the place out from time to time, but never come back with anything. And those weird coyote sightings or something."

"How many minutes did we get here, Fabian?"

He wiped the sweat from his brow and pulled at his collar, looking over his clipboard. "We blew up a reel. Cut it in half, clean it up. Probably four minutes. Gives us another four at least but some room. Whaddya think?"

"I think we'll go back for lunch and a drink and then you and Shrug will get that local color. Charlie and I will check out the lab. Still have a few hours of good light. Might have time to get some moody shots on the creekbed here later."

"I saw a Mexican place right on the main drag," Shrug said.

"Half the restaurants on the main drag are Mexican," Jody said.

"But they're all good," Ollie added. "Go to Juanita's and tell 'em I sent you. They'll treat you nice."

"You don't think Fabian's too mad, do you?" Charlie asked.

"He's too resigned to be mad," Watkiss replied drily. His head still spun a little from the pitcher of margaritas at lunch. He wondered how long it would be before Fabian's manners would let him and Shrug get away from the gregarious Juanita. She'd seen him in his suit and asked where his family was from then proceeded to talk the table's ear off for an hour while the kitchen served their best. Ollie hadn't lied about that.

"I mean about me coming in hot on this show."

"Are those regrets, dear?"

Watkiss threw the brake on the Volvo at the chained-off side path. There was spur from the canyon road, the same that Ollie and Jodie had skidded off a couple months back, this one leading to the facility that he'd talked about. It felt like a nothing place, somewhere nobody was supposed to be.

"Not really regrets. Just that, well, I know I can come on really strong and…"

"You're a beautiful comet. Burning as hot as you can. The problem is that doesn't last. I simply don't want you to burn yourself out. I understand this is not the most regimented crew you've worked with, but we do know what we're doing." He drew his hand over and placed it on her shoulder, rubbing gently.

"Oh that's nice."

"Your shoulders are like granite. I didn't think you were this stressed." He worked the muscle beneath his fingers as best he could, given the awkward angle.

"I just have a lot on my mind. KABC has been on my agent. That means he's been on me." Her eyes were heavy and reluctant.

"What are you saying? That you want to go?"

"No, that's not it at all, John. I just see how much this show means to you. I don't exactly understand it, but I see that." She reached around and took his hand, resting it on her cheek. Half-closing her eyes, she looked away and leaned into his touch. "I just want you to be happy."

He thought about the unicorn again and his heart caught. Fabian was hard on her, but he was being territorial and maybe rightfully so. There was, however, a very clear note ringing through the office that Charlie and Watkiss had only become involved because Charlie wanted something and she was willing to give in order to get. But she hadn't needed to. She was smarter than just about everyone else in the show, and certainly more driven.

"I can take care of my own happiness, Charlie."

It was a statement that he wanted to believe, anyways.

"I'm just tired of people thinking that I'm sleeping my way to the top. Just want to be…"

"Hey, I don't think that. I am not going to question your taste in older men, just count myself fortunate."

She sighed out heavy and turned so she could look at him directly. "So, I just wanted you to know, if I end up going somewhere else, that it's not you or this show. If anything, it'll make it easier for me, for us, to be together." Her stare went bright. "It won't even be a question then."

"You understand that if everyone could see just a little of this side of you, they wouldn't have any doubts."

"I'm not interested in being vulnerable so that someone can turn around and take a bite out of me. Fuck that."

"Such language. You kiss your mother with that mouth?"

"No, but I can suck you dry with it."

"I'm never going to get used to how… direct you are."

"Good," she said with a sly grin. "I have to be able to surprise you somehow."

"I'm surprised every moment you're with me."

She kissed him quickly along his lips then punctuated it with a quick nibble. "Come on. Let's go get some shots of this mysterious factory. Maybe we can turn it into something."

The road was strewn with chunks of beer bottles like the bodies of huge insects, cigarette butts and condom wrappers left out in shoals of vile confetti over cracked asphalt. It hadn't been maintained in some time and was just a local lover's lane now. The chain was a half-attempt at keeping the kids out. No signs warning off trespassers or actual law enforcement presence. Just a length of chain between two concrete posts, flagging and all but laying on the ground. The hill rose up past the posts, such that the end of the road couldn't be made out from where they stood.

A few hot minutes of walking over the detritus and worn tire tracks brought the two of them to the top of the rise. Off in the distance sprawled out Yucaipa, a patternwork of houses and buildings that looked small at the feet of the San Gorgonios, haze of basin smog covering it all like a rusty veil.

"This is really California, isn't it?" Watkiss asked.

"What?"

"A bunch of mountains and desert scrabble that someone got talked into planting a metropolis in." He wiped the sweat from his forehead and took a heavy breath. "It's like there's no there there."

"I don't get it," she replied. "I look out there and it's not all that different from where I grew up, just less green. Seriously, John, you sound like those executives you pretend you hate."

"I was just observing the nature of the mirage."

Charlie shrugged. "When you've lived in a mirage your whole life, it feels pretty normal. Come on, let's check this place out while we still can. We'll be the first in a while, I bet."

"How so?" Watkiss hefted the camera back to his shoulder. It was lighter than the other, but still more than he liked to be carrying around in the heat.

"All these beer bottles have been here since before the last rains. They're all half caked in mud and stuff. There's no new ones thrown down."

"Kids have been staying away?"

"At least for a while. Maybe there is something to all this bigfoot stuff." She shrugged.

"My dear, are you becoming a believer?"

"I believe in getting a good story." She continued her march up the rest of the hill, sensible shoes on her feet, fashion be damned. They'd be out of the shot anyways.

It felt later than it should've, sun low on the horizon yet still pounding, ground warmed from the day bouncing the heat right back. The place was an oblong of concrete tilt-up construction, one of the many examples of instant industrial architecture that popped up all over Southern California in the last decade and a half. This one was two stories, windows and doors along the lower floors only. It didn't look like a retail or even an office front, rather a remote industrial space.

"No customers here," Watkiss noted.

"Million of these places in Orange County. Go up in two weeks and it seems like they've always been there."

"Well, not this one."

"Abandonment doesn't suit some buildings."

It was true. The windows were dirty or mud-covered where they hadn't been kicked in. Though there were boards up behind those that had been.

"Not totally abandoned, Charlie. Look at this."

Watkiss pointed out one of the hastily-repaired ground floor windows. KEEP OUT was scrawled in thin black lettering, crumbly like crayon.

"Someone still values their privacy?"

"If they don't mind missing some other basic services, I suppose."

They walked around to the back side of the building, in the shade between the thicketed hillside and a strip of asphalt too small to be anything other than an access path.

"Tire tracks here, faint," Watkiss pointed them out.

"And look, there's a door propped open over there." She indicated the far corner of the building, where an exterior door and been wedged open with a fist-sized rock at its base. "Someone is squatting here."

"Self-locking from the inside? Maybe."

There wasn't anything around, just the calls of distant doves and other critters rustling through the underbrush.

"What do you think? Roll a little?" she asked. "Do I look okay?"

"You're glowing."

She smirked. "It's going to look like sweat, John."

He fiddled with the camera and pulled a focus, standing some fifteen feet from her, back to the door and waiting.

"Hold on, step over about five feet. There's an obscenity written in mud on the wall. Don't want to get in trouble with the FCC."

She sidled over and set herself up.

The doves stopped. All the critter sounds stopped too, as sharply as if someone had just halted the playback. There was a scuffle of feet somewhere on the hillside and scattering of rocks, but too many to be a squirrel or lizard.

"What was that?" Charlie looked around for the source of the sound.

"Don't know. Coyote? Goat?" Watkiss pulled the focus and set the exposure as best he could by eye. He wished Shrug was here.

"We don't get goats here. Deer, yes."

"Go ahead, just improvise something. And… rolling."

"This is Charlie Davenport for *Quest4* and we're investigating follow-up sightings of the Southern California Bigfoot, also called the *Scarman*. We're at an abandoned industrial site outside Yucaipa, where local citizens have reported *strange* lights and figures with *glowing* eyes." She turned to walk the pathway between the building and the hillside.

There was another scuffle, but this one came from inside the building, something moving and shifting within.

"Did you hear that?"

Watkiss paused the film feed and lowered the camera. "Yes. We should probably go."

"You're right. We should go *inside*." She took a step towards the door.

"The bigfoot isn't going to be living inside a building. And I don't have a light to burn to get a good exposure."

"Faint heart ne'er captured fair maiden!" she said as she kicked the door open with a shod foot.

Watkiss winced and waited for a reaction to the screeching. Nothing. Not even a skitter from within.

"Come on, let's go."

"Just a few minutes."

Stupidly, his heart was racing, whether it was from Charlie's fearlessness or the possibility of stumbling into a vagabond camp or a warren of misanthropes armed or not. He wanted a cigarette suddenly. When he had been busy and focused, the craving wasn't a problem, but needing the distraction and the excuse to just stand and breathe quietly swept over him.

The inside of the building smelled like electricity, like machines broken open and their insides wafting out voltage and lubricants, time turning industry into ruin. The back door had led into an unlit workspace scattered with shelving and banks of what could have been filing cabinets, regular and repeating shapes—half-lit at best.

"Hold up. I've got a flashlight in here." Charlie rummaged around in her oversize purse. "Can't have actual pockets so I have to haul this around." She snapped it on and the circle of light hit her from beneath like scary story time around a campfire. "Gaah!"

"Positively terrifying, Charlie."

She swept the beam around the room slowly. "Can you get this?"

Watkiss shouldered the camera and set the shutter for as low a lighting situation as possible and prayed a little. "Maybe? Stand there. Shine the light on you."

He took an exploratory shot. "No idea if this will work, but we're committed."

"Okay, get this stuff." She led him with the flashlight beam.

It stabbed through the must and murk of the room, light revealing not filing cabinets, but banks of instruments and dials. On one wall was a bank of computers, devices the size of refrigerators with big reels of tape mounted at eye level. Some of the equipment was burned and scarred. But none of it was dusty.

"This is valuable electronic gear," Charlie said. "Too expensive to just be abandoned out here."

"You see they're cleaned-off, right? What's it say on these things? There's some writing."

Charlie sneaked over to the bank of machines across the room, circle of light shrinking down as she approached. She leaned in and rubbed some dirt off of one of them. "'IBM for Method/Move.' Does that mean anything to you?" She let the light slide down to the floor after reading the nameplate.

Watkiss tried to get a shot with the spilled light up from the floor, but it wasn't even going to pass as an artful blur.

"Be a dear and bring the light back up?"

"Oh shit, John. You should see this."

John froze and peered out from around the eyepiece. The flashlight pointing at the floor showed tracks in the dust. At least one set of them was human, men's workboots. Then there were the others. They didn't look like footprints so much as they did smears, something shuffling over the floor. There was hesitation in these, as if it was fighting itself over every step, and a kind of epileptic instability, repeated motion that felt like record skips as drawn out in dust.

"What are these?" he asked.

"Big feet," she replied.

"Or a prankster's idea of a joke. But on whom?"

She turned in place and swept the light back over the rest of the floor. The same marks had been made over and over, wandering aimlessly, some parts of the floor all but swept clean by it.

And then there were the machines bound by wires and cables in some chaotic web, seemingly unplanned and random. Plastic and rubber sheathing snaked across the floor, tied to one another and to the bank of computers, finally binding an array of small and bent pylons, like miniature electrical towers laid out in six points around the room.

"You're getting this, right?"

"Keep the light steady. Up and down on one of those." The thought of a magic circle flashed through his mind. The wiring was haphazard but the placement of these structures was not.

The towers were asymmetrical and bent, assembled in the dark and out of the wrong pieces. But there was an underlying order to the arrangement that sent a chill down him.

"Those are live wires," he said. "Back out very carefully."

They held their breath the entire way back, time frozen but for the thrumming of their own hearts.

"What is this place?" she asked. "What are—"

"Something we're not supposed to know about, I'd say. None of this looks right. But it's not what we're after."

The grumbling roar of a poorly-tuned engine grew from outside and both stopped in their tracks.

"Quick, out the other side. There has to be another door leading out," Watkiss hissed.

"A window if we have to."

They both ran through the building, past abandoned desks and work benches, all thick with dust but all smeared half-clean. Whatever had made the tracks had been here too, exploring, investigating.

There was a muffled yell from where they'd come from, a sound of shock and dismay, more sorrow than anger. It only pushed them faster.

Watkiss became aware of a flickering hum, like a television stuck between channels but electronic guts still thrumming. The air itself began to crackle too, swimming with static, sodden with and heavy as a sudden thunderstorm. Walking through the sound consumed effort, climbing a slope that wasn't there.

"What is this? It's awful."

"Here. There's some light. Maybe we can get out through a window or something."

Turning a corner, they came to the room with the boarded-up window, dusk light leaking around an imperfect seal. They beelined towards that, dimly aware that the electric sensation in the room was stifling and cloying. There was a sour smell of wet paper gone to mildew and rot. Miscommunication leading to heartbreak and relationship decay.

Charlie pulled at an edge of the board and tried to shimmy it free. It hadn't been nailed in, rather bricks were piled up before it and the whole thing just propped up.

Behind them, a man's voice called, colored with worry. "Hello? Where are you, Lois? It's Robert. You remember me, right?"

"Help me with this!" Charlie hissed.

Watkiss lowered the camera to the ground with haste, trying not to damage it. He then reached around her, pushing a row of bricks at a time off the stack, heedless of the noise. He felt sweat and heat underneath his suit coat and wondered if he'd be able to clear the space before falling over.

Wet static filled the room, the sensation of drowning. They both felt strangely weightless, divorced from place and sense, yet still fumbling with the thing that blocked their escape.

Watkiss noticed the light first, a sort of flickering underwater thing, semitransparent flesh and bones making strange shadows. There was a sound of machines, broken ones, gears mismatched and chattering on one another, teeth clattering but no words coming from it.

"Charlie. Stop."

"LOIS!" called the man's voice from somewhere deep in the building, closer than before.

The light, flickering and muddy, moved, as if the source of it had just turned in place, responding to the man's voice.

Watkiss stood there, afraid to turn and see it. He could feel Charlie holding her breath and taut with fear next to him.

"What is it?" she whispered, pale.

"Something right there. I'm going to turn and look."

"No, don't," she said and her voice was so tight it crackled. Her fingernails bit into his arm. "It'll see us."

"It already did," he said. "It was right here."

He craned his head around and saw something just leaving the doorway. It looked like a strange double-exposure photograph, a cheap special effect like the kind that showed up in every episode of *Spaceways*, two images layered upon one another with some oil lights projected on it to make it weird. But this one had depth. It was there. He could have fallen through the spaces suggested by the ripples, fallen forever.

There were two figures superimposed on one another into a vaguely human form. It was surrounded by a nimbus of energy that rippled and swirled, sheathed in uncounted luminous streaks of capillaries pumping blood that glowed. The whole of it seemed to be continuously coalescing out of something larger and more insubstantial, a strange reverse sublimation from vapor to momentary solid, precarious but persistent.

Watkiss saw the hollows of its eyes just before it turned from him and Charlie. Those spaces were filled with guttering light, impatiently boiling, spitting luminous mist outwards and upwards. There was no sense of an actual face, only smoothly-eroded features and two eyes looking like they'd been gouged out of clay by bullets.

"Lois? Where are you?" The voice was strained, urgency clear even in its hesitation.

As the thing moved off, Watkiss was hit with the impression of multiple beings existing impossibly in the same time and space, fighting one another to even manifest there. Something else seethed beneath that, the sensation of gritted teeth, blood flushed with rage, of an impatience an intolerance for even having been made to exist.

"My god," he whispered.

"What is it?" Charlie asked. "I just saw the shape for a moment."

The winnowing light of the thing shuffled off, towards the other voice. There was no reply, only a distant clattering, clicking, of pieces not quite falling into place.

Watkiss picked up the camera and shouldered it. "Come on," he said.

"Are you crazy?" Charlie demanded. "We don't know what that thing is!"

"It's a unicorn, dear. We don't get to see them very often. Come on." He moved slowly but without hesitation through the doorway and Charlie followed as close as his own shadow.

Something moved past the boarded up window outside. It blotted out the purply dusk's light for a moment before moving further around the building with soft footpads.

The source of the light around the corner shifted and dragged around. The thing inside was moving, faster.

"Oh, Lois. Oh thank god." The man's voice was lightened in relief. "You're… Oh, no."

Watkiss wanted to stop. The heartbreak in the man's voice brought him physical pain. He felt Charlie stop and tense up a step behind.

"What the hell?" he asked.

"Keep going."

"You're not supposed to be like this." The man's voice stabbed at the both of them. "What happened to the settings? The field, it must have…" The voice tailed off to a sad echo in the laboratory. Then there was a clattering of metal on concrete, sharp and hard. "No no no no no."

Softly, under the man's voice, there was the seething chitter of the thing. Its light pulsed and swam, holding steady in place, but still betraying motion.

"I brought a cake. See? I thought it was right this time."

More jarring sounds, metal screeching.

"I BROUGHT YOU A CAKE!" The last words slurred together into something sorrowful and angry.

Watkiss edged to the doorway of the room. Indistinct whorls of light played over the interior walls pulsing and alive.

"It doesn't matter. We have to get you back in the field."

The hum started very low cycle, very quiet, growing in strength as it sped up like audio feedback building and growing into a squall of noise. Before reaching that crescendo, the sound leveled off and was punctuated with clicks and pops, the crackle of electricity. The pinkish light of the thing was pushed away by something more regular and colder.

"Nnnuh," came the reply, echoed and seemingly coming from two voices blotted into one another.

That sound made Watkiss want to fall to his knees or turn around and run, screaming into the mountains. It was not a sound made by human lips at all. It was a fumbling semblance of language. Charlie's hissed intake of breath betrayed her fear. He couldn't flee and he couldn't push forwards.

"Come on. You'll fade out."

There was no vocal reply, only the shuffling of feet around the corner. It sounded as if there were more than two people there, multiple pairs of limbs scuffing on the concrete.

Watkiss continued forward. This what they'd come here for. This was it. The unicorn was right there, getting ready to lay its head in his lap. All he had to do was to shoot the pictures. He snapped the motor on and hoped he couldn't be heard.

"We don't have much time, Lois. Please."

"knnt."

"You have to. I know it's hard. It's hard for me, too."

There was a final, definitive chirp as something scraped hard on the floor, grinding as bone on bone. The quality of the machine hum changed.

Another octave of sound kicked in. It vibrated through the room, clarifying, removing the muddiness and sense of free-floating disconnection.

Watkiss came around the corner so he could see. The man was bathed in an eerie and flat glow, but not like from the thing they'd seen earlier. Instead, it was overlapping arcs of barely-visible energy ionizing out of the air. It looked like parts of alien alphabets or ones long-lost. The arcs flickered and pulsed, not solidified. They went from a near opacity to translucence to almost not even there, pulsing and almost alive.

A tall and stoop-backed man in shabby clothes and beard worked at the bank of machines. Tape reels spun and stopped, spun and stopped, a halting flow of information as the works flowed to life. Behind him on one of the tables was an opened box, folded down flat. Inside that was a cake with frosting flowers and something that Watkiss could not see written on top. Something about that stabbed him hardest.

"'What the hammer, what the chain?'" the man recited, fueled by anxiety and worry. "'In what furnace was thy brain?'. Oh, I can never remember the rest."

"Blake," Watkiss mouthed back to Charlie who looked at him, perplexed.

"'Furnacebrain.' Why?" she asked.

Watkiss shrugged as he pulled the focus on the camera and prayed for a shot, anything. "It's a good name."

The thing, the Furnacebrain stood there behind the screen of shifting energies.

It reached for them with a limb that was single at the upper arm, but split twitchingly into two human-ish forearms, one slighter and more distinctly feminine than the other. It scratched out a semicircle on the energy field, leaving glowing flinders that dropped to the floor like wood sparks.

"'Fearful symmetry,'" the man said as he fiddled with controls. "There should be two, not one. Two. They should be split."

Watkiss recorded, panning from the man to the Furnacebrain in its cage. He realized that it was looking at him now, twin eyes of flame boring right through the camera lens into him. Watkiss felt anxiety and fear welling up inside him and more he felt anger, anger at being here, anger at his dream flailing, anger that the unicorn was being led to put its head in the lap of the maiden so that it could be killed, so that its horn could be harvested. He pulled a shot on the cake and tried to zoom in on that, but the lens wasn't good for it. It just showed the flickering and swimming light of the thing and its cage.

"John. It sees us."

The thing jabbed at the wall holding it in. Ripples and cracks cascaded out in the air as if it was stone being jackhammered. Shards of energy made solid and impotent plinked to the floor. One of the pylons sparked at the surge.

The man turned from his work to the source of the sound and then his eyes went from there to the outstretched arm of the Furnacebrain and its picking at the wall.

"What? What is it, Lois? What's got you agitated?"

His eyes went wide as he saw the reflection of the light in the camera lens and finally made out Watkiss and Charlie huddled by a shelving unit.

"Who are you! What are you doing?!" He crossed from the machine to the room.

"We're from television," Watkiss said.

"Get out of here. You're upsetting her!"

"She?" Charlie asked.

The Furnacebrain stopped in mid-tap and whipped its head to the other side of the room. Immediately after, something outside hammered on the outer door. It was something big, strong enough to make the metal safety door jump in its frame. The hammering continued.

"Oh no. It's found us," the man said as color drained from his face. "But the field. But the field was down. Oh no."

The pounding became more insistent, a tattoo of fists on metal hard enough to bend it crosswise. Furnacebrain crossed the boundary described by the energy field, getting as close to the door as it could. Its arms and legs split from one another, going from overlapping at the elbow to overlapping at the shoulder. The same happened with its legs, splitting at the hip. Even the torso and head seemed to try and rip away from its counterpart. The posture was swelled in aggression and fingers on all four hands worked in anticipation, clawing at the electrified air.

"You have to get out of here!" he shouted. "We have to-!"

"Who are you!" Watkiss shouted. "What's happening?"

"There isn't time!" the man replied. The spittle from his yell glittered for a second before hissing on the field. "There's no time! He's here!"

A final blow echoed against the door and then stopped. The room hummed. Watkiss collected himself enough to speak.

"Wha-"

Watkiss never got to finish the question. The door groaned as whatever was outside began instead of hammering, to pull on the handle. Sounding like the lead voice in an industrial chorus, the metal whined and moaned before a chunk of the door simply snapped off. Half the handle and bar mechanism came off from the outside then disappeared. The chunk clattered to the ground out of view.

Then two sets of long and misshapen fingers came in through the hole opened in the door. They came in together and unfolded gracefully like a reversed prayer. Both hands opposed, the fingers braced and pulled.

The door did not last long, shrieking as it was pulled from the frame, bolts snapping and useless.

"Get out. It'll kill you."

"John. Come on."

"Just a few seconds. I can get the shot."

The door dropped away and hit the asphalt outside with a chunking sound. Then it came through, bathed in the twin lights of the Furnacebrain and its energy cage. Another humanoid form. This one was tall, taller than the biggest man Watkiss had ever seen (a giant at the fun-fair when he was a child, seemingly big enough to reach up and pull the sun out of the sky). It had to hunch down to squeeze past the empty doorway, doing so with what felt like resignation that the world would always be too small for it. The thing was not massively muscled, instead it was gaunt (the burned body he'd seen in the seat of a crashed car, thinned by heat and flame). Its face was empty as the Furnacebrain, only it had eyes that did not glow, just black globes (pools of oil from the refinery spill of his youth). Its skin was wrinkled and rippled (raised welts and scars, raised welts and scars).

"The Scarman," Watkiss breathed "My god."

"That? That's it?" She whispered.

Cleared of the doorway, it strode into the room and all was silent but for the cycling hiss of the Furnacebrain's prison and the reassuring whirr of the camera. Watkiss tried to calculate how much film was left but had no idea now. The Scarman's steps were tentative, as if it knew something was here, something that it wanted, but not precisely where. Without a neck, it had to tilt its entire body to scan the room.

>CRAK< went the field. Furnacebrain had hit it with all four hands at once, leaving a physical mark in the energy like a bruise that glowed.

"Get out of here!" the man yelled. "Go on! Get out, Wren, you freak!"

The Scarman paid him no notice, instead walking closer to the field, where it had been attacked. Those horrible burned yet flexible fingers reached out to touch.

"This isn't fair!" the man protested. "I brought a cake. It's not supposed to be like this."

The Furnacebrain slammed bodily into the walls holding it. Its whole form shuddered, losing something fundamental in its structure, warping from the effort. The Scarman all but jumped at the sound like a child would startle.

The room itself palsied, wracked by gigantic and unseen hands, gravity itself being shaped.

"What the fuck?" Charlie asked. "My whole body, just…"

The wave of not even nausea but something beyond it wrung Watkiss, dropping him to his knees. It was as if a hand rippled through his soul, leaving behind only disruption and a wounding. Not so much an injury but the memory of an injury uncovered and experienced anew. An unhealed scar, forgotten until now.

The man bent over for a moment and then drew himself up, drooling. "Leave us alone," he cried. "It wasn't our fault."

Watkiss didn't know what that alluded to, if it was the body they'd found or something else.

The bent pylons began to glow red-orange at their extremities, all at once. Afterimages of crisscross and smoldering metal flashed behind Watkiss' closed eyes. The hum that had filled the room was faltering, crackling like tape backing up in the playback.

"It wasn't our fault. Nobody wanted this."

The Furnacebrain raged against the wall that held it, sensing weakness. All four arms flailed wildly, but only because the thing seemed unstuck. Unstuck not in place but in time, scanning back and forth like footage being scrubbed and scrubbed again until it became abstraction. It whipped its head back and forth. Soundless, it screamed with its eyes instead.

The field, all of the arcs of energy, became mismatched and misaligned. Pieces no longer interlocking, the works became something even less than abstracted shapes or words that could have been if only Watkiss knew the language. A pylon flashed from orange to red to white in seconds, cascading down to sparks and slag and a purple flash.

The machine stopped. The hum instead became an absence, a subtraction, until it disappeared. The room went dark but for the guttering glow of the creatures locked in their horrible embrace. There was no communication, not even a pretense of it as there had been before. Furnacebrain brought its rage like the only gift it would ever have to give.

"Charlie, get up. Can you get up?" Watkiss struggled to his feet and tried to help her. Tears streamed down his face but he couldn't say why. There wasn't any physical pain other than a barked knee. Something was flooding out of him, dredged from his recesses and all upwelling to his conscious mind. The unhealed scar and its source.

"Feels like my insides have been scooped out with a fork." She hauled herself up on his arm. "God, why am I crying? What's happening?"

The man who ran the lab let out a wail that Watkiss would wake up remembering for years. Something was being torn out of him, or perhaps it was a realization entering him that whatever experiment or treatment he was attempting here was not only a failure, but would never succeed. It was not only sorrow but a rage cooled down and made sharp and hard so that it could cut through anything. He stood and cried again, face veiled completely in tears so that it shone in the weird light.

The Scarman and the Furnacebrain were locked in not even savagery, but antithesis to an extent that there was room for no other feeling. The oil-slick globes of the Scarman's eyes pulsed, reflecting the glow of the other creature. It was fully stoked, all of its energy blazing. The twitching thing reached forward with its face in a weirdly human stance of defiance.

"You are nothing and I am free," Furnacebrain said in a voice that seemed to echo out of depths far greater than itself, hauled up from a horrible vault of pain forged into hate. "I am free of the prison and I will be free of you."

Two of its arms grappled with those of the Scarman and the two other clawed at its opponent's body, shrieking as it did, gouging out something dark and tarry.

If the Scarman hurt, it did not show in any meaningful way, eyes staring ahead dumbly.

"You are stupid." Its voice echoed weirdly in the closed room, too big for the place. "You are stupid and I was here before."

Pivoting off one foot, Furnacebrain turned in place, dragging the other monster off its feet. Then it spun, hurling the huge body across the room. The Scarman flew until it collided with the bank of machines. Activated, tape reels spinning spastically. On others, the casings were wrecked, insides exposed. Machines sparked and smoked. The Scarman dragged himself to his feet, weaving drunkenly.

"And I will be the only one left," the burning thing said from the awful hollows of its mouth.

Strobing bursts flashed from the failing pylons and power cables burst into flame, lines of insulation like melting pythons, serpentine infernos.

"No, Lois. Not those!" the man, whoever he was, shrieked and pulled at his hair. "The anchoring module!" He spun from the debris of his machines to the writhing figure, limbs melting into one another and then apart, horrible coals of eyes burning.

"Little fool. She is not here. There is only-"

The thing flickered and warped, as if drawn in sand and wiped away momentarily, features jumping and twisting in some unseen wind. Its eyes continued to burn hatefully, sparking just the once. There was no fear of recognition, just anger that something was being taken away.

"Fix it!" Furnacebrain ordered, words slurred into an angry howl. "Fix it or you will-" Its body shook again, or was it that the whole world around it shuddered?

"I'd need years," the attendant said. "It wasn't supposed to be like this. I brought you cake."

"Fix me!" The burning creature took two quick steps and picked up the man by his jacket, lifting him bodily and shaking.

A thin and blackened hand closed around one of Furnacebrain's, gently. The other took the man by the back of his coat and held him firmly. Its body twitched and flowed, bending in ways that no body, not even this one, was meant to. It was silent, glaring with its terrible eyes, eating everything it could with its sight. The steaming flicker surrounding it smeared and bled, dripping away before turning to vapor. It was stuck between channels, between states, neither here nor there, neither being nor not.

"Lois, please, come back," the man begged.

The Scarman gently put him on his feet.

"It's me. It's Robert. Come back."

The Furnacebrain or Lois or whatever it congealed upon itself, shedding bits of energy in crackles that oozed and dripped. Then its body bent to a supplicant form and kept going, falling to the floor. The twitching and energy discharge stopped. The eerie glow of the melted pylons showed only a hardened cinder of something that could have been bones. The whole mess of it steamed.

Robert knelt before it and wept like he was bleeding out his very life. Slowly and patiently, the Scarman lifted a hand and put it on the man's shoulder.

Tears welled up in Watkiss' eyes and streamed down his face, burning as they dried. He couldn't say where it came from, whether it was the monster that had died or the monster who reassured the man. It was the most human thing he'd ever seen. He turned back to Charlie whose eyes were red and tear-lit, too.

"I'm happy. I'm sad. I'm a mess," she said.

"And you call me the romantic," he said, drying her eyes with a gentle swipe of his thumb.

The melted cables and pylons flickered with live flame and that began to spread, licking across anything paper or wood left in the place. The Scarman shook Robert gently and pointed him to the door, lifting him effortlessly with his other arm. As it strode across the room, it stopped to look at both Watkiss and Charlie, staring with oily black eyes that reflected the flames. It beckoned with its free hand, curling a finger towards itself.

Watkiss knew that this is what Marky Dupree saw under the bridge, this horrible thing that had nonetheless saved his life. A shiver ran through Watkiss, recognition of a soul inside a withered husk, a human life lived out in a vessel of misery. The sensation was divine and unmediated as it coursed through him.

Then it carried Robert out through the shattered doorway, dancing just a little to fit through. Watkiss took Charlie's hand and took her through it as well.

Outside, they could hear the sound of smooth feet over the broken scrabble of the hillside and the sound of Robert weeping as he stared back into the building, flames licking out the open door.

"Happy birthday, Lois."

Watkiss wanted the story more than he'd wanted anything, but seeing the hurt of that man and feeling his own wounds unhealed but revealed still fresh, he couldn't bring himself to ask the first question. And neither could Charlie.

The last few seconds of the video flickered out in the edit bay and the three of them sat in the dark. John coughed on his cigarette.

"Who else has seen this?" Charlie asked. "Anyone? Who fucked us?"

"Shrug just brought these back. He said it's just the one reel. That's the only reason they let him have it." John stubbed out his cigarette. "It was wrecked so they let us have it."

"It's not a total loss," Fabian said. "We kind of have a shot of an empty lab. And that thing at the door. A few seconds of that. And two minutes of abstract, psychedelic weird."

"Oh, and the cake," she said with acid. "We fucking got the cake."

"Robert would have been very happy with that."

"Roll it back. I want to see it again." She gritted her teeth together hard enough to hear.

"You're going to cost yourself a fortune at the dentist, dear."

"How can you be so calm?" She slammed the console enough to make the ashtray jump. "How can you be so fucking calm?! The footage is ruined!"

"It's not ruined. We have you outside the lab and the lab and…" He pointed at the monitor. "And we have this."

The image on the screen was blown out and reversed, with only the vaguest sense of a humanoid figure at the center of the inexpert shot.

"Furnacebrain doesn't film," Watkiss said. "It wrecks film."

"That's still a stupid name," Fabian said. "Won't catch."

"Doesn't matter. It's not going to catch. There's nothing to hook it to."

The video rolled and there was an inverted afterimage of a figure and some arc-shaped distortions moving over one another.

"It looks like Kandinsky on Quaaludes," Charlie said, despairing. "Maybe we can narrate over it."

"Narrate what? Convince people that they're seeing something when they're seeing a bright nothing?" Watkiss rubbed his temples. "We got the doorway right?"

Fabian rolled it back to the hands sneaking into the fissured door and ripping it back off its hinges. The weird emanations from the Furnacebrain made the image crawl and trail, emulsions disturbed in the exposure.

"Kinda?" he said. "Look, you can tell those are hands. And you can tell that's a body coming through."

"It's all bright and psychedelic. Maybe we can use it. But it'd be better in shadows and sort of a suggestive darkness. That sells better for the audience."

"Beggars can't be choosers."

"Okay, fine. Then let this be the reel that saves *Quest4*. Let's get Ken in for rewrites on the dialog and see if we can put this to bed."

"This won't change any minds, J."

"It doesn't have to. That's the beauty."

Fabian shrugged and stared making marks on the tape for ins and outs, working together a flow, or at least a suggestion of one.

"It's not fair! We saw it! We were right there!" Charlie protested. "Nobody's going to believe this."

John looked at her and said "We already believed it. Every person we've talked to on camera was braver than you right now. Every one of them. They opened up to us and told us what happened, where and who they were when they saw the unicorn."

"UFO, John."

"It's an expression."

SUICIDE JEWELRY

The first thing Lucy did when she got to Los Angeles was to fix her lipstick. She lay down on the sun-warm sidewalk and got in close to the hubcap of the parked Porsche to check her face in the distorted reflection. The black and severe hair still caught her by surprise. Her lipstick matched at least. She worked it a moment, filling out the curve in the pitted chrome. People flowed around her without even a perceptible change in pace as easily as a river around rock.

Most of them.

"Do you mind?" growled a pinched biddy dressed for Sunday.

Maybe it even was. Lucy wasn't sure.

"Not at all," she replied without taking her eyes off the warped reflection. She closed her lipstick and pocketed it.

Sunday schoolmarm harrumphed a reply that sounded more like dry phlegm and trotted off. Lucy stuck out her tongue to the reflection, almost touching the hubcap with the tip. Then she coughed at the smell of the city and gutter damp with something that couldn't have been rain this time of year. She pushed up off the sidewalk and dusted her palms clean, clutched close by the reckoning that she didn't know anyone over here. There had been rumors that folks came to LA, sure. There was always talk about it. Rochelle and her boyfriend swore they'd make it someday. Not so much as a postcard or word up the grapevine about her. Or anyone else who'd left home to come here. In more than a year.

But at least they'd done more than talk about going and actually did it. More juice in that than a hundred brave words over beers and Stoli. They'd done it.

Just like Lucy Emerson AKA Lorissa Licht had. Too many nights in shitty bars screaming her lungs out backed up by a band that was barely more enthusiastic than the drunks and deadites in the crowd. All the lights and fog in the world couldn't make people care, so she saved on stage effects by using those caged work lights, scattering them so they burned there like fallen and guttering comets. She held one in her off hand to light her face from below and turn her mouth not into an instrument but an opening to a smoking Gehenna.

It had almost worked, too. She'd built a small following that would crowd the stage no matter what dingy dive she played in and she'd played them all, gotten stiffed in them all, barely clawed past the hollow gaze of the folks who'd given up life to drink there.

But she wasn't going to get any further than that unless she struck out for bigger places. Or at least other territories with unknown pleasures.

Trouble with the unknown was being unsure where to start. The crowd continued past her and she took their measure, eyeing the street fashions and how clothes hung differently, folks clutching cups of fast food restaurants she mostly recognized, but didn't quite remember. Unfamiliar cars sputtered and groaned past her on Broadway, all of them spitting out smog and she wondered how anyone could actually live like this.

She was going to have to learn how to. It almost was home but not, the differences catching her like splinters in her fingertips. She looked at the reflection of her now-raven hair in a square-cut bob, but for a fingers-width that fell past her shoulders out front. She looked at it and was caught outside of her own expectation.

"Right. This is who I am," she said to the reflection. Then she fixed on the silhouetted figure who hovered off to her left. He'd been standing and watching as long as she had herself. Only his eye was hungrier, more approving but somehow even less believing.

She'd figured there were going to be weirdos but had hoped she'd have gotten more than five minutes before she'd had to deal with one. Without thought, she squared her shoulders under the surplus trench coat she'd dyed bruise purple. The words kein zuhause außer hier were painted out in tight blocks of white strokes. She tightened her fist over a set of keys that she'd never use again.

"Look," Lucy said. She turned in place and faced the guy "Go find someone else to creep on!"

He didn't take the step back like she'd wanted. He was motionless but for his eyes. They went wide and green like he'd seen Marilyn Monroe walking the streets in a nighty. Shock overpowered everything else, but she saw a flash of an abstract sort of wanting something beneath it. Maybe not for her exactly, but for a lost something. Brief and terrible recognition took over after, coming through like makeup now wiped off.

"Oh my god." Baby mice weren't as quiet.

"What?" She tightened her fist and shook it a little.

"Has anyone ever told you that you're a dead ringer for Lux Nova, the singer?" He said the name like it was one Lucy should have known. But there were lots of singers out there. That's what kept things going – an endless supply of girls willing to do whatever to get ahead.

"I'd be lying if I said 'yes.'" She shifted her weight but did not release the keys from her right hand. "Who is Lux Nova?"

"Was," he said.

Lucy imagined that he was dressed fashionably, leather suit jacket but no fringe or beadwork, turtleneck sweater that was too tight and pants that were the same. She thought she saw a scar or welt atop the collar on his left side. It looked itchy, like something picked at and never let to heal.

"She was almost a big thing."

"That's too bad. She quit singing?" Lucy tried not to think too deeply about quitting herself.

"She, ah, quit everything." His expression went from reckoning to a over-cooked dread, graying his complexion.

"You talk like you knew her."

"I thought I did," he said. "Toby." He extended his hand. "Toby Farmer."

Lucy looked at the hand as if it were holding a still-gasping goldfish in it.

"I'm very sorry I stared at you. That was rude." He pulled his hand back, dead slow. "I was just caught off-guard."

Lucy let go of the keys and stuck her hand out where his had been. "Lucy Emerson. I just got into town and am wiped out. I didn't mean to snap."

"You meant to, but it's okay. I deserved it." He took her hand and his was cool and dry. "It's good to meet you."

"Same." She withdrew and wondered what his story was. He vibed producer or agent, but not one of the successful ones. One of the hungry ones who breathed in air and breathed out promises. But Lucy could breathe promises too. And it might be good to have a friend in a strange town. At least for a little while. "Look, you can make it up to me if you want. Buy me a drink?"

Roaring and backfiring, a couple of bikes rolled down the boulevard, bearded and grimy leather-clad riders whooping wildly. Toby didn't even flinch at it.

"Yeah, sure. The Criss-Cross is right across the intersection there." He pointed past a tall, adobe-colored brick building older than Lucy's grandparents, to a corner lot across Second Street and a once-tony bar that had seen better days.

Lucy though about day drinking and must have made a face unconsciously. She mopped up her expression.

He shrugged, all wobbly. "I mean, it's a little early, but yeah. Yeah."

"Delightful." She patted the fender of the Porsche and said "Thanks for being my mirror," then followed Toby over to the blinking red neon of the Criss-Cross Club.

Lux Nova was a singer who'd made the rounds, going through backing bands like Janis Joplin had gone through whiskey bottles, draining them dry and tossing the empties into a pile that littered the better part of Sunset Boulevard. That was, if you took Toby's recounting at face value. Lucy didn't have a good reason not to. When he talked about Nova, he wasn't talking about an act that he'd lost by getting signed to a better, more-connected agent. He'd lost a limb, just managed to hide that fact until he got a couple old-fashioned in him. And the bartender had poured like he was mad at the boss.

Nova finally made a connection with a band and reworked material, somewhere between punk anthems spat in the face of lined cops and liturgical material meant to harrow and kiss damnation. She would transfix. She would shatter. And if she felt it that night, she'd rebuild all that was broken. But it wasn't a thing that could be put on vinyl or tape. It was all magic that happened live. Nova burned like her name and you can't hold onto something burning for long, Toby joked.

Then he breathed in through broken ribs like he was about to spit blood. In the red cast of the little bar, his tears were sanguine. Lucy pulled out a ragged and lace-trimmed handkerchief, usually a stage prop, and wiped his face with it. If he knew he was crying, he wouldn't admit it.

"She was really something, huh?"

"More like everything. I just wish… I didn't know how troubled she was. Or I didn't want to admit it."

"So, what, she left? She signed to Harper or maybe Death?"

Toby blinked. "What?"

"You know, another label. I figured…"

"Oh no. Lux Nova killed herself."

"Holy shit."

"Sorry. She OD'd," he added as an afterthought or correction, dabbing over the misstatement. "I knew she used even after I gave it up. I just didn't know how bad it was. Heroin."

"Sure," Lucy lied. "I just thought coke was what the cool kids were doing."

Toby shook his head without laughing. "Lux didn't do anything because it was <u>cool</u>. She had a mission. Think she was saving souls one night at a time. Just she needed to work on hers and never found the time or inclination."

Lucy put her hand atop his, resting on his thigh. "Hey, I'm sorry. I didn't know. I figured you were maybe her agent or something. Nothing more than professional."

He swirled the last of the bourbon-washed ice in the glass where it looked like molten glass cooling. Then he drained the drink and chewed the ice thoughtfully.

"I didn't either. Not until she was gone." He flexed his fingers under hers.

"Did it happen long ago?"

He stiffened like there was something bitter in the ice. "A couple years. There are people who still scrawl her name on lampposts and call in for 'Never Forget' on KXLU or even KROQ. We got that single out the week before she threw it all away." His hand tensed into a fist and he shot forward, leaning on the bar hard. "Hey, can we get another round here?"

The bartender watched him with his good eye and took a moment to get moving.

"Please," Toby added. "Just, please."

The bartender nodded and grabbed the Wild Turkey bottle like he was going to perform some violence with it.

"I better not," Lucy said.

"Then watch me drink. Or just talk to me while I do."

"You know I don't just go into bars with dudes, right?"

"Don't worry. Neither do I."

The fresh drinks arrived, looking more like grenadine in the jukebox light.

"So," Toby asked after a hefty belt. "What do you do, anyways?"

She shrugged and shrank in place. "Do? I just got here. I don't have a job."

"Yeah, but you planned to have one, right?" His skin glowed, but at least he wasn't weeping. "Movies? TV? Dancer?"

Lucy tried not to be hurt by him not asking whether she wanted to sing or not, especially after talking about Lux Nova for the last hour and she'd been thinking about how Lux was doing exactly what Lucy had been trying to. Like there was a space already cut out for her, a road already paved and waiting, just needing someone to walk it.

"I'm a singer," she said, after taking a hit from the drink. It went down hot.

"You're a what?" Toby asked, leaning in like the bar noise was too much for her to get over.

"A singer," she said. Louder this time.

"What?" he all but yelled.

"A SINGERRRRR!" Lucy projected the shout, filling her chest with it, not for tone-shaping, but for raw output.

He laughed and then she did, both slipping out of themselves for a moment. She was just someone new in town and he was just a guy who'd remembered to be nice to her. After being weird to her, but at least he'd tried.

"Yeah, I figured you were. Just wanted to hear you project." He took his drink to half with a slug. "What sort of stuff you sing? You don't look ratty enough to do punk. Not angular enough for new wave."

"Maybe I'm just dressed to be out and not for the goddamn stage."

"You wanna be famous, you know you gotta be ready to do the stage face all the time. You gotta put it on and keep it on. So what do you wanna do?"

"Scary shit." Lucy rolled the drink between her two open palms, welling the condensation at its base. "I wanna be a vampire."

She snatched up the drink and took it down then wiped her mouth with the back of her wrist. "I want to shout the truth in someone's face and scare them to death with it."

"Tall order."

"I've gotten the regulars at the Nile Club to give up seats they've held since the bar opened. I figure that's a start."

"Maybe it is at that." He studied his drink but did not finish it.

***

Toby popped the cassette into the deck at the back of the rehearsal space. The walls were ratty off-white, probably had never been clean, scuffs and marks worn into the paint by frustrated or bored or triumphant musicians over the space's history.

"You own this place or what?" Lucy asked, setting her bag down. It lay on the industrial carpet like something coughed up by the sea.

"My friends Gary and Ty use this for their band. And I know the guy who runs the place."

"They're not gonna mind?" Lucy asked. "I don't want 'em just bursting in in the middle of this."

"I'm not asking you to take off your clothes, Lucy. I just want to hear you sing."

Something turned around inside her, whispering that this was a mistake and she knew it was. The same thing that had talked her out of shows in the past or even coming out of that little room in the big house she'd rented. The little voice that said no.

"You wish."

"Figure of speech." The hatch on the tape machine closed with a plastic CLACK. "I'm not going to mess with the settings or anything. Just go over and let it rip." He pointed at the stand-up microphone.

Lucy slid the mic down to her level and stood in front of it and froze. She tried to think about what to sing that would make an impression that she could even remember after a couple drinks on an empty stomach. Her skin crawled with worry. She tried to climb over the no in her mind.

"We've got all afternoon." He was joking and not.

She breathed loud enough that it was probably going right to tape, then she let her breaths get deeper, like she was falling not into sleep, but nightmare. Each one ended a little more ragged, with a twitching at the end. Then she drew in a final breath and held it.

That thing you gave me
Won't ever forget
That thing, going to the grave
I'll always regret
I'll always regret
I'll always regret

Then her voice rose to a scream, one unfamiliar even to herself and she spat the rest of the lines to her own song "Black Gifts" but like she'd never sung it before. She filled it with fear. Here she'd just come to this stupid city with no friends and no plan, desperate to go anywhere other than where she'd been, to leave the familiar behind. She breathed and shouted her song into something new, soaring then growling then begging then holding a blade that could cut through anything and that blade was her voice.

Lucy finished the song and stood there panting for breath even as the back of her throat was bubbling hot tar. She'd given something that she didn't even know she had.

She looked up over at him and he stared back at her, eyes wide as if he'd been walking through a glittering trainwreck, energy and power and shattering devastation unmaking a thing and leaving beautiful debris in its wake.

"I might've fucked up the words some," she said with a soft rasp. "I just lost myself there."

"I'd say more like you found yourself." He stabbed the controls with an extended finger. "Holy shit. Where'd you say you were from?"

"I didn't." And she didn't have an easy way to say it, either, so she left it dead.

"Well, you're here. And if you can sing like that four nights a week, maybe we can get that somewhere."

"LA is just fine for a start."

"LA is not going to be ready for what hit it." He looked at her, flensing past the skin and going deeper. "You got a stage name?"

"I'd gone under Lorissa Licht. Kinda goth-y." She cleared her throat and tried to hum some of the numbness out.

"And?" The expression on his face bled to bored.

She tried to hide behind the mic stand. "Well, that was it. I was worried about the material more than the whole persona."

"Hmm." He hit the eject on the tape and maybe it was all over just like that.

"You're acting like you've got a better idea."

"Maybe I do." The cassette went into a case and then into a jacket pocket as easily as a lost business card.

"Well, what kind of idea?"

"You know why people dress up and put on makeup and do their hair weird, right? All that punk stuff?" He crossed his arms before him.

"To stand out. To be individual."

His head shook slowly. "That's not enough. It's to make an image. To pretend to be someone else, something else, way bigger than themselves.

Then the audience tacks the legend onto that. Ain't nobody wants to build a myth on just a regular Joe or Jane. They want something bigger. They crave it. They think they can control it, not knowing they themselves made it."

"Okay, mister psychology. So I work on an image." She waved her hand from her hair down. "I'm more than halfway there. And I'm not even in makeup."

"Right. But who are you going to make yourself up to be?"

"I dunno. I'll figure something out."

"How about we make you up so that nobody could look away." He stepped in closer, quicker than she could react. "Then people drop their defenses. They let you in. And then you can melt them with that goddamn voice of yours." His eyes rested on her throat.

"Okay, but who would that be?"

"This might sound weird, but how about a revival act?"

She shook her head, not getting it yet.

***

Lucy had thought that he'd just been shining her on, that whole thing about Lux Nova and her being dead ringers. But once back at his place in the lower reaches of the Hollywood hills, looking through the collection of flyers and photos and posters he'd kept from managing Lux, the resemblance was more than casual. It clawed its way over to uncanny. Every page turned chiseled out another little detail that Lucy couldn't shake.

Lux Nova could live again. Why not? What hell could hold her? What heaven would keep her prisoner and not let the destroying angel fly free? The legend wrote itself and ran the headlines.

Lucy traced Lux's profile in an 8 by 10 glossy and a chill crawled down her spine on a thousand tiny little legs, each of them topped by a little prickling hook that caught and dug. She wanted to throw the book in the fireplace. She wanted to keep looking. Another page turned and there Lux was, only half-draped in flowing white cloth, one breast exposed as she grasped a spear and brandished it across her frame. It was more than the face. Lucy recognized the body and all its markers, but for a weird scar a few inches below her own navel.

She had a cluster of moles across the small of her back that she was acutely conscious of and thankful that no pictures seem to have captured Lux from that angle.

Toby came in with two glasses of wine to join the bagged hamburgers that sat on the low table before her.

"Red for beef, right? I'm sure the burgers are mostly beef."

"I never drink… wine," She said with an accent then a giggle, mostly to distract herself from the weird sensation of seeing pictures that could have been her being the performer she could have been if only she was brave enough. The space between her and Lux disappeared for a moment and Lucy felt prickly dry ice fog and the shouts of fans who demanded damnation and release.

She caught herself with a start and grabbed the glass, taking a big enough drink to make her gasp.

"Hey, you okay?" Toby asked.

"Yeah, sorry." She coughed onto the back of her hand then rubbed it against her t-shirt. "I'm just really tired. Been a longer day than I thought."

He sat on the couch next to her and it creaked audibly. "Estate sale find. I just love old stuff, odd stuff. Got a history."

"Might even be haunted?" She took a second drink, this one more measured.

"No such thing as ghosts. Not even in LA. But hey, if you can convince someone to pay more because something's haunted? That's all right by me. Elvis acts do big money. People want to see the same thing remade over and over."

She stared at the page open before her and ate the image up, eyes blue and wide. "You really think that I can do this? I mean, the voice stuff, I can sing like that 45 you played." She tapped the picture with Lux and the spear, Lux the Impaler, and sighed. "I don't know about this."

He slipped a laugh. "You're kidding me, right? It's like I'm sitting right next to her again, looking at you."

Lucy felt herself freeze, despite the bolts of wine. "You and she weren't…"

Toby caught himself between breaths. "Not like you think." He took a very focused sip of wine and tilted the glass back, legs sketched out in the kitchenette fluorescents. "Loving her was like loving a tornado. Good way to get ground into the dirt."

"But you did anyways, right?"

"Yeah. I did." He sought out her eyes. "This fucks things up, huh?"

"What things? I'm not planning on sleeping with you. You're cute, but don't get ahead of yourself."

"Even wanting to be around me, much less letting me manage you." He set the glass down roughly but didn't spill it.

"No, that's fine, Toby. I'm just trying to get a handle on this." She opened the bag and pulled out the first of the foil-wrapped hamburgers, still warm but cooling quickly. She held it out, waiting for him to reach out. "But you bought drinks and this fancy dinner and you at least act well-connected enough to fool me."

"I appreciate your confidence." He took the food from her and she reached back into the bag immediately after.

She waved around with her free hand. "I don't know this whole world," she said as she pulled out her dinner and tore into the foil. Something told her that she shouldn't have said it so she focused on the fast food.

"What?"

She took a bite, unable to wait any longer, not remembering how long ago her last meal had been. "LA. The music scene." The bite went down all corners somehow.

His expression softened some. "Okay. Hey, it's okay to be worried about this. It's a world of difference going from… where <u>did</u> you say you came from?"

"Lawrence, Kansas." It was a lie but only she knew that.

"Holy cow. Yeah. That's nowhere."

"Hey. There's a college there. It's not all wheat farms."

"Sure."

"There's soybeans too. And some corn, despite what Iowa would tell you." She took another quick gulp of wine. She tried to keep the lies neatly stacked.

"Okay, so it's a place." He leaned in some. "But it's not LA, is it?"

"Nope. After being here a bit, I can say that it's like no place I've ever been. And, I'm sorry if I sound like an ungrateful asshole. This all just happened kinda fast. I mean, I was on the Greyhound this morning, stopping in Vegas I think. I'm barely caught up on that." She stretched the tension out of her back, torqued in ways that she didn't know had been possible.

He watched the quick contortions, maybe calculating the curve of skin and flesh beneath the ragged black and denim.

"I'm not ready to deal with being Lux Nova and my damage and maybe making your dream come true."

"Look, let's just do no pressure, okay? Sleep on it and we figure stuff out." He finally took a bite into the drippy cheese and burger.

Lucy chewed the bite in her mouth, finally tasting it. She nodded and swallowed. "You know a place where I can stay?"

"Other than here."

She nodded. "No pressure. You just said it yourself."

"You don't believe I'm a perfect gentleman?"

"There aren't any," she said grimly. "Not where I came from and I'm sure as hell not here."

He leaned back on the couch and it creaked like a lab door from a horror movie. "Good. You're getting smart. Even if you walked right into a bar with a guy you didn't know today."

"I didn't drink that much."

"And you ended up in his apartment."

The food boiled in her stomach. He was right. And she'd just fallen right for it. "Not for the night. Besides, he's kinda cute. Even if he's a little broken up over falling in love with a genuine star. Just what I saw in the photos gave me chills."

"You got no idea. And I'll tell you a little more. After I call my sister make sure you can crash at her pad." He watched for a response. She saw that out in the open, that he'd let her right off the hook she'd climbed onto.

"That'd be very kind."

"You say that before seeing the place. It's downtown. I mean, worse than you've seen already. But she's cool."

"I don't know how to repay you for any of this."

"I'll think of something." Then he smiled at her.

"Don't do that," she said. "I was almost believing you were a nice guy, then you pull this."

"Okay, twenty percent." His smile went billboard bright. It was a good one, charming and disarming enough that Lucy wondered if she was wrong or right about him or even wanted to be. The answer was definitely yes.

"Standard terms?"

"Standard as it comes." He stood up, leaving the half-eaten burger on the table, far away from any of the precious memorabilia and walked over to the phone hanging on the wall with its weirdly coiled cable.

***

The sidewalk glittered in the slanting morning sunlight, catching edges of broken glass or shreds of Styrofoam containers. Industrial malaise and shutdown had given way to the crush of organic decay as pieces left out of the machine broke down. Seeing it even in the glamour of morning magic hour, Lucy was glad they'd come in at night. The neighborhood was feral and only now going through the first stages of being tamed, still squirming out of any attempt at domestication. Some of the buildings were being refurbished, encased in scaffolding and draped plastic like a dirty chrysalis. Soon it would cleaned up and made safe for money, but not today and not for a while.

"Morning, Lucy," Toby said as he met her outside the security door. He all but vibrated in place barely containing an eagerness that Lucy recognized in herself.

Someone cadaver-thin and dirt-wreathed slept on the sidewalk. At least, Lucy hoped he was sleeping. "Yeah… morning." She fixed on the figure and wondered why this was even allowed.

"Don't do that. Nobody likes to be stared at."

"If they're dead they don't care."

"Staring at the dead is just plain rude." He half-turned and indicated a path around the blockage on the sidewalk. "Yeah, just one of the downsides of goddamn Reagan shutting down all the mental hospitals. Sheriffs just dump people here in downtown where nobody important gives a shit."

The thought of asking him who Reagan was surfaced in her and she pushed it away. Maybe he was just a loudmouth actor like the one she knew.

"This place is terrible." She pulled her jacket around herself, despite the morning warming early.

"It's not so bad, once you get used to it." He led her up the street to his Buick, squatting heavy on the asphalt. "I'll get you to a better place than this." He leaned hard on the door to get it to open.

"So, anywhere?"

"Hush. We're going to Pasadena."

Lucy sat and fumbled for the seatbelt and quit.

"You're not belting up?" he asked as his clicked.

"I've come all this way. What's a seat belt gonna matter?"

"You wanna die?"

"Nah. Don't care." She couldn't help but laugh at herself.

"How punk."

"Punk rock isn't supposed to care. Would Lux Nova worry about a fucking seatbelt?"

"That's the spirit." He cranked the engine and it gnashed under the hood before turning over.

"What's in Pasadena, anyways?"

"There's some pawn-." He stopped and re-comported himself. "Antique shops there. There's some things for your stage image that we'll need, and I'm pretty sure we'll find them there."

"What are we looking for? Props?"

"Suicide jewelry."

"Now that's a band name."

The groaning turned to a chugging heave as the Buick pulled away from the litter-strewn sidewalk, leaving a lingering gray cloud behind. Lucy didn't speak for a long while as the car lagged up Hill Street to Arroyo Seco, just watching the ragged panoply of downtown give way to something that looked like a place folks sent picture postcards from. That she might send back home.

***

It wasn't an antique shop but a junk store, detritus of misfortune and chains of bad decisions all coming to an end in the debris of this place. Lucy could smell the desperation soaked into the walls like those roadway motels that never got cleaned out quite well enough. Ill-formed plans and schemes bleeding out somewhere in the desert, leaving a scent that clung to the carpets and the plaster all mildewed and complaining.

The woman behind the counter wore a smart suit, fitting her tightly as a custom coffin. The silver and black brooch shone on the choker she wore, a filigreed gothic tick. Its legs were bent like fishhooks, ends biting down but not drawing blood. She had Marlene Dietrich's perilous cheekbones and lazily-closed eyes above them.

"Oh, back so soon, Toby?" she breathed. She didn't look at Lucy at all.

"Just wait here," Toby said, leaning in to whisper. "She's very particular. Go ahead and look around. But. Don't. Touch. Anything."

Lucy swallowed a shudder. "I can just wait outside." The flop-sweat smell was in her nose and mouth. She couldn't escape it, so she tried cutting herself loose with an excuse.

"No, it's okay. Stay in the store." He patted her on the shoulder like he might his kid sister then strode over.

Lucy ate her disappointment at this sudden boundary. Maybe he was just flirting with the clerk to get a better deal. Either way, his charm turned up.

"Good morning, Felicia, you're looking lovelier than ever." His voice started up high then slid down to something more friendly and conspiratorial.

Lucy couldn't hear Felicia's replies or even see her, blocked completely by Toby's back. She turned and scanned the shelves, piles of old hi-fi equipment with bays of dusty television sets below that, even giant radio sets some with tubes visible in their open backs like misshapen light bulbs. One of them was crowned with a sound horn, organic curves suggestive of a lily or some other flower, an orchid maybe. She racked her brain as she tried to remember.

The opening of the horn flew wide and dark, lightless within. Faint texture of brushed bronze suggesting clouds and weather in the light, a funnel storm. Something stirred inside, skittering like static foaming over a distant ocean shore. Lucy leaned in closer, hearing only the disintegrating signal whispering out of it. Phonemes bubbled through, tongue-speaking and meaningless, but almost almost almost forming something. Something spoken and urgent. She placed her ear close to the opening, holding her breath for utter silence.

Something was there. Hazy and indistinct as the city through smog. Shrouded. Harder corners scratched through, words coalescing. Words without meaning, only sounds and sounds and-

"Becoming is harder than you think."

Lucy felt something thin and hard, like impossibly large spider legs or a fingernail touching the outside of her ear. It reached out from the depths of the horn. It dragged across her skin, catching on the fine hairs there. The touch was not claiming, rather probing, testing, marking a boundary, tracing that.

She screamed and jumped back, almost falling onto the keys of a gap-toothed electric organ straight from the pages of Sears and Roebuck. She caught herself but her heart was still shrieking in her chest.

"Fuck," she whispered. "What the fuck."

The opening was black and empty and too big. Maybe she could have imagined something like the thinnest fingers imaginable, only with too many joints and gray skin, just moving to a repose in the dark, only a glimpse allowed.

"Excuse me!?" Felicia barked. "Don't touch unless you're buying!"

"I'm fine," Lucy said. "It's fine!" she said, louder. She tried to will the grimace from her face, but it felt etched in.

"Hey Lucy, come on over. She's got something to show us."

Lucy stared at the radio and wanted to smash it open, to find whatever was curled up inside. But she couldn't afford to, and doubted that Toby could either.

"I'm watching you," she whispered to the radio and that was the only sound in the room.

"There's something in that thing," she said to Felicia in her coffin-suit on the other side of the counter. "Something."

Felicia stared with a pitying distance, forced to acknowledge Lucy directly.

"Mice, dear. Those old radios are excellent nest sites, provided they're not plugged in." She then stood up and began to walk around the back side of the counter, fingers up and beckoning that they follow.

She came out to the main showroom and sauntered them over to a corner laid out in almost a serene fashion. It was painfully clean and open in comparison to the rest of the place, where junk and kipple was stacked haphazardly and allowed to gather vermin. Here there were glass cases well-lit and laid with beds of midnight-blue velvet, texture so lush that it demanded touch that the glass denied.

Lucy realized that she was not choking, but she was short of breath and cool. Like she'd just risen from a cold pool. Whatever it was didn't seem to bother Toby or Felicia. This was finality, submission and enervation and it was everywhere.

"Here are the pieces you asked about," Felicia said in a cool tone.

Toby's eyes scanned over the assemblage, quick as a burning oil slick.

"This is what you were talking about?" Lucy asked. "The suicide jewels?"

"Suicide jewelry," Felicia corrected with a sour note. "Some other sellers won't talk about it. They're old-fashioned and superstitious. Not me. If it's what the customer wants, well I aim to deliver." She tapped her red fingernails on the glass and they resounded far louder than they should have been. "If you can pay."

"I can pay," Toby said. "If you have what we discussed. I don't see it."

"Patience." She pressed a button and the trays slid up and backwards on a conveyor belt while a motor droned. "Ah, here."

The machine stopped and Toby gasped when he saw them. Lucy pushed to get a better look into the case. Before them lay the collection of a flattened ovals of black and teardrop-shaped pieces of carved glass. They were joined by a thin silver chain, one that seemed too frail to bear the weight it bore. At the back of the chain rested a clasp shaped into two interlocked hands, each one forming a circle. A heart-shaped red charm hung at the bottom of the chain, but not a cartoon outline, an anatomical human heart carved of thick ruby glass the color of the Criss-Cross club's neon sign. Felicia took the necklace out of the case with some ceremony and held it up so the light could shine through. This revealed a black scar, opaque and impenetrable, cut through the heart shape.

Joining the necklace was a pair of earrings, more black teardrops bent by some unknown gravity. There were also bracelets, these made of interlocking beads the same color as the red glass of the heart.

"Sold only as a set," Felicia warned.

Lucy's heart jumped at these. She'd seen them before, but only last night, in the photos from Lux Nova's performances. These jewels had rested on her neck, pierced her, hung on her wrists like hesitation wounds. They were thrilling. They made her want to throw up.

"I'm amazed you have these. The last place spat at me when I brought them up."

"You went to Willoughby, didn't you? The person who sold me these told me where they got them. You could have called me first, Toby." Her smile was a joyless slice.

"How long did they own them?" Toby's eyes were wide with something like greed.

"An entire week, I think. I knew they would be back quickly. Night terrors or something. But, caveat emptor," Felicia said with a grin that was too much tooth against slash of red lipstick.

Lucy wanted to smash the glass and take them all. She wanted to run out of the store and out of this place, never to return. Both extremes pulled at her so hard she felt herself fraying. Coming here was a mistake. There was talk about that, how things weren't always great when you ran away. Sometimes you were unlucky enough to find exactly what you were looking for. But she'd never believed it.

"Hey, stay with me." His hand felt heavy as a dropped sandbag.

She shrugged out from underneath it. "Yeah, I'm fine. Just… Are we going to do this or what?" Her eyes flicked from his to the jewels and lingered there before coming back.

"Someone's impatient," he said and began to raise his hand, as if to stroke her cheek to chin.

She pressed her left onto his wrist and it was pinned to the glass with a thunk. "I just want to get started with this, okay? This was all your idea. You want to bring Lux Nova back, then let's do it."

Felicia watched but said nothing. Caveat fucking emptor.

"Okay, yeah. Yeah." He reached into his inner jacket pocket like he might have a gun to rob the place instead. "We'll take them," he said to Felicia and her studiedly distant gaze past Lucy.

"Normally it's all sales final, but you're such a good customer." She pulled a key from a cluster on a retractable chain fixed to her belt and sent it home.

"They won't be coming back." Lucy wondered about this and if it was an act or if and how often Toby had been here buying and selling junk. Lots of folks got by selling when things got lean and buying back when high on the hog. Maybe he was just one of those. Maybe. "A case would be nice," she added. "Can't exactly wear these out on the street. Besides, my ears aren't even pierced." She grabbed the lobe on her left and shook it as if to display its intact status.

"I'll be darned." Toby looked closer. "I never noticed. You okay with changing that?"

"I guess I gotta be if I wanna play the part."

"Some parts you don't get to play," Felicia said as she snapped the jewelry case closed and worked the latch on it, feeling the metal, not looking anywhere but at Lucy. "Sometimes you have to commit."

He handed her bills to account for the given price.

Lucy said "Don't worry about me."

"I don't plan to." She put the case in Toby's hands. "When is the first show?"

"Ask her."

Felicia continued to look past the would-be star.

Lucy ran fingers through her hair, still stiff with black dye. "I've got to go blonde, right?"

"It would match your eyebrows more closely, yeah," said Felicia with a bite. "Maybe just a good wash or a wig?"

"Only my hairdresser knows for sure, honey." She tugged on Toby's arm, pulling him a little closer. "Let's get out of here."

Toby dropped her at the rehearsal space with a bundle of clippings and photos, the Lux Nova single and a handful of tapes, all aspects of the identity she was aiming to absorb, if such a thing was even possible. Becoming another.

"We can look at some video tonight when I'm done," he said as he walked her past the row of doors, muffled squalls of noise thumping behind some of them.

"Only mostly soundproof, I guess." She tapped the graying plaster of the hallway. "You sure I can't come with you? I don't wanna hang out here by myself. Maybe I can go back to your place?"

"Oh, *now* you want to go to my place. Listen, if you do vocal practice there, you're going to get my lease torn up for the trouble. You'll be fine here. Besides, it'll be good for you to be seen by the scenesters who come by. Just don't let anyone get too close a look."

The door flung open steps from their reaching it. Three sweating rocker rats stepped out in single file, black t-shirts and jeans worn tight to fraying. All of them were close enough to teenage to still feel gangly, more tall boys than video-ready Greek statue physiques.

"This shit is nowhere. We're just spinning our wheels," one of them said, voice seeping from beneath a sea of shaggy hanks of hair that fell nearly to a Motörhead t-shirt that was sizes too small.

"Ty's a flake," grumbled one who slung his bass guitar over his back like some medieval broadsword. He paused after, looking Lucy up and down like she was perched in a shop window for him and him alone. "Hellooo nurse."

Lucy took a step to him like she was a knife. "Buzz off," she growled. "Unless you want to become a dues-paying member of the fan club. Looks are free until I poke your eyes out."

The other two hissed sharply and the bass player laughed. "Okay, okay. I'll catch you later, blackbird." He waved as the three of them stalked down the hallway, their jokes only for their own ears.

"Next time you see me, it won't be me!" she called to his denim backside sauntering out. She spun to Toby. "You know that guy?"

"Only vaguely. Those three are new guys in Dreamless." His lip went tight and sad. "For as long as they last. I like the original duo, but that whole creative differences thing?"

"You mean they all fucking hate each other?"

"Yeah, that part."

"So, you were gonna jump in and save me any time, right?"

"The second that it looked like you were going to be in any trouble. And don't think I noticed you sizing him up."

"Not normally my type."

"What is?"

"Nobody I work for." She stared straight at the door, waiting for him to re-open it.

"What about with?" He pulled at it hard.

"Maybe." She stepped through ahead of him.

The two men in the room were half-hugging, heads touching and one arms around the other. It wasn't brotherly or friendly, but it wasn't anything Lucy hadn't seen before either. Being in weirdo outsider bands meant running into all kinds. Guys were sometimes into guys, wasn't a thing that made a difference to her. It was other people's damage to get worked up about that.

"Oh, shit," Toby blurted out. "Sorry, guys. I didn't."

The taller of the two pressed back and shook his head, more drained than angry. He might've been in his thirties, older than the dudes who just left by a fair bit, not dressed to hang out on Sunset, just street clothes that fell to the side of black and plain.

"Hey, Toby. It's okay. Nothing _you_ haven't seen before." He paused and looked over Lucy. Then he took a step closer and dug in. His eyes went wide and his face paled. "Holy wow."

Lucy didn't know what to think about that other than weirded out.

The other one shook off his exhaustion or funk or whatever had been eating him to notice. He had long curly brown hair, well-kept though sweaty. He was a little younger, a little thinner than his friend, but still older than the others in the band. He was domesticated but somehow hungry, wilder than the scarecrows who'd just left. Those guys were sidemen. He must have been the front-man.

"You're Ty, right?" Lucy asked.

"What," he said. Then his eyes fixed on her and he did the same as his friend or lover just had. "Yeah, I'm… Yeah."

Unease settled on her like sweat after running in her nightmares. "Oh, you think I'm… Lux, right?"

"This is Lucy," Toby said, firmly enough to set it in stone. "These are my friends Gary and Ty. They're in an outfit called Dreamless."

"Goddamn, are you sure you're not?" Ty asked. He walked around her, looking her up and down. "If I was a believer in the miracle of resurrection, I'd say this was Lux back in the flesh."

"I'm *Lucy*. But the way you guys are carrying on, I have to wonder."

Toby stepped up and beside her, trying to drag the spotlight off. "She's new in town. I'm trying to get a showcase set up for her. So I should step out and do that. It's cool if she practices here for a little bit, right?"

"So long as you keep paying your share on the rental space, sure thing." The bigger of the pair, Gary, was packing up a keyboard into a carrying case, making ready to leave. Something about him was off, motions deliberate and precise enough that he had to be concentrating on them to avoid thinking about something else. Lucy knew it was her, but not why.

"Hey, you don't need to hurry out, okay?" Lucy said. "I was hoping to get some feedback on my material."

"Your *material?*" Ty repeated, twisting it into a ridiculous question. "She sounds like you, Gary. All technical." The last word maybe was meant with loving derision, but somehow the loving was left off. Lucy knew that he was probably a lot of fun to be around after a couple drinks, so long as you weren't the subject of his observations.

Gary set his jaw hard enough to see the muscles bunch on the side of his head before speaking. "Stop it, Ty. This bullshit attitude is what's wearing the guys' nerves down. Not everyone has to think like you."

"Fine," he replied, body still stiff as steel. He turned to Lucy. "So, you wanna talk about your art?"

"That's not a come-on, is it?" she asked, purely out of reflex.

"Yeah, you've probably been swarmed by dudes using that as an opener. But the truth of it is that I like sucking dick probably more than you do. So you've got nothing to fear."

"That's an exaggeration. But he will on occasion," Gary snapped and Lucy laughed out loud at that.

"Guilty," Ty said then licked his lips and ended with a bow. "Tell me about yourself."

Lucy just took the cassette from Toby's pocket and pressed play on the tape unit.

Storm clouds passed over the skylight, throwing a pewter-silver cast that dimmed as rain gathered in first circlets then sheets.

Toby just melted back and said something about having to make some deals, knowing Lucy was in good hands. She and Gary and Ty spent the afternoon listening to tapes and listening to her singing, not to match, but to find the same vein to tap. She wasn't going to be Lux Nova, not exactly the same way. But they could work the same seam. They could have shared experiences and desires. The desires. That was all of it. The intention. Wearing the mantle of the shattering angel, the demon who heals and weeps and wails.

She dug for the same pain and rage and strength that Lux must have. She sang until it hurt and then she sang some more.

***

The rain pooled on the skylight now urine-yellow in the sodium lights from outside. Gary and Ty had to take off as they'd been at it for a couple hours before Lucy had even started. They'd urged her to come with; Toby could get her from their place. It was right by. Gary was the last to leave, weighing something unspoken but thought so hard that Lucy had no problem guessing what it was.

"We can talk about that later," she said. "But I don't think I have an answer to whatever you're gonna ask."

Gary only nodded.

She hugged each of them and waved them off, whispering thanks because that was all the sound she could make. Part of her wanted to go, maybe work on things a bit more. All of her understanding of music was sweat out in practice and fumbling and without any understanding of the theory behind it. Gary could hear something once and play it back then explain why it worked or didn't and what could be done to fix it. That was a gift she couldn't put her arms around. She could just sing and she wondered if that was enough.

The door closed behind them and she flicked off the lights. There was a square of soft and gold radiance under the skylight. She loaded up a tape marked "CELLAR DEMOS" with a smudged date like a melting lipstick kiss. It was one of the few she hadn't heard that afternoon so she slotted it.

She picked up the case carrying Lux's jewelry, knowing that it was what she had been wearing when she died. When she killed herself. She figured that it was important enough, perhaps even sacred enough, not to lie about or take lightly. Lux had worn these on stage and back even in the dressing room where she'd died. Some place called the Last Prayer, a new club then, only weeks open, but a sure-fire way to get on the map for the ghoul cool set. It should have been a tragedy, but from the stories written about Lux, it seemed as inevitable as the planets working their orbits, all part of some big machine that Lucy or perhaps even Lux herself couldn't see more than a fragment of.

Lux's voice, disembodied and disinterred, pulsed from the speakers to the dirty walls and back again, echoing louder than it should have, rippling and fuguing. Maybe it was an effect of the tape warping over time, but Lucy didn't believe that. It was Lux's voice, something was happening within it, wrapping around Lucy and itself so that beginning and end lost meaning. There was only the moment being stretched out in sound.

She opened the jewelry case without realizing it, feeling as the clamshell hinge yielded. Lucy searched for the tiny jewels in folds of velvet, sudden heat rushing around her chest and neck. Her face burned beneath her skin as fingers closed on the first earring, tracing up it to the pin and clasp like a tiny metallic flower. She removed it and brought it to her left earlobe, only dimly aware of the mechanics of her actions, not guiding them herself.

The song rose not to crescendo but to a howl that was stripped of anything other than fury. There was no grand design. There was no truth beyond the instant that she and her were in. Lux screamed then her mouth closed, murdering the shout in mid-syllable, teeth clicking like nails hammered into a crucifix.

Lucy pressed the pin through her ear and felt a hot gush on her fingers and down her neck. It burned for only a moment then cooled quickly, cloying and close.

She waited patiently for the next song to begin so she could do the other.

The word LUX stuck to the mirror, written out smeared and deliberate, each letter a fingertip width in her own blood. It was almost right. Missing something. Lucy worked her index finger against her right earlobe and re-wet it. Bright spark of pain as fingertips brushed the post. She then added a block letter E to spell LUXE. Extra-fancy. Complete. She took a step back and stared at herself in the cracked glass, the word superimposed over her face, erasing her. Her reflection was faceted in cobweb circles like a smashed insect eye. Blood ran down her ears and neck on both sides, much worse on the right side somehow, red seas curling brown.

"Can't make an omelet without breaking a few skulls, right?"

The earrings glittered like the scales of undersea creatures, things that had never seen the sunlight but still somehow shone. She admired them in her reddened fingers, hissing when she tugged on one by accident.

"It's called piercing for a reason, dummy. You'll get used to it." Her own voice came back to her strange, bounced off the tiles of the close room.

She wadded up the last of the tissue from the stall, wet it and did her best to scour the stain away. It only mostly came off, leaving a faint trace of blush on her skin. She kept working at it. A good look for the stage, but a little freaky to walk around in.

"Hey, where are you? Lucy?" came Toby's voice from down the hall, lost and echoed. "Hello? I know I'm late but…"

"There's no Lucy here," she said as she came out, not quite cleaned up. "But Luxe has arrived." Her voice was full-throated past the pain. She smiled and showed off the earrings, the piercings still seeping a little. "You like it?"

He stared, words lost. "You psycho." He hissed out a breath after that.

"I beg your pardon. I'm getting in character."

"You're really going all the way?"

"I'm trying to," she said, coughing at the scratch in her own throat. She hadn't felt like this since smoking the remnants of a pack of unfiltered Fatimas in half an hour on a teenage dare.

"Sounds like you did better when you weren't trying to."

"Yeah, sorry," she rasped. "I was practicing with those guys. They're nice, at least once Ty gets over himself."

"That's insecurity that makes him a jerk." He looked at her once more and shook his head. "Just unbelievable. I still can't get over it." His fingers drifted to the scar at his throat, the same scar in the heart-shaped pendant.

"Well don't. You're the one who has to sell this act."

"And sell it I have. I think we can get you a show on Sunday."

She felt her lips pull back tight and then willed them back into something closer to pleasant. "Sunday? That's a dead night."

"All the better."

"Where's the venue? Here, keep talking while I finish up." She wet the tissue wad but it only disintegrated in her fingers.

"You should leave it. Good stage presence."

"Where?"

"I tried for the Last Prayer, but you gotta know someone who knows someone in there now. Like the goddamn Freemasons or something."

"I don't want to start back there. Not after… You know."

"That's why it would have been so great. Run head-first at the legend."

"Which part of it?"

Lucy tossed the pinkish pulp at the can and missed, leaving a splat shaped like a question mark at its base. "*Where*, Toby?"

He stepped back as if he'd seen a snake. "A place called the Riptide in the Westside. New, hungry. They want something different without any of the headaches of the meathead crowd that the hardcore acts have been bringing in. They're interested in something arty and theatrical."

"Arty? Is that what we are?"

"So we're a we?" he asked?

Lucy muttered. "Not like that, but a partnership."

"What we talked about is more like KISS meets Brecht, so yeah. Arty and theatrical."

She dried off but still felt sticky and shrugged that off to nerves. "Sunday? That's not a lot of time to get the act ready." She followed Toby into the hallway to see him staring at a point on the opposite wall. "Specially if you're gonna space out."

"Yeah, sorry. This is happening real fast is all. Taking a second to think about things."

"<u>You</u> think it's fast? I got here yesterday."

He switched his stare to her. "You were ready the second you got here. Here." He tapped her just under the collarbone on her left side. "You left home because you were ready."

She didn't move his hand. She let it happen. "I lucked out and found someone who saw something in me. At least twenty percent of something." Leaning back, she let his finger grab air and watched his expression. "Now can we go back and get my things from your sister's place and get something to drink? My throat is killing me. Something trying to claw its way out."

She took a couple steps down the hallway, leading him.

"We could get drinks at the Bounty. Winston Churchill used to go there. True story."

"Maybe whiskey in some tea, but I don't wanna get loaded tonight. Or tomorrow. Doing shows hung over fucking sucks."

He closed the door behind them.

Lucy looked at the streetlight planted in front of the place, cast iron and enameled so often that any detail in the metalwork had been blunted into invisibility. Taped to it was an assortment of flyers and tear-away sheets printed on paper that fairly glowed in the yellow lamp. One caught her eye, clean white paper and block lettering in fat marker strokes. LUX NEVER REALLY DIED, it said in stacked letters. There was no indication of a venue or date or anything else. Just the message like it was the gospel truth on a Sunday morning. She stared at it and felt an icewater thrill run down her spine as clearly as the blood on her neck moments ago.

"Did you do this?" she asked as she snatched the flyer off the pole.

"What? This? This is advertising."

"Just the slogan. And it's spelled wrong."

He raised an eyebrow. "You figure how?"

"It's spelled with an E at the end. We're updating it. And the name will be Luxe Licht. I've even got an idea for the logo, too. Would make a cool tattoo or jacket patch."

"Oh, okay, boss. Anything else I should know?" He forced a smile but the light threw a cast of jaundice over it, sickening him.

She grabbed the flyer and stuffed it in the pocket as a souvenir. "Just that if you're gonna pay for a street team, make it count. Get audience through the right door."

"You sound positively like a businessman."

"Being the greatest singer in the world ain't shit if nobody hears it." She shoved her hands in her pockets. "Did that already and it was no fun."

***

Lucy turned off the playback, fumbling the button twice. The screen froze in a paralyzing blur of video noise and a shape or a woman abstracted and bent as if in supplication before violence received or given.

"Okay, that's enough," she said.

"You bored?" he asked through the haze of weed smoke.

"No, not that. Just." She grabbed the joint from the corner of his mouth and held it between her fingers for a moment, considering a blinding hit.

"Thought you weren't gonna get wasted."

"Half high from being in the same room as this." She parked it closer to her lips. "I spent a lot of time being in Lux's head over the past couple of days. I want some space for myself. And this isn't working out right."

"You gonna smoke or stare at it?" he asked.

Her ears still dully ached and it would help but she instead passed it back, dizzy enough from being in the same room.

"Hey, what's up?"

She stared at the screen, drawn back to the not/her up there in the video. Seeing Lux in motion had been a blast of alienation because it was like looking through a bent mirror. That could have been her. That could be her right now. Tonight. Was there room enough in her for two?

"I just don't know that there's a lot of room for me in this. It's like I'm just pretending something. Like I'm goddamn Beatlemania for an artist who was an outsider weirdo at best." She took a big hit and waited for it to velvet hammer her. She blew out blue smoke on the exhale. Balancing the fact that she shouldn't have done it with the sensation made it even sweeter.

He reached over and she passed the cigarette.

"It's still gonna be you. We're just going to do the Lux thing to break the ice. Unless you want to keep it going."

"Yeah. No." The dope wasn't hitting but something else had, the weight and seriousness of things fell on her like molten lead, smothering her by inches. Her breath labored as the feeling flowed into her through her skin and mouth. She leaned into him. He reclined, pushing the table away to make more room. The carpet was tacky on her, club-floor sticky and she just lay there with her head on his chest. She felt only his pulse, like he was holding everything in suspension, down to his heartbeat.

"This isn't anything," she said.

"Sure it's not," he replied. His arm went around her, fingers resting on her collarbone, where they had before. The first kiss came down on her neck after a moment and she let the chill of it make her feel something besides trying to chase someone else. Another and another. She half-closed her eyes, still seeing the frozen image on the screen, the woman she was trying and afraid to be.

The kisses on her neck stopped as his hand traced an arc from her neck to between her breasts and further down. She could feel his head turned. He was watching the screen too. She was sure of it.

But it had been a long time. And he was gentle. And she was Lux or Luxe, burning there in his arms as her hips buckled to his touch.

The image on the screen burned itself in, between her eyelashes as his touch erased the both of them, at least for a slow moment.

***

Lucy put the necklace on last. It was heavier than she'd thought.

"Hold still," Gary said as he worked the clasp behind her neck. His hands were bigger than Toby's and she tried not to be surprised by that. "So, how'd he take it?"

"Huh?" She asked without turning from the mirror in the cramped dressing room. Her eyes lingered on the blonde hair at her crown then drifted to the heart pendant.

"Toby's not here. You asked him not to see you before the show?" Gary stepped back, almost into the wall. The cast of the fresh, mint-green paint made him look pale, his eyeshadow and liner turning to sunken coal pools.

"He, uh." She traced the line of the necklace with a black-painted fingernail. Then her hand closed to a fist, holding onto nothing. "He didn't want to see me. Just dropped me off and that was that. Business shit."

"Maybe he was freaked out by the wig." He ran a hand over his own fading hair, spiked short and sharp. "With that blonde wig, it's just weird."

"The wig. Yeah. Un-fucking-canny." She drew in a tight breath and had trouble putting it anywhere. Something had taken root in her, taken up room. "I didn't know a damned thing about Lux Nova a few days ago. Now I see her in the mirror. Just her."

Gary's hands went to her shoulders, his nails dark green and metallic like insect shells. "Toby doesn't know this. I kept it quiet because he got--"

"What?" She turned from the reflection she couldn't match and looked to him.

"He got kind of possessive about Lux, once he finally saw her. Saw her as Lux Nova, that is."

"Like jealous?"

His shoulder shrugged under the leather vest, irregularly dotted with roughed chrome studs. "Maybe. I mean, I get like that with Ty, sometimes. Jealous. But there was more to it."

"Okay, so he's jealous. Good to know." She thought about what had happened between them two nights ago and how after that, there was not even a sense of intimacy. Conquest sometimes just leads to boredom. But Toby wasn't just blowing her off, either. She figured it had been nerves on his part as much as hers. Watching boys pump and dump was an all-too-familiar thing to her growing up. And perhaps he had what he wanted and that was enough for him.

"Maybe. It's like he took ownership of Lux's career. But the fact is she <u>had</u> one before they met. She was just Leslie Randall back then." His eyes misted up and got heavy.

Lucy fumbled around on the cluttered and shallow make-up table for a clean kerchief, finding only the one she'd brought with her when she came to LA days ago. She remembered it smelled like home.

"Here."

"Thanks." He dabbed at his eyes with the delicacy of a surgeon. "Took me half an hour to get made-up. Big fingers."

"You okay?"

"Yeah. Just a lot of memories coming up. Thing is, you only see Lux Nova, this goddamn force of nature. And she was, once she got on stage. Once she figured out who she was. You never saw her as, just, Leslie Randall. Just a human being. Just a kid from Reno."

Lucy took a deep breath for the first time in the last two days. She felt like she'd been tiptoeing on eggshells since then and now she'd just decided to walk no matter what got broken.

"Thanks, Gary." Her breath went ragged. "I'm sorry she died. I'm sorry that I even agreed to this."

"You can't be her. It was dumb of Toby to set you up for it."

"I agreed."

"<u>You</u> didn't know better. I've heard you sing and you're every bit as good as she ever was. I think your head's screwed on tighter. She had a lot going on and not all of it good. But not all of it was her damage."

Lucy thought of asking him whether or not Lux really committed suicide or if it was something else. Gary was already staggering under a load of unwelcome memories and she really needed him together to play keys and rhythm tracks behind her. There was no way she could go onstage alone and do this. And she was alone, even if the ghost of Lux Nova had been invoked over and over since she'd come to LA.

The necklace caught on her skin and bit sharply, enough to make her start. Her ears throbbed at the same time and the bracelets went tight. All at once she gasped and breathed in so hard her sides stitched.

"Aah!" Her voice was all dead air.

"You okay?" His hands went around her upper arms, strong enough to keep her from going limp, just in case.

"Yes. I'm fine." She shook herself off. "Just nerves acting up."

"You'll be great."

"Thanks, Gary. You were always a good friend."

Lucy told herself that it was just the sound filling her that lifted her out of her boots. She kept saying it though she knew it wasn't true. A weird separation had split her from the world like sleepwalking or jet lag or the perfect balance between wired and wasted when she could be in a scene and at the same time see everything in it, stripped to its component parts. Everything was easy, like she was being given the answers, being told what to say before she had to say it. An imaginary friend had alighted not only on her, but in her. It was inspiration, breath. The breath of life itself.

The pulsing from the keyboard sounded like the hum of power lines amplified to a level that it became tangible, sound you could walk on, dance on, not even have to touch the ground. There were two tones, one a long-period cycling drone that burrowed through skin and flesh and bone; one above it, a heartbeat strung out in a never-ending marathon. There was no sound from the crowd at all, no whispers, no distraction. They clustered like pilgrims after a journey, awaiting revelation.

Lucy wondered if any of Lux's fans from before would be there, acting as doubting Thomas, asking to put fingers in stigmata for both the perverse fleshly thrill and to disbelieve. To knock down their own god. She could feel the slight pull of the lines attached to her black over-robe and hood, folded back to reveal her platinum blonde locks. They shone in a way that no natural hair should, more like film-noir femme fatale than mere human. She looked out on the stage and saw Gary hunched over the keyboard stand, blue light making him and the room cold as a glacier sea. The north where things and people were banished and made forgotten.

She pressed the button on her hand control. It flashed a red light in his eye line. He raised his hand and closed it into a fist that told the light-man to bring up the spot, to pin Luxe Licht with the beam. A hundred breaths drawn in at once sucked the air out of the room as she strode onto the center of the stage, plodding bootsteps like Death's pale horse marching up then coming to a stop. She could see nothing past the glare of the spot as bright as noontime sun. She walked into it without blinking, without a twitch of her blackly-painted lips.

The electronic pulse sped as she moved to her mark on the stage. Sound cycled faster and faster to a point where the wave was holding the entire place in suspension, in levitation fueled by expectation and the delicious not knowing what was going to happen next. She raised her arms as if to lead a prayer.

The techs read the cue perfectly. They pulled on the nylon line attached to the shoulders of her satin-black cloak. The breakaway seams gave just as they were supposed to and her wig tumbled free. The Lux Nova costume was stripped away, revealing Luxe Licht and her black hair cut at vampire angles, her white dress straight from Weimar decadence. The light caught her jewelry and exploded in glistening scintilla.

She sang in Luxe Licht's voice, she sang about promises, syllables stretched to operatic dimensions, atomizing power behind them, a song of destruction and rebirth. She should have been immolating, her voice a rasp of overexertion. Instead, it was the easiest thing in the world, power not hers flowing through and leaving some behind before it kissed exaltation to the crowd gathered before her.

It could have been hours or days.

Lucy/Lux/Luxe knew that her staying before the adulation of the crowd was a vice that only fools would willingly pay for. They wanted more and would have picked her clean for it if she'd stayed. She dropped to her knees and lay in a shape of prayer on the stage until she felt the spotlight fall off of her. The swell of the keyboard roared against that of a single electric guitar left to rest on an amplifier, coalescing into a wall of noise that pushed the audience back bodily in the darkened hall.

The lights snapped out and the shadow flooded back in.

Gary dropped half of the cloak upon her and she wrapped herself in it then disappeared to the side stage and the green room.

"I got you covered," Gary hissed. "It's clear."

She said nothing, only squeezing her friend's hand as the tears streamed down her face, melting her makeup, blending black and white into something altogether new.

The door thumped twice, hard enough to rattle the latch. Lucy watched it from the mirror. She scrubbed at the white stage makeup with a cotton pad wet through with baby oil.

"Who is it?"

"It's Toby! C'mon and open the door!" The voice was clipped with impatience. Breathlessness hit her then and she told herself it was post-performance emptiness, not anything else, not what Gary had talked about before the show.

She got up and released the bolt and opened it enough for him to slide through. His body raked against her fingers on the edge of the door and the second he was past, she slammed it shut.

"You're taking this mystery thing a little far, aren't you?" he asked. "And we talked about an encore." He tapped a couple roses wrapped in cellophane against an open palm and the motion of it reminded Lucy of a switch being readied.

"We talked about a couple things before you disappeared, Toby. I had to make some calls on the spot." She turned back to the process of revealing, though she was hard-pressed to remember where she'd left off. A spot sheened with faint freckles on her left side, yes. "Were you even in the audience?"

"Yeah, I was there. Entertaining one of the critics from *The LA Times* and *No* magazine." He tapped the roses again, hard enough to shake petals free. "Temperamental s-o-bs."

"So, what did you think?" She worried away a matching spot on her right side.

"If I didn't know any better, I'd have said that Lux faked her own death and just took the last couple of years off."

"But <u>you</u> do know better," she said with a bite. "You weren't fooled."

He moved in close behind her, not that there was anywhere else to be in the tight space. He smelled of sweat and smoke, enough beer that he must have waded through it. Leaning down, his face hovered in the mirror, just off of her shoulder.

"I saw you up on stage like the sun rising at midnight is what I saw. So did everyone else."

She saw a dreaminess in his eyes, a dream wrapped in something else but no so tight as to hide it away entirely. There was fear there, welling through razor cuts so fine that they were invisible until the tension of the skin broke, squeezing out red that welled into runnels. She saw the pulse in his throat, his carotid dancing by the three-fingered-scar that lay above the collar of his shirt.

He moved to kiss her neck and she let him have only the slightest touch, no matter how much she'd liked it before, the times they'd paced around each other and fell to kisses, fell to undressing and tasting and reaching for the part of the other that they only revealed at the end of things. Lucy tried to understand this knowledge, how it could encompass time that she had not spent with him, before she'd even come over. There were memories in the maze of her head that had not been. If they had, she would never have let herself be so vulnerable a second time. She would not be again.

Toby said something from the other side of the ocean. She heard sounds but not words.

Lucy's heart had within it a second pulse, a counterpoint to her own, a rhythm that was familiar yet made strange as her own voice sent back to her on a tape recording or echo. She listened to thoughts in her head that were not her own. The jewelry was burial-cold on her. A trickle of blood ran down her right ear, hotter than any spotlight.

"What?" she asked.

"Not very friendly," he repeated, laying grit to the voice. "Not after a couple nights ago."

"I'm not in the mood." She scrubbed around her cheeks and jawline, leaving the heavy eyeliner in place. "Just want to get cleaned up." As she said that, she felt flashes of her body stiffening, radiating out from her wrists and neck. "Oh, fuck I'm bleeding."

Her gaze skimmed over his reflected face and his fear was gone. Only because something had chased it out, leaving room just for itself. It wasn't jealousy so much as it was a hunger.

"Just so long as you don't leave me," he said. "You can't ever do that."

Lucy tried to staunch the blood and knew that she'd heard that exact sentence from him before, years ago. It couldn't have been her, but it was. In a small room, like this one, adorned with lilies gone bad and stubs of candles and graffiti layered upon itself so that it became a new language, a record of another history. She knew it was in the dressing room in a place called the Last Prayer and she was tired of Toby's shit, Gary had been right and the night had gone great and everything worked and Toby hadn't understood it. He knew only what had been and what he wanted to hold onto.

She knew in that moment that Lux Nova hadn't committed suicide, not even unintentionally. The doctored heroin hadn't killed her, but the jealousy and fear had. Lucy knew that Lux Nova had carved out a final note in Toby's neck, a reminder that would never quite heal right. Lucy felt Lux flooded away after the sharp silver jab, a swooning and dreamy crash into nothing.

But Lux was here.

Toby's hands rested on her shoulders. "You're a mess, Lucy. Falling apart."

She struggled to get the second voice and memory, the second her, into some semblance of control. But she couldn't remember who she was. Lucy or Lux or maybe neither.

"Leave me alone," she said to herself.

"Not friendly at all. And after all I've done for you." He crouched down, eyes at a level with hers in the glass. His façade burned away, finally revealing, finally showing what he'd wanted all this time. He wanted to express what he could not himself through her. She wasn't any more than an extension of him, a tool.

But she was. Lux was Lucy was Luxe. She couldn't be his. She had to be her own.

"Have you ever thought, Toby, that maybe you don't know better?" She took the cloth off her ear and left it to dry, the blood having left something on her like a fingerprint or a hallmark.

"About what?" he grinned and ran a finger through her hair. His eyes followed the lock up back towards her scalp. He was inspecting.

"About who it was on the stage tonight." She breathed through gritted teeth.

"A bright new star, that's who. One that I'm going to own this–" He stabbed the thought dead.

"Go ahead. Say it." She turned in the stool to face him. "Say it."

"This…time. Wait."

Maybe he felt it too. Maybe he knew what Lucy knew, that Lux inside Lucy was whispering to her. She'd never died, only waited.

"Lux didn't overdose." Lucy didn't even need to ask it. She was as sure of it as she was sure that the sun would rise tomorrow.

"That's not true," he said, too loud. "She OD'd. It was… It was horrible."

"Toby, I. Lux didn't OD."

Something ate at everything in Toby, picking out bits of him, down at his foundations. She watched it peeling away the space behind his eyes, becoming blacker and blacker, light being worried out of them. Light blotted by something much deeper. Something that would not let go so easily.

"No," he whispered. "She died."

"Maybe. But that's over." Lucy or Luxe moved in closer, close enough to smell the bitterness of his sweat, every bit as rank as the smell of that junk store in Pasadena. "I thought you'd be so happy." She breathed him in. His wound seemed all but fresh, skin unevenly torn by fingernails, not a suicide but a homicide note. Her finger traced the part of it left visible. Blood from her ear made it weal.

He made sounds that were not words, little catches at the back of his throat, bigger than they should have been. Sound of him being hollowed-out, scraped clean.

"Aren't you happy I'm back?" she asked. She brushed her lips on his neck and his skin beneath hers was desert-dry. "You always liked this. You don't like it now? Don't you like this?"

Her kiss opened wide and wet, tongue moving between lips, over the cold expanse of his skin and the roughness of the mark she'd left upon him years ago. He didn't move, only barely enduring the moment.

"You're dead," he whispered. "You can't be alive." He was shrinking back from her, hand on his neck fingers working strangely, as if to make sure he himself was still there. That he wasn't the one who was dreaming all this. "You're not her. Black hair. Look at you." His finger raised as if he was in nightmare, slow and leaden, unable to find its target.

His eyes went wide and dim. "Black hair," he repeated.

"Oh, this?" she said with a laugh. "The roots are already showing. Such a shame to cover up this natural color, don't you think? Blonde all the way to. My. Toes." She leaned forward, showing him the crown of her head, laying the locks flat and pulling them tight.

There in the part shone the faintest streak of gold beneath the black, a seam of radiance.

"You see?" she asked, staring him in the face. "You see it?"

He said nothing, only letting out a yelp that lasted for as long as it took him to slap his hand over his mouth. He kept pointing as he stepped backwards. She moved to keep the space between them the same. He paled at that.

"Don't. Don't ever stop running, Toby. Or I'll catch you!" Lucy stepped in, barely raking him with the tips of her fingernails.

He went pale and bloodless. But not without some strength, as he ripped the door open and muscled into the hallway and down it, knocking over waiters or lighting techs, whoever was unlucky enough to be between him and the outside.

He ran, stumbling and clamoring over tables and chairs pushed back into the former dance floor, falling through smoke haze lit like veils, like detective movies. He fell through them on his way out the door, pushing it so hard that he spun without balance and fell off the curb onto Wilshire Boulevard.

Even this late, there were a lot of cars out, driving quickly and carelessly. Or maybe distracted by the lights and the promises on the marquees.

Lucy heard the distant screech of rubber and road that ended with a thud and crumpling like a bass note buried deep. She peeled off her old face and left it behind on pads that were black and oily as the street outside.

CLUB CLOSED: PRIVATE PARTY

Roscoe spent his first night out of prison drinking beer while sat on the bumper of the car that once had been his. His brother Greg had taken over its care when he went up the river. Can't drive a Dodge Magnum to prison. Too bad, 'cause it probably would have aged better there. The bumper chrome bubbled with rust. Rust in Los Angeles. How was that even possible. The finish gleamed as if it had been buffed with steel wool and battery acid. It still ran, just barely. It had gotten them out here. Whether it would get them home was beyond guessing.

They were parked in front of Lucky's Liquors in Van Nuys, pouring Mickey's big mouths down their throats one at a time. The flies were out and big and fat, buzzing like drunks at closing time as they orbited the purple bug lights. Once in a while, one would hit the electrified mesh--a suicide commando clearing the lines for its buddies.

Thing is, there was always more flies. That bug light wasn't ever going to short out. God hadn't made the fly big enough to do it. Four years behind bars taught him that. You can throw yourself against the machine over and over and over and all you're going to do is get broken down. Roscoe should have learned it when he was fifteen. He only thought about it once at twenty-five. Thirty-five and two-time loser and the lesson was maybe going to stick this time.

He wanted a straight life and hated himself a little for that. Wanted the straight life, but didn't know how to live it. He was all but breaking the law drinking in public in the very parking lot of the place he'd robbed six years back. Not just he, but they. Greg was there on cover, like he always had been, aiming the scattergun as much as he needed to. Not much at all. Pointing one of those towards the same wall as your target was usually enough to get them to stop screaming or reaching for the alarm bell or doing anything you had specifically told them not to do. Good thing it was that easy, 'cause that's about what Greg was good at.

But Greg didn't have to be good. He was lucky. And when something goes wrong, you want lucky. Skill only delays you needing that good luck that gets the red light to turn and the cop smashes into a streetlight or sedan gunning things early. Sometimes skill is enough. Roscoe was wondering when that would prove itself to be true.

"Dang. That was a big one," he said, glassy-eyed. "Made that light flicker." He put the fat green bottle to his lips then finished the beer.

"Spectacular. But still a poor excuse for a first night out."

"Maybe you could think of something better to be doing instead?"

"I could see if Marianne was busy."

"Roscoe, if she wanted to be seen by you, she'd have visited more than once." He hurled the bottle at the trash can in the corner of the building's façade. It smashed against the rough cinder block and made a little music as it did.

"You weren't even aiming were you?"

"Don't need to."

Greg was right. Marianne's one visit had been a mincing and awkward goodbye that took fifteen too many minutes. But Roscoe wanted to be wrong about that.

"Sometimes it helps to try a little."

"Save that for the rubes. You and me, we're outlaws. Doin' as we please." He slid off the hood and jumped to his feet, looking every inch a reprobate, a guy who didn't make rent because he didn't sweat it. There was always going to be another place to live that your reputation hadn't caught up to.

"Speak for yourself. I gotta see my parole officer tomorrow. You do have a bed for me to sleep in, right?" Roscoe worked his shoulders and then pulled at his waistband. His trial suit was too tight, even on years of prison food. His back ached and unless he slept tight, he was going to be a wreck.

"You gonna really do this straight thing?"

"I better. Next time they're gonna lose the key or just toss the switch on me."

"Aww, you ain't that kind of criminal."

"I'm not any kind, any more."

Some dude roared down the boulevard behind them, pipes all but blown so that it sounded more like a demon's howl than an engine.

"What if I told you I got us a job? Easy five large. Each. One night."

"I'd tell you I ain't interested."

"In. Out. Paid. Boom."

"That last word puts a scare in me, Greg."

"Hey, you think I don't feel bad that it was you not me for that last one? Of course I do." His eyes went all glossy but that was most of a six-pack in half an hour more than any sorry feelings.

"I wasn't saying that. Just that those days are done."

"Talk to me about it after you see your PO and try to get the shit job they're gonna wave in front of you. Talk to me then."

Roscoe didn't say another word to him that whole night and didn't feel bad about it. They drove back to Greg's place on Riverside, sullen and silent.

That next afternoon Roscoe pulled the door shut behind him, so hard that it shook nails loose from the frame.

Greg kept on reading his well-loved copy of *High Society*, not even turning the page. "Went that well, huh?"

Roscoe grabbed a hard-boiled egg from the bowl in the fridge and the second-to-last Budweiser and sat down on the rat-bit sofa.

"So tell me about the job."

It was a place in Hollywood, a place where weirdos went. Weirdos even by Hollywood standards. Some kind of dance club, bands played there. It was a whole scene called the Last Prayer Club.

"But the name ain't important. We ain't going in through the front."

"'Course not. That'd be dumb. What's the grab?"

Greg's eyes glazed over with his own particular eager thoughtlessness. "It's, get this, a private party. A particular kind of rich weirdo having a bash there. Won't be more than ten people inside. We won't be there long enough to even count them."

"Money? Jewelry? Valuables?"

"All that. But we're just there to lift one particular thing. Anything else we come out with is ours. Ten grand upon return to the rightful owner, who is pissed the hell off."

Roscoe crunched up the leftover shell and stuffed it into the bottle's neck. "So this is grand theft property return? What happens when they call the cops?"

"That's the beautiful thing." Greg's eyes gleamed with that easy money. "These people don't call cops."

Roscoe shook his head and smacked the empty down hard. "Those folks are either connected or they have guns."

"Another beautiful thing. They don't carry. They do like weird and spooky shit." Greg's fingers waved before his eyes like a sideshow hypnotist and he giggled. "But no iron." He waved his fingers like he was casting a magic spell.

"What? They're spooky?"

"You know, skulls and Halloween all year. They look like horror movie hosts. But they ain't armed."

"But they are rich?"

"You don't rob poor people, dummy."

"So let me put the picture together," Roscoe said as he stood up and began to pace the closet-like living room. "There's a private party of weirdos, with money. They dress up like vampires."

"Like Elvira, man."

"Elvira?"

"Oh I forgot, you don't know." Greg went into a leer that would have made Casanova faint from horror. "Yeah, she's on TV on Saturdays. You are in for a treat."

"Okay, back to this. Your connect wants us to go in, steal a ring and whatever else we can shake loose and then walk out? We get paid when?"

"Oh, did I say he's gonna pay us then? Hold on." Without further word, Greg leaped up from the Laz-y-boy chair that looked like it was upholstered in decay. He ran back to the back bedroom and came out with a big manila envelope that he upended onto the coffee table that was older than either one of them. Bundles of neat but not new twenties tumbled out, each one hitting with a satisfying solidness.

"He paid you ahead of time?" Roscoe's words came out tinged with equal parts wonder and fear.

"Yeah, so it's like we *have* to do it!" Greg idiot-grinned as he thumbed through five hundred bucks like it was nothing, like he was clipping coupons. "We gotta be the luckiest guys in the Valley right."

Roscoe didn't like it. There was nothing to like about it. Nothing except the ease of the payout. And that wasn't a thing he liked either.

There was an air of inevitability about things, inescapability, foolish as outrunning gravity or swimming against a crashing wave. You have to swim into those or they'll swamp you hard.

"When?" he asked with resignation.

"Real soon."

The mask was a thin piece of vacuformed plastic painted in garish greens. The gun wasn't all that much better. Roscoe stared into the wrinkled paper bag, child's mask balanced on one knee, empty eyes staring straight up.

"Where did you get this?"

"A guy."

"Okay. And the mask? The Creature from the Black Lagoon?"

"Halloween was months ago, Roscoe. Did what I could."

"These things will just get us killed. Maybe better to do it without them."

"The masks will stick. Just put a dab of spirit gum on your nose."

"Wasn't talking about those. We gotta get our own bullets, man."

"Why? These came loaded." Greg frowned at the prospect of more work.

"We don't know what kinds of rounds are in these. Could be old. Just put a fresh load in there to be sure."

"Okay, yeah. Smart. You always were smart, Roscoe."

Roscoe started up the Magnum and thought a moment. "I know a guy. Knows his guns and ammo. He's a prop master for one of the studios. He can help. If he's still around."

He was. Greg waited for Roscoe as he shook hands with some wiry, surfer-haired guy in jeans and a cut-off KISS t-shirt as they stood in the yard of a nice little house in Burbank. Roscoe and the guy talked for a moment then he swapped a grocery bag all wadded up for a thin sheaf of bills. Roscoe almost danced back to the car.

"Yeah, Clint came through. Take a look in there." Roscoe jammed the bag into Greg's waiting hands.

Greg rummaged in there and saw a bunch of loose brass cylinders and a couple of orange-coated plastic shotgun shells. "Couldn't we have just gone to Valley Guns?"

"Not as a felon. Which I am. And you may as well be." The Magnum's engine rattled to life and they drove over the hill to Hollywood, smoggy sunlight filtering through the afternoon. The 110 gummed up like drying blood and the both of them listened to the radio over the growl of a sea of thwarted engines.

"You put those shells in, Greg?"

"'Course I did Roscoe. Of course I did."

"Anything special about this ring that the guy wants back?" Roscoe asked. "Must be a real hum-dinger to drop ten large on. That is if we didn't just run off with the money."

"We're not like that."

"But that guy doesn't know that. And just how does he know you to hire you on this?"

"Oh you know, word kinda gets around. I've been keeping busy since you went up. Lots of irons in the fire."

"Uh-huh," Roscoe said. "The ring?"

"It's got a black diamond, set in white gold. Looks like a tear. Lots of sentimental value."

"Easy enough." He said it once more.

They parked back behind the building as the sun was setting and waited for the night to really settle in. Waited for everyone to get to the party.

Then they put on their masks. Greg's looked like some big-brained mutant, sunken eyes and exposed convolutions like cottage cheese.

"Go over the plan."

"In. Grab the ring. Out. Boom."

Roscoe sighed. "Let's just skip the boom if we can, okay?"

"Hey, I'm the brains here." He pointed at the exposed cerebral matter on his mask. "My job. We need to shoot, we shoot."

Roscoe put on the mask and didn't argue.

They stalked to the back door, propped open with an empty beer crate. A yellow slash of light fell onto the parking lot from the kitchen. The sounds of the street had fallen back. Someone was singing in Spanish alongside a radio as dishes clattered nearby. Greg nodded and Roscoe opened up the door wide then they stepped through.

A tall and young Mexican man stood next to the stainless steel basin, white undershirt and tight black jeans, all wiry energy. A long watch chain suspended from his pocket halfway down his thigh before looping back up. He turned and looked at the two men coming through the door and half-smiled before they even raised a weapon. His hands came up relaxed, cool.

"That's good," Greg said.

Roscoe looked him over. "Where's your hair net, man? Health code. You want this place shut down?"

"Oh, yeah." The kid smiled crooked. "Yeah. Sure." He pulled something out of his back pocket and wedged it on all cockeyed. Maybe his first time.

"Better," Roscoe hushed.

There wasn't anyone else back there, just the kid in the narrow galley that served as storage and fire exit. Crates of liquor bottles were stacked up like a library of debauch. Music oozed and bumped out in the front of the club. It was dirty as an oil spill washing all over Malibu, suntanned bodies stuck with cloying muck.

"Rock sure got weird since I was away."

"I told you these dudes were *out there*."

"This sounds like a funeral for god."

"Maybe it is. Devil shit."

Roscoe swallowed the rock in his throat. He glanced back at the kid watching them by the door to the main room and then shook his head slowly, indicating with the pistol barrel to turn on back around. The kid frowned like he wanted to watch, being sent off to bed early.

"Loud or quiet?" Greg asked.

"You're the brains."

"Loud, then. Make a statement."

Roscoe weighed both options. Both were likely to un-impress people who played with skulls and listened to the sound of the world being ground under the wheels of huge and terrifying machines. The beat could make the dead get up and dance all sinuous and skeletal. No difference either way, just put your weight on it and commit.

"Loud it is," Roscoe said. "Give 'em a show."

Roscoe kicked the door to the front open and yelled "Nobody move!"

"Okay motherstickers! This is a fuck-up!" Greg added.

"Holy shit, man," Roscoe whispered. "At least try to do your job."

That was when they got their first look at the room. Roscoe didn't even know where to begin. Maybe it was the walls that seemed to eat light like the flocking on a blacklight poster, just endless pooling shadow. There was piping and stripes, strings of shining barbed wire hanging from ceiling to floor giving the vibe that the whole room was some kind of prison. A colored light from below shone into a chandelier that was made not of jewels but of uncounted shards of broken glass, all the edges uneven and jagged and ruby red casting beams that threw bloody suicide slashes onto the ceiling and floor.

Arms sprouted from the corners of the room, mannequin arms, the fingers covered in rings that all glinted in the terrible red light. Roscoe remembered a movie he'd seen as a teenager, with people in a house all hiding from something coming to get them and just terrible arms and hands clutching in, reaching for them. He felt the same way, heart in his throat. He thanked god he was wearing a mask because he'd burst into cold sweat at the sight of all this and if Greg had any sense, he'd have too.

Before the two men was an oblong table heaped over with festively-wrapped packages stolen from how many parties leaving how many heartbroken children. There was bunting of black lace along the table so it looked more funeral than festival. The jarring contradiction of party and damnation stuck in Roscoe and he figured he was never going to shake it, not in years.

If they made it out in one piece.

He counted eight people in the room, five women, three men, all varying sorts of strange. It didn't matter what color their clothing, it was either black or red in the light of the room. Some of it was shiny, more scale than fabric. Everyone had jewelry that glittered from within, earrings too, enough that Roscoe wondered how that much could fit on one earlobe. The place was a hothouse for strangeness. They belonged here and only here.

"Hands up! Now!" Roscoe barked.

One of them, a pale woman with flowing black hair and a headdress that glittered darkly stared ahead, through the both of them. And then she smiled.

"How delightful!" she cried. Her hands clapped together so quickly that Roscoe couldn't even track it. He heard the sound ring through the room, seconds too late. "We're being robbed!"

Hands moved under the table and Roscoe tightened his aim in response. "Nuh-uh. Everyone stay put. Hands out and up."

The woman in charge took in the room with her eyes, not moving at all. Finally, one of her hands moved up and the other moved crosswise, hovering over her mouth.

"Do what he says," she said, lips concealed. The voice penetrated Roscoe like the jailhouse shower, needles wherever it hit. "We are being robbed. But it will be all right."

Nobody relaxed. They lifted their hands just slowly enough to make Roscoe know they were being mocked.

"I regret that we don't have drinks for you already poured," the woman in charge said, voice suddenly pleasant and warm. "Feel free to get something from the bar in the next room."

"We won't be staying," Roscoe said, soft as sandpaper.

"Hey, a snort of good stuff would go down real nice," Greg said to his brother. "We got time. It's not like they're gonna call the cops, right?" He wove the barrel of the shotgun in a short but gleeful arc.

"Oh! How terrifying," she cried. "Please don't threaten me. I'll do *whatever* you ask." Her lip quivered but only for a moment.

"See? We got time."

Roscoe wanted to say a hundred things, mostly that letting Greg be the brains was going to get both of theirs kicked in. But now was not the time to show the rubes that they were not serious.

"We don't."

"How sad," she said. "You were the first real surprise of this party. Well, the second, since Anton chose not to come. Very rude." She had the faintest whisper of a lisp, something that made her seem more childish than she actually was. Roscoe was trying to figure out exactly how old she was, but the answer slipped from him. Her clothing was almost dark fairy princess stuff, evil Sleeping Beauty, but her bearing and command of everyone else in the room was nothing a kid could pull off.

"Who's Anton?" Greg asked.

Roscoe had to hold himself back from backhanding him, pistol and all. "We don't care who Anton is. Let's do what we came for and go."

"So exciting."

"Ariela," said a brown-skinned woman with darker eyes than Roscoe had ever seen. She had her hair done up in braids and they looped around like a hangman's knot at the ends. "Stop."

"Oh Alondra, can't you tell? We are safe so long as we do what these two very dangerous men say."

The woman named Alondra bit her tongue and in that moment, Roscoe knew exactly how the two related to one another, because he'd been living it since he got out of jail. Greg was on something like power. It happened. Some guys got a gun in their hand, particularly a big one and they thought they were ten feet tall and made of diamond. Or maybe that was just the luck.

So was this woman, and Alondra was clearly the common sense of the two.

"Quiet a moment," Roscoe ordered. "Look, lady."

"Reina. Queen," the pale woman corrected, with lips black enough to fall into. "But you may call me Ariela since you have me in your power."

She smiled and Roscoe wondered if the woman had ever been in any-one else's power.

"We want the ring," Greg said. "Right now."

"Right. The ring," Roscoe added. "Just hand it over and we'll be out of each other's hair."

"Oh, you're not a bother," Ariela said. "In fact, this is thrilling. I can't remember the last time I felt in danger. Can you, Alondra?"

Alondra said nothing, only shaking her head with irritation plainly visible.

"This party has been the corpse of a movie star. Beautiful but lifeless," Ariela said to those gathered.

A tall man with a pompadour that gleamed hard and perfect scowled in response. His hands and arms crawled with tattoos, the likes of which Roscoe had never seen, not even in prison. His arms were sleeved in ink to his shoulders and his hands seemed to be made of them. He flexed his fingers in a weird sequence and Roscoe made himself look away.

"¡Tacíto! ¡Basta!" Ariela's voice cut through the room.

He half-bowed, eyes still on the gunmen. "Solo estaba pensado en ti, mi reina."

Ariela raised an eyebrow then asked "¿No crees que pueda manejarme solo?"

"Por supesto que no."

Roscoe knew enough Spanish to follow what had gone on. But he still didn't quite understand it. What had she stopped the tattooed guy from doing? Something with his hands, but there weren't any weapons in them.

"Cut," the queen commanded. "You will go with one of these men to get them some drinks. And refresh mine while you're up."

Someone tall stood back from the table, hands up, arms graceful. At first, Roscoe had mistaken them for a woman given the way clothing their clothes hung, but he wasn't sure.

"I got this," Greg said. He brought the barrel of the shotgun up. "You go get us some drinks, man." His eyes bore right into Roscoe from behind the mask. "We'll have a little fun. We got time."

Roscoe bit his tongue clean in half. The last thing he needed to do was to argue in front of the crowd and give them a reason to think they weren't a unified front. Even if it was goddamn stupid what Greg was trying to pull.

As Cut moved from around the table slowly, Roscoe leaned in close to his brother and whispered "The longer we stay, the less likely we ever leave, you get me?"

"That queen chick knows the score. They won't do anything."

"Yeah, she knows the score. That's what the fuck I'm afraid of. Be careful."

"Go. Walker Black if they got it. Just bring the bottle." He gave a gentle shove.

Roscoe had gotten that once for Greg, on his 21st birthday. Spent way too much on a bottle that was gone way too quickly, but even a bonehead like him should be able to appreciate the finer things once in a while. Life could be short. Very goddamn short.

"Want a straw with that too, genius?" Roscoe poked the mouth hole of the mask that was only a little bigger than a quarter tipped on its side.

"If they got it, yeah."

Roscoe stalked out, following Cut as he or she or they swung their hips on an arc that would have made Monroe envious. "Hey, Skin," Cut said as they passed through a doorway. "Wake up, we're gonna need fresh drinks."

The two of them passed into an empty club floor, one end walled off by hurricane fencing, with a raised bar to the side. It felt like a fortress in a hostile landscape, scarred and bitten from nightly assaults. Given what was going on in the private room, Roscoe was glad he wasn't here on a busy night.

The man behind the bar was made of muscle, every striation cleanly cut under his skin. There were dudes who did this in the yards, but they usually went for chunky mass, not absurd definition. Skin looked like his had been stripped to show the working beneath.

"'Bout time. Glad I'm not working for tips tonight." His front teeth were the same color as the trays the prison commissary used, only much much shinier. "Who's the… guest?" he asked.

"Creature from the Black Lagoon," Roscoe said. He didn't wave the gun, but kept it visible and unmistakable.

"He and his partner are the entertainment," Cut quipped.

"We sing, we dance, we hold up bars."

Skin shrugged. "Beats working. What am I getting you?"

"Johnny Walker black."

"Fine. How you want it?"

"Bottle."

Skin glanced at Cut who nodded without hesitation. He shrugged again like it was in his job description. "Your tab, man. What else?"

"The queen-"

"Wants a paloma," Skin said, without letting them finish. "With a splash of Cointreau. I got it." He stood without moving. "Well?"

"Well what?" Roscoe demanded.

Skin stared at Roscoe with dead-eyed obviousness then sighed. "You have a gun. I'm a bartender. I need to reach out and get fresh glasses from under the bar. I don't want you to shoot me."

"Yeah, yeah. Go around and let me in." Then to Cut he said "Stay right there."

Roscoe came back behind the bar and looked around, not seeing scatter gun or even a place to put one.

"You're brave. No cover?"

"I'd have told you, but you weren't going to believe me."

"You're right about that. Go ahead."

Skin opened up the refrigerated cabinet beneath and pulled out a faintly-greenish bottle of soda with Spanish written on it in a familiar script.

"Hold up," Roscoe said. "Is that Coke in a bottle?"

"Oh yeah, hard to get now. They got that new flavor crap. Queen won't allow it in the club. I have to pretend that we don't serve it."

"New flavor? What?"

Skin's eyebrows, his only visible hair, went up. "You living under a rock? Shit's all over the news, people can't stop talking about it."

"Man, I've been in prison since before that movie star became president. Kinda out of touch."

"Coke ain't Coke anymore. That's how fucked-up the world is. Tastes like that other stuff."

Roscoe shook his head and wondered how many other dumb little things that he'd once depended on for the world to make sense, how many of those things were gone.

"Gimme one of those," he said, suddenly parched.

"And I thought the JW was going to set us back," Skin sighed.

Cut grinned and nibbled their thumb. "He's got a sweet tooth. How cute."

"Not cute. Just been upriver for a while. Catering isn't exactly top dollar there."

"Did you get out for good behavior or bad?"

Roscoe didn't answer as he watched Skin pour out almost half the green bottle into a highball glass rimmed with salt. Must've been grapefruit, a sort of pinkish translucence to the soda. He tipped in some from a bottle of tequila with a silver label and then topped it with a float of Cointreau from a squat rectangular brown bottle, all in the space of a few seconds. He pulled the scotch down and took the cap off without being told to.

"Yeah, tough to open these one-handed."

"Thanks."

"Hold on, lemme pop that Coke for you." Skin lined up the bottle with a metal ridge bolted to the bar and flicked his wrist, neatly snapping the top off with a hiss. "Hecho en Mexico, man. That's where you gotta get the real thing."

"Yeah, brings a tear to the eye."

"Hey, on your way back, can you tell that dishwasher to maybe bust his ass a little and actually wash some dishes?" Skin said this to Cut and a little to Roscoe, too. "Seriously, wave that piece in his face. Kid's useless. Consider it a favor, huh?"

"I'll see what I can do."

"Thank you, Skin," Cut said with a cloying sweetness as they took the queen's drink and the bottle for Greg. Roscoe was trying to think up ways to keep him from getting a hit of it. Things were all but out of control, if they ever had been in it.

"Seriously, first night of a job and you'd think that you'd want to make an effort." Skin all but spat out the words. And they stuck in Roscoe's head for no reason at all.

"What's that all about?" he asked Cut.

"I guess the new dishwasher isn't all that. Maybe lacking discipline."

"And he's never worked here before?" There's luck and there's coincidence. They're also not the same thing at all. Luck happens without an explanation. It's just there. But coincidence usually lines up with a plan that's not necessarily your own.

They sighed. "How should I know? I'm not in personnel."

Cut's walk back was noticeably more restrained. Roscoe took a quick second to tip his mask up with the back of his gun hand and then a fast swig from the bottle. It bubbled so hard that his nose stung and eyes watered. It tasted like a hot summer afternoon and chasing out the dust with a soda stolen from the icebox. It tasted even better than that.

"Alondra is gonna be so pissed at you," Cut said. "I'll tell you that for free."

"Let her be mad. And let's stop and talk to that dishwasher. There a back door to it?"

"You have to go through the party room. And if I don't get this to the queen still ice-cold, you'll have to explain why."

"Fine, but make it quick."

Cut pushed the door open back into the mad tea party. Greg was seated next to the queen at the oblong table, leaning back on two legs, jocose with the gun slung across his lap. She had her hands out at the pile of presents, unwrapping one of them slowly and with ceremony. The paper shone like skinned goldfish, glittering and torn.

"What the hell, man?" Roscoe demanded. "What in the map to hell is going on?"

Greg tightened up, but only a little. "Oh, hey, Roscoe. We're all watching Ariela unwrap some presents."

Why not, Roscoe asked himself. Why not just give up. At least his mask was still on.

"Get up," and it took Roscoe his entire will not to blurt out Greg's name here "and at least pretend you know what you're doing."

"He knows exactly what he's doing," Ariela said. "He's very entertaining. Have you heard any of his stories?"

"I'm in half of them, Your Majesty."

"Delightful. You should sit and tell me one from your perspective. Perhaps it comes out… differently." She looked up from her half-opened present and locked her blue eyes onto him. Her smile was enigmatic but knowing, playfulness balanced upon a knife's edge ready to split it open and reveal something much more serious beneath.

"Your paloma, queen." Cut placed it down in front of her and Ariela admired the rippling condensation on the edge of the glass, how the salt on the rim melted and caught the red light.

"Maybe later, your majesty. I'm going to check on something in back," Roscoe said. "You. Cut. Come with me."

Cut fanned themselves with a flattened hand and pursed cheeks that needed no rouge for their definition. "I'm thrilled."

"You needn't worry, Roscoe," Ariela said coolly. "Everything is absolutely under control." She peeled back another strip of metallic paper with deliberate and trying patience.

That's what's so fucking terrifying, he thought. He was filled with the awareness that his own pulse was racing and had been the entire time, even making small talk with the bartender.

"Just... Just watch her," he said to Greg. "And maybe get back to the ring, huh?"

"What ring?" Ariela asked without looking away from the sheet of gold leaf.

"He'll tell you. Come on, Cut."

"Whatever you say." Their smile did nothing to reassure.

Roscoe took them by the upper arm and led them both back to where the dishwasher was stationed. "Someone's going to tell me what's going on and I think your queen is crazy or playing at it so I can't trust her. You seem pretty normal."

"Well that's disappointing."

"Not square, but like you're not playing games."

"That's no better."

They came through the door to the storage galley and looked down towards the giant stainless steel basin, piled to one side with glasses and small plates all covered with indiscriminate smears and lipstick smudges. The kid was leaning against the wall, staring at a watch he had on a chain that led back to his pocket. His pants were so tight, Roscoe had to wonder why he needed to take it out to even read it. Something faintly stirred in the water, dishes just dropped in carelessly, maybe.

"Hey!" Roscoe yelled, and the kid didn't even jump at that. "Ain't you supposed to be working?"

Undercover, he's undercover, Roscoe thought. If he's a dishwasher, I'm a model citizen.

"Ooh. Rough," Cut said, Roscoe's grip tight from anxiety.

The kid looked up, satisfied with whatever he saw on the timepiece. "Not until break's over. Union rules, comprende?"

"Do I look like I care? Go wash some goddamn dishes, huh?" He halfway brought up the gun, not playing around.

"Okay, okay. Calmate, okay?" The kid tentatively grabbed a glass and pressed it into the suds like he was giving a shot. It would have taken all night if Roscoe had let it.

"You wouldn't have lasted five seconds in the Folsom kitchen," Roscoe growled. He let go of Cut's arm pushed them back. Then he shoveled the pile of dishes into the water. They went in like a building collapsing, slurking under the surface and the suds.

"Get to it. Bartender's waiting."

The kid wiggled around the glass in his hand, lips and eyes pulled back in a suppressed grimace. He was in discomfort and not doing a good job of hiding it.

"That looks painful," Cut said. "Do it some more."

A muffled cheer went up from the party room, surprise and glee and genuine shock beneath it. Roscoe kept his eyes on the kid, not looking towards the distraction. The kid watched him, face reddening some.

"Can I take my hand out? Shit's too hot."

Roscoe took a step over and thrust his left hand into the water and the soap. He felt the heat, but he'd felt far worse, knowing that he'd get beaten if he didn't keep up on the quota. Little pain or a lot, his choice. Little pain was manageable.

"What is that, Cut?" he asked without any strain in his voice.

"My guess is the cake just arrived. Pineapple vanilla, hibiscus-flavored frosting. That took some doing."

"Could this get any more weird?" Roscoe muttered, exhausted.

"We're only getting warmed up, honey."

"I'm pullin' my hand out," the kid said. "Don't freak."

"Yeah, yeah. Wimp."

The kid wrenched his hand out. Roscoe was already off alert, barely keeping from laughing. Yeah, this guy wasn't a threat to anyone other than the boss he was stealing time from.

"Okay, just get those-"

Roscoe saw the gun in his hand, glistening and trailing soap bubbles that went rainbow-colored in the light like diamonds, dripping diamonds. It was up and out before anything could be done. Raising his own would have just been a very brief request to get shot.

"Just stand right the fuck there," the kid said. His voice had changed, dropped and deadened. "And you, too, freako."

"Goddammit," Roscoe muttered.

"Only my friends call me that," Cut spat.

"Enough, puta. And you, drop the piece."

"I drop this thing and it's likely to shatter. Got it cheap."

"Even better. Drop it."

Roscoe stared at the gun the guy was holding as he crouched down. "I'm just lowering it, okay?"

The guy's piece looked like a surplus 1911 Colt. Good gun. Could put most anyone six feet under fast. A small rivulet of water trickled out the barrel and splashed to the floor like an old man's urine stream. Maybe the kid had it out and had to stash it fast. Didn't matter.

Roscoe's gun clicked to the ground and his spread fingers pulled off it.

"Slide that shit away," the kid no longer a kid said.

"Yeah sure." Roscoe pushed on the gun and it skittered back towards the galley hall. "Hey, buddy. I hope that's not a model B you got there. 'Cause it won't shoot for shit if you so much pass it over a glass of water. Design flaw." He held his crouch while the guy thought about it.

The kid's face loosened just a bit, tiniest of furrows going up on his brow and his ears pulled back a little. Then his eyes went to the gun, no longer trusting it.

"Hey you-" he didn't finish the order to fetch the other gun.

Roscoe launched himself out of the crouch and into the guy's center mass, left hand coming up to deflect the weapon out. He hit the lighter man, leading with the right shoulder and reaching to keep the gun out of play.

The kid brought up a knee and he had a kick like balsa wood. Folsom was a miserable hole, but it had taught Roscoe how to take a hit or three. This one barely rated. His hand found the guy's wrist and he locked onto it, pushing back until the kid's elbow locked.

There was a metallic sound behind and Cut yelling something but there was no time to take any moves.

"Drop the gun, you punk, you stupid punk!"

The kid didn't say anything intelligible in reply, just a stream of spat consonants as he tried to work out of Roscoe's grip. Roscoe doubled down and slammed once, twice, then heard the gun clatter to the stainless countertop and the kid just deflated there.

Roscoe shoved him away from the basin, sprawling to the back door.

"You stay put!" he growled as he snatched up the Colt and leveled it at him, unconcerned about the weapon's wet or dry status.

"Motherfucker. You lied." The kid's voice came from the floor, where he was busy kissing the cracked tiles.

"And you're the dumb motherfucker who believed me," Roscoe said, panting. "Just stay there a minute."

"OKAY YOU BITCH! TURN AROUND SLOW!"

Roscoe hissed out a faint curse before answering. "Come on, Cut. I just saved all of us a gigantic headache." He turned around in place anyways. He didn't know Cut, if they'd have the guts to pull the trigger at nearly point-blank range. They probably didn't know what they were in for. But that didn't mean fear wouldn't make them squeeze. Then the game would really be up.

"How… How do I know you're not with him?"

"Who? This dry fart?" Roscoe gave him a kick and the kid yelped. "I've only known him ten minutes and I want to put him in a hole."

Cut was holding the gun squarely but uneasily. Their sharp little face was scrunched up in concentration or deliberation, Roscoe couldn't tell.

"Ariela has a lot of enemies. Maybe you're one of them."

"Maybe he is. I've never heard of your queen until we busted into the place. This is not personal. Just a job."

Music sprang up, filtered by the walls but the sound of bright brass horns sliced through.

"What the sweet hell?"

Cut shrugged. "Las Mañanitas. Kinda funny when you think about No Tomorrows."

The joke was lost on Roscoe.

He took a step forward.

"Hey! Get back!" Cut yelled over the music.

"Not gonna," he said. "In fact-"

He dashed towards Cut, who wasn't in on his joke, so they probably thought he was just insane.

"No! Don't!" Cut screwed their eyes closed.

Roscoe's hand went around theirs, his index finger between the hammer of the gun and the barrel. It might hurt if Cut freaked out, but a lot less than the alternative.

"You don't want to shoot me. Honest. Let's be friends instead."

"You can never have enough friends, I always say." Cut withdrew their hand, taking time with that. Roscoe's blood went hot in his veins. It'd been a long time since he'd touched anyone or been touched at all.

Roscoe took the gun from them and slid it into his back pocket.

"You have such lovely skin, such texture," they said.

"You say that to all the dudes, don't you?" Roscoe then took the kid's gun and stuffed it into his back pocket. "Let's get back to the party, okay? Help me with this guy. I want to see if anyone recognizes him."

They threw the kid through the door first, just as everyone was finishing up the song, holding that last note while Ariela stared into a single very tall candle that stood from the center of a cake on a covered tray. Her lips were pursed as if to blow and she frowned when the gunman hit the floor and splayed out in the red room light.

"I didn't ask for a pip-squeak," she intoned with some disappointment, glancing up from the crashed figure on the floor to Roscoe. "Take him back. Far too small."

"Colt makes everyone the same size," Roscoe said as he took the gun from his back pocket with his left hand. "Don't worry. It's far less dangerous than this one." He indicated his own handgun in the right. "Just so we're clear."

"Cut, what is the meaning of this?" Ariela asked and then pursed her lips as if to blow out the candle. "Quickly."

"So, Roscoe went to check on this guy, who was fucking around not doing dishes, and then he pulled a gun on both of us. They wrestled. That was exciting. And Roscoe got his gun."

"How tedious," the queen said. "Roscoe, why didn't you just shoot him?"

"I only shoot people I'm robbing. And that's just if things go bad."

"Would you say that things are going well?"

He shrugged. "We're all wheels down, rubber on the road still. This long into what's supposed to be a fast job? I'll take it." Roscoe looked around the crowd. "Where's Gre-… my partner?"

Ariela blew on the flame. Instead of dying out, it flicked and grew as if taking strength from the breath. Her face glowed with it, as did the faces of everyone gathered. They stared into the flame seeing something that they kept to themselves, finding some private comfort or answer in it. She drew in another breath and the candle flame was extinguished. Or she breathed it in. Roscoe swore he saw the tip of the fire lean towards her just before it went out and a clawing wisp of smoke hung there instead. It had leaned to her like a pet being called.

"Gregory? He's right there." She pointed absently, as if she was much more interested in the shape of the smoke than the man who was supposed to be covering the room with a shotgun.

Of course they know his name, Roscoe thought. *Sure.*

"Hey, uh, Roscoe." Greg was sitting off not far from where Ariela had pointed. His mask was tilted up on his head like a demented hat. "You didn't bring a straw, so I had to do this to drink." The shotgun was still resting on his lap, no more threatening than a bouquet of daisies.

"For the love of god, tell me you didn't finish it. Here, take this." He pulled out the pistol and walked it over to his brother. Greg rested it beside the shotgun.

"He's been sharing. He's a good boy." The queen pulled the candle out of the cake and laid it to one side with great ceremony.

This was so far out of control that the only sane response would have been to beat feet for the door, get in the car and drive as far as the Magnum would go without crapping out. One gunman on the floor, his brother somehow held prisoner by these lunatics and Roscoe well on his way to completing the set.

"Ariela, esto ha durando demasiado," Alondra said. "Deja de jugar a este ridículo juego."

"Esto es lo más divertido que he tenido." She took a deep breath. "And it's my birthday. It should be fun." She leaned hard on the last sentence, somehow regal and petulant at once. It was not unattractive.

"Pardon my interrupting whatever game this is, but don't you have any interest in why there's a gunman sneaking in here pretending to be a dishwasher?"

Alondra watched the exchange, moving slowly and without sound, crossing behind the table to the chair where Greg was seated uneasily. Pompadour was drinking from the bottle of Walker Black with a smile on his lips as he watched this all unfolding. Roscoe saw glimpses but so quickly that nothing could be done other than register them.

"The pip-squeak? A gunman?"

Roscoe stepped over to the kid and hauled him up to his feet. He weighed about as much as a bag of wet feathers. "She asked you a question."

"So what?" His sneer was defiant yet empty. "Least I'm not here to rob her."

"Enough. Who sent you?"

"You oughta know. We're all in this together, right?" He leered at his tormentor. "You and me and Gregory. All on the same team. Just give me my gun back, huh?"

"Yeah, I'm not with him," Roscoe said, jabbing his thumb at the kid.

Ariela frowned. "I think it would be more exciting and dangerous if you were."

Kid's gonna kill us all. Fuck. Roscoe thought to himself. Amusing or not, the game was just about played out.

Alondra was close enough to Greg that she could snatch away the gun if she was fast about it. There were no eyes on her. She leaned to improve her grip.

"Ahoooooaaaa!" Tacíto whooped half-drunkenly and crashed into Alondra. She toppled forward, falling just short of Greg and his scatter gun and the kid's weapon. Greg was aware enough to catch it but impaired enough to make a clean grab on the flying shotgun impossible. He swatted at it feverishly but came up empty.

"Nobody mo-- fuck!" he blurted. Both the weapons slid out of his lap.

"Grab the gun!" was all Roscoe was able to get out before the back of the kid's head smashed into his front teeth. Then came the elbow to the ear. Red pain, redder even than the light of the room, blossomed from split lips and the side of his head rang with a high-pitched tone like radio static set to deafening.

The kid was out of his hands and scrambling for the shotgun. He just knew it.

"A show! How delightful!" the queen squealed. "Get up, Alondra! You'll miss it!"

Greg fumbled for the gun, clambering in a panic with eyes wide, hyperventilating. Roscoe made a blind swipe for where the kid had been, grabbing only empty air. He tore the mask from his face, since it had gone cockeyed. There was a rose of smeared blood on the inside around his lips.

Skill only gets you so far, he thought. But this wasn't even skill. Skill would have sent him out the door when the queen refused to accept she was in danger and maybe she never had been. But he certainly was. He thought about running, just going in a flash.

But then there was Greg. Dumb, lucky Greg. He'd have been hamburger or whatever happens to hamburger when you run it through the grinder ten more times. And Greg was the only one who'd come see Roscoe more than once. Greg was the only one who'd met him at the bus station. Greg was the only one who'd taken him drinking after. And Greg was the reason he'd gone to Folsom in the first place.

Because Roscoe knew that Greg wasn't cut out for this life at all. He was just lucky. But when good luck runs out, it isn't that it leaves you, it's that it turns into bad luck.

All those thoughts swirled through his head before the mask hit the floor and before he heard the sound of the pistol's hammer coming back.

"Okay, mother fucker," the Kid rasped as he leveled the gun barrel, pointing it up just a little to get right into Roscoe's eye-line. "This is enough of your amateur hour bullshit."

"He hasn't been here even fifteen minutes," Ariela corrected.

The Kid gritted his teeth and winced at that. "Loco bruja."

"There isn't any other kind," she added.

Roscoe knew that word wasn't just woman, but witch. A thought stuck in his head like a rusty nail in a sneaker sole.

"¡Callate, Ariela!" went out over his shoulder, then he turned to Roscoe. "And you, buddy, you go line up over there with your idiot friend."

"He's my brother," Roscoe growled. "And if you touch him, I guarantee, it'll be your last fuck-up."

"Stupid must run in the family. Move! And you. Moron. Bring me that shotgun."

Greg did as he was told. That was his problem. The kid shoved the pistol into his waistband after lowering the hammer back into place. Roscoe noted that he wasn't all stupid. Even if he had traded up to another weapon loaded with blanks. But there was no way of him knowing that.

Roscoe took his place with the others, helping Greg up to his feet. Alondra stared daggers at him as if it were his fault that an at least semi-professional killer was holding a shotgun on the birthday party. For her part, Ariela didn't seem to mind at all.

"I thought you two were far more entertaining that the pip-squeak. He's just boring."

"Boring? Your majesty? I'm the one who's going to give you the best birthday present ever. A one-way trip to hell." He might have been professional, but he was goofy enough to spit lines like he was in a matinee show.

"Who sent you?" Alondra asked. She brought her hand up towards her mouth, turning it crossways.

"Stop. I know your tricks well enough." He put the scatter gun barrel enough in her direction that would have taken her face right to the bone. "Just be lucky I'm here for Ariela and not you. But that time might come. Are you afraid?"

"I'm not afraid of little boys," she said, not even bothering to snarl it.

"Calm yourself, sister," Ariela said. "This has stopped being fun. I'd like to enjoy my cake. If you tell me who sent you, I'll let you walk out of here without you having nightmares for the rest of your life."

The Kid stared for a moment and then he began to laugh. "Other people might fear the mighty Queen of No Tomorrows, but I'm not one of them. Your tricks are only that. You can't open the door to the Míctlan that my grandfather feared. But I can." He tipped the gun barrel, aiming squarely at Ariela.

She remained seated, more interested in the cake and the hole that the candle had left, looking uncomfortably like an entry wound. Roscoe couldn't shake that. She was breathing deeply but regularly, calm. He'd never seen anyone like this before, so utterly without regard for harm or even the physical nature of the world around her. She'd have crossed the 405 at rush hour without looking anywhere other than straight ahead.

"Look at me, bruja!" the Kid ordered. "I want you to see me last."

"You don't want that at all," she said. "If you do, you'll not see me, but your Grandfather brought back from the lands of the dead themselves."

"Do it!" he shouted hard enough to make his voice crack.

She turned to him, slowly, as if giving him every excuse to get out of the way. Roscoe could only see her in briefest profile as she looked up, her eyes not quite meeting his.

The gunshot went off, loud but not loud enough. The smoke was thin. Not black powder or cordite, but something else, pink as sunrise. There was the briefest flash of spark from the barrel and then a shower of color. At first fast and then very slow, like a thousand little parachutes of red and yellow and blue opening up, all metallic, all in a cloud of glitter. It was confetti, a riot of it.

"Clint you goddamn clown," Roscoe muttered. "Blanks, not this crap."

Ariela shrieked "¡Feliz cumpleaños a mí!" as the dots of color fell ridiculously around her and the ringing sound faded.

The Kid stood there, unclear on what had just happened and when it finally dawned on him, he racked up another shot as quickly as he could and fired again. More thin smoke, more color, more confetti. No death at all, but a party. He lowered the gun and his lip quivered as he urinated forcefully in his tight pants.

Roscoe dove forward and decked him for the second time in a night, before he could load up another shot or reach for the gun in his waistband. There was no way for him to have known it, but his gun was the only one with real bullets in it. Hopefully the blanks were less obvious than the confetti shot, what the hell was that even?

The pool at the kid's feet had spread out, shaped like a continent of realized fear. Roscoe relieved him of both weapons, pocketing the pistol once again and holding the shotgun down at the floor. There was no need to cover the kid. He couldn't do anything other than stand there and whisper to himself.

"Es verdad. Es verdad. Todo es verdad."

"No sabes lo que es realmente cierto," Ariela said to the quivering man. "And you, thank you so much for saving us," went out to Roscoe. "I am in your debt."

"You're welcome," he said, not believing that he'd had any part in it. But at least she was thanking him and not cutting both him and Greg to ribbons.

Then she turned to regard the ruined cake, covered nearly completely with confetti and inedible. "But is it art?" she said with a giggle. "Win or lose, one must keep playing."

Alondra came to her side. "¿Tu estas bien?" She took the queen by the shoulders and looked her up and down, untouched but for a scattering of color and smoke-smudging like misplaced makeup on her pale skin.

"Estoy bien, hermana. ¡Fue divertido!"

Alondra shook her head with a smile. "Hay veces que todavía te conozco."

"Me conoces lo suficiente bien."

Roscoe stomped over to Greg, who was deflated in his chair, mask ridiculous and halfway on his head. "I know. I fucked it all up."

"This was fucked-up well before either of us was involved, little brother. But we better get out all the same."

His eyes glazed over with tears. "I'm the worst outlaw."

"Nah, man. You're good. You've kept out of prison. That puts you ahead of a lot of would-bes."

"But the ring? We gotta get that."

"You see any rings on any of the queen's fingers? That was a setup." He pointed towards Ariela and then realized that not only she, but all her entourage were watching them. All but for Tacíto, who stood behind the Kid, pinning his arms. The tattoos on his arms seemed to move in the weird red light. But Roscoe knew that couldn't be happening.

"Oh shit," he whispered.

"'Oh shit,' indeed," the queen answered. She pointed at Greg then Roscoe with a finger that seemed too long, jet black nail as shiny as fresh paint on a new car. "I'll get to you, but I have more pressing business."

She turned back to the Kid and the way she looked at him, Roscoe wouldn't have been in his shoes for even a second, not for every score promised and then denied him. Not for Capone money. She wasn't angry, instead anticipating, almost hungry. There was no slackness in her skin, no softness, as if she'd been carved from marble to a face of simmering and demanding wrath being held back by a net of will that was all but snapped.

"You ruined a perfectly lovely, if not dull party. I'm sorry, everyone," she said with a shrug of apology, mostly to Cut. "It's my fault for being so particular. And you wanted to please me so hard that you squeezed the life from it like a little canary bird.

"But that's no excuse for ruining it." She licked her lip just a little, tongue-tip scarlet against the black bow.

Roscoe wanted to run, to pick up Greg and carry the both of them as far as he could. Maybe they'd make the car. Maybe they'd make the galley. But no matter how hard he thought about it, he couldn't budge his foot. It just wouldn't listen. Maybe Greg was the same or maybe he'd just defeated himself.

"Asegúrese de que no pueda moverse, Tacíto."

"Mi reina." The shorter man flexed a little and the Kid grimaced but did not make a sound.

"Cual es su nombre, pequeñita?" She looked at the cake, maybe hoping that it could fix itself if she thought about it hard enough, and maybe she even could.

"Tomás Augusto Ximeno." He stood there perspiring in a rictus.

"Mucho gusto, Tomás."

The kid Tomás said nothing. Tacíto whispered something for only him to hear and then he swallowed hard.

"El placer es mío, reina."

"Bien. Now, as this concerns them, let's continue in English, yes?" She waved back behind her, vaguely indicating Roscoe and Greg. The attention made Roscoe want to shrink even further.

"Okay."

"Do you know these two? You said you did, but that smelled like a lie to me."

"I have never seen them before."

She dipped her chin down once in a half-nod and then turned to look directly at him. "Who sent you to see me with that gun?"

"Mi reina, nosotros no podemos saber que esta minitiendo ahora," Tacíto said.

The queen looked to Alondra and she nodded back reluctantly. "That is true. Tomás, answer."

He said nothing, lips pulled down in a scowl, as if he were suffering unseen pain coursing through him. "I can't say."

Ariela grimaced, no longer even filled with hate but shrugging disappointment so heavy it pulled all of her down with a sense of drudgery. "We tried it my way, with pleasantries. I asked."

Tomás shook his head, perhaps from whatever was eating at him, perhaps in response to Ariela.

"We will try it your way. You will beg to tell me and perhaps I will even listen." She stood back from her chair and walked slowly towards where Tomás was being held.

"Lights!" she said with a snap.

The red lights dimmed down to a simmering nothing, only the vaguest sense of shapes outlined from lamps spilling in from the hallway. The notion of just barely seeing things made them far worse than total blindness. A handful of the partygoers pulled out and held up lighters, all ignited in silence.

Ariela held her hands before her, just above head height, index fingers on either hand extended and nearly touching. She drew them down in arcs that almost matched, each fingernail scratching out a trace in the air. They left a disturbance, a streak that caught the light like an imperfection in glass seen side-on. Both her fingers passed one another and met up on the opposite side, forming overlapping circles that hung in the air, a shape that should not have been there.

"¿Que hay detrás de esta ventana, Tomás?" she asked, neither smiling nor frowning.

Roscoe's eyes had adjusted to the gloom and he could see more clearly, but then he realized that it was not his eyes adjusting. Instead it was the etched circle in the air glowing with a reddish, purplish color that would not fix. It flowed and bent with a strange pulse.

"¡Te diré!"

"Más tarde lo harás. Dime que ves."

Tomás' was weeping. The big tears were the truth behind every bully, every gunman hiding behind a piece of iron so they didn't have to feel another thing or show how much the world had ground them down day after day. Some dudes in the can cried like that when they realized they had to get out, that they couldn't stay in the ordered chaos of those four walls. Roscoe hadn't, but he knew what drove them.

Ariela reached into the top of the hanging circle with her black fingernails. They drove sparks from the pulsing line, sparks the color of blood. She set her feet and shoulders and then she pulled down, ripping the circle out of the air with a shudder that felt like a big wave at the beach, unexpected and stunning.

"¡Abrir la ventana!" she shouted.

Something rushed out, darker than the dim of the room. The glow from the circle was gone and something much blacker came in its place, unfurling and unfolding, tendrils or fronds of plants made from shadow. Feathery, lifeless shapes manifested themselves and they licked over Tomás' face like flame eating a burning building. They left no marks on him, but he flinched from them all the same.

The pressure in the room had changed, cold weight upon Roscoe like two weeks in the hole that he got once for tripping a guard though it was the guy's own fault and that injustice just made it sting more. Concrete got no kindness, not in Folsom winter.

Tomás screamed and it might have even been a word. All that came out was unreasoning fear, the fear of fever dreams, the sound someone makes when they give it all up and run headlong into thoughtlessness. He didn't scream so much as the scream was pulled out of him. Then he wept as he dropped to his knees.

The fronds or limbs or whatever they were played over him one last time, one last caress from the pit, the un-place that they had been called up from. They withdrew with a startling and gentle deliberateness. Curling sections folded and drew in on themselves, becoming flatter and flatter until they disappeared from view. Ariela held her hands out in front of her, flat. Then she drew them together and what had once been there was gone.

She snapped her fingers and the lights came on, not the red lights from the shattered chandelier, but the room lights, as if a play that nobody knew they were participating in had just ended. Roscoe had no sense of isolation, no weight of solitary. He could only barely remember the most fleeting glimpse of the shadows that had been there a moment ago. The only real evidence of it was Tomás, kneeling in his own issue.

"It looks like we've taken all the fight out of Tomás," Ariela said. She walked over towards him, trailing a train of shining blue-black fabric behind, so deep that Roscoe felt as if he could have dived into it.

Ariela knelt down besides the defeated kid and drew her fingers down from his slicked hair down his cheek and whispered to him. He spat an answer as a teetotaler would have spat a mouthful of whiskey. Roscoe could not pick out any of it.

He watched as Tacíto observed the proceeding with care. His eyes were still hidden behind wraparound shades, though he sweat a little. Maybe from holding the kid down. Maybe.

The queen stood and told the others to come, pointed to the Kid and then pointed to the back door, through the galley hall. They all moved quickly, deferentially, disappearing the ex-gunman and then themselves, leaving only Tacíto and Alondra behind with the Queen. They argued briefly, but whatever Ariela had thought before, she thought. She glanced at the two of them and Roscoe felt something let go, something that he could not see but had been there. His body startled as if he was having a falling dream, catching himself on the edge of sleep.

Greg gasped quietly next to him.

"You okay?"

"Yeah. I guess. Feel weird. You?"

"I'm okay. Just how long is that gonna last?"

"Until the queen gets bored."

Alondra pointed out towards the door that kid had just been carted through, hard enough to make her noose-braids jostle like a gallows rope in the wind. Ariela shook her head in the negative and made a gesture that encompassed the room then folded her arms in front of her for a moment before lifting a single finger up.

The discussion was over. Roscoe could hear Alondra's teeth grit from where he stood.

"Thank you ever so much for your patience," Ariela said with a brightness. "Do you know why you're here?"

"We came here to steal a ring, ma'am," Greg offered and Roscoe could only shake his head at that.

"Oh, that's right. You did, didn't you. And I forgot to wear it altogether." She tapped out her fingers one by one as if counting them.

"And are you going to be wanting your money back, too?" Roscoe asked.

"I'm quite sure that I don't know what you are talking about. You were both *very* entertaining."

Roscoe was at a loss as to what he should think of things. Had Greg and he been hired as a distraction or had the robbery been an enticement to flush out an attempt on her own life? He didn't know because it was an unknowable thing. The queen was never going to tell them, even if it amused her to. There would be no path to certainty, no more than who killed JFK or that random joe found dead on the riverbed under Sixth Street.

"Can I share something with you, majesty? An observation from a simple ex-strong arm man."

Her smile could have lit the city with its gracious patience. "Nothing would please me more."

"The biggest jobs are all inside jobs."

"Isn't that what makes them the most delicious? The deceit, the trickery?" Her face crinkled beautifully at the thought of it, the glee boiling up through her smiling mouth and eyes.

"And the blanks? How did you know?"

Her smirk was unreadable. "It is best not to dwell on these things. If you would, please leave the pip-squeak's pistol on the wash-basin. You won't be able to use it here."

"What's going to happen to him?" Greg asked, innocent as a lamb.

"What I told your brother applies doubly here, Gregory. Don't think about it. It is not your problem any longer. You've done your job beautifully. Your stories are so funny."

"Did he tell you the one about Lucky Liquors?"

"Perhaps another time," Ariela said. "And thank you for making this birthday so memorable. So thrilling."

She extended her hand and it was small and perfect, pale porcelain skin with nails like black shards of nothing. She held up her hand in offering.

Alondra coughed with a broken glass brusqueness.

"Oh, right, shit," Roscoe said. He bowed and kissed it gently, awkward in his own body for the moment, drowning in the ceremony of it.

She offered it to Greg. "Oh, no thanks, ma'am. I hardly even know you," he replied. "But you sure are pretty. Even more than Elvira."

Ariela's eyes widened, just for a moment, lit up with a sudden and startling enthusiasm. "I just love monster movies, don't you? It's so nice to… fake believe for a while."

"Don't you mean make believe?" he asked with an innocence that babes couldn't pretend to.

She shook her head then withdrew, reservation frozen where something more carefree had sneaked out. She clasped her hands into one another and stood without saying a word, resplendent in blue black that fit like water fit the shoreline.

"You should go," Alondra said.

"Happy, ah, birthday, Your Majesty," Roscoe said as he grabbed Greg before he could say something else and shatter the very thin ice they were skating along.

"Felix cumpleanos," Greg said without the ñ sound, mangling it.

Ariela had already turned back towards the table, brandishing a knife above the cake for a moment and then setting it down with a gravity best described in measures of sorrow.

The Magnum was sitting in a blue-white pool of streetlight like an ice floe in an ocean of darkness. They both got in and collapsed into the seats, all the pent-up energy and nerve bleeding out of every pore and breath until they could do nothing for a few moments, only exist. Roscoe just kept thinking about an oncoming train barreling down and then running through the both of them as if they hadn't really even ever been.

"You okay, Greg?"

"Never better. Though I'm confused about the ring still."

"Don't be. It's settled."

"But that guy. The one who set it up."

Roscoe cranked the engine and it complained before rattling to life. "The guy probably works for her."

"Oh. Okay." He sat there and thought about things for a moment. Then his face stretched out in horror for a moment. "I just remembered, I forgot to do something."

"What?" Roscoe asked, dreading the answer. He edged the car out of the spot of light and into the dark.

"I never did swap out those shells like you asked. See?"

He dumped out the bag that Roscoe had gotten from Clint. The cartridges were all silver-jacketed. The shotgun shells were marked in bright orange plastic. For safety. Roscoe stared at them, even picking up one of the stunt shells and holding it up in the light to make sure.

He hit the gas and never looked back

THE CINDERHAUS

The song ended and as if cued, the lady's spurs jingled almost deferentially as she crossed the threshold. Silver. Ornate. Flashes of light and sharpness at her ankles. Clasps like a hand encircling her just above the tops of her shoes. She was maybe in her fifties, perhaps older. Well dressed and kept, walking with shoulders squared back like she was being followed by a bodyguard who'd make King Kong think twice. Walking in like she owned Third Hand Books. Because she did.

Cait knew her only as Rose Gill, but she supposed the woman had more names than that. She owned an odd scattering of businesses in Los Angeles and Palm Desert and maybe even Santa Barbara, wherever old money went to relax, ready to be served. The Third Hand Bookstore was one of the smallest gems in the crown that she wore, but it was the one Cait knew best. As well as she could learn the ins and outs of a place in six or so weeks.

The PA in the store filled the place with a low-cycle hum, the noise of the record change. Then the needle dropped and the record hissed for a moment. "In the Flat Field" by Bauhaus started up, drums of pursuit and jarring guitar sketching out borders of new territories. Probably too loud.

Rose stood there, taking in the sight of the shop for a moment in the late afternoon sun. She half-smiled, satisfied, then let that melt away as her expression went to one of dissatisfaction and a faintly shaken head.

Cait moved to turn down the volume a bit. Too late. The store had been empty but for her and Grace loitering somewhere in the back room, probably playing with the fog-grey cat who didn't have a name and wouldn't have come to it anyways.

"Sorry, ma'am," Cait said and tried to hold her blush down. "You're Mrs. Gill, aren't you?"

Rose looked her up and down, taking her in from auburn hair to black Converse, the in-between wrapped up in jeans and long black blouse, ruby-red sweater jacket over that. Even though judgment was reserved, Cait felt under-presented.

"Miss," she said by way of answer. "But please call me Rose. And you could only be Cait."

"Yes, ma'am."

Grace materialized out of the back room, holding the grey monster like a stuffed toy. Cait's expression told her to step back and disappear.

"Oh, please. Just Rose is fine."

The call to informality did nothing to calm Cait. She'd only worked here a short time, but she'd never been late, never missed a register count, never had to be told how to do something more than once. She'd learned who could safely browse without supervision and who was just there to try and lift anything valuable from the open shelves. Roy, who ran the place, was even okay with Grace coming in and hanging out, helping enough for pocket money. Employment came and went in cycles and he'd been at a slack tide for some time, so he was more than a little permissive so long as things got done.

But Roy was not here and Cait wasn't sure where Rose drew the line, informality or not.

"Well, is there something I can help you with?"

"I need your expertise on some items for sale that I may or may not be bidding on tonight." She tilted her head as if to glance down the stacks and then smiled. "Have your friend and the cat come out up front to watch the door and the till. And let's us talk for a moment in the back room."

"Grace," Cait called back. "You've been promoted."

Grace stood behind the register like Cait had just tossed her the keys to the Jag parked outside, but feeling more fear than opportunity.

An hour later, Third Hand was closed and locked up tight, with an apologetic yet threatening note taped to the inside of the front door: SOR-RY, CLOSED EARLY – GUARD CAT WILL EAT YOU.

Cait was waiting in front of her apartment building for a car to come get her. Grace had gone wherever she did once the sun went down. She was always cagey about that, to the point of evasiveness. Cait's makeup was barely dry and she was trying to come down from the panting pace she'd had to run to make the new timeline for the evening. So much for *Bride of Frankenstein* at the Vista.

Instead, she was going to the Cinderhaus auction.

As the invited guest of Rose Gill.

She'd heard about it, but had never been, even when she was at her most active in the world of antique books and other crimes. You were only ever asked to come. You couldn't just wander in. The venue changed every year and Cait hadn't even heard when this year's would happen much less where to even look for it.

But then it had been a very long year for her.

Settle down. Just relax. You're being let in and they can't toss you out. But it's wild. Not even Rory Soame had gotten invited when he was my blind. Maybe they'd tumbled to the fact that he was a fiction. Maybe he had never rated.

The car coming up the drive was like none she'd heard before, liquid purring betraying untapped reserves of power just waiting to be called upon. The twin pairs of headlights came on like early dawn, hitting Cait with tangible heat. It was an old, old car, coffin-shaped body and curved outside fenders and running board that flowed organically with a hypnotic grace that felt like motion even when standing still.

Cait stared at the relic, all silver-painted and lacquered, with sheen showing hot spots of light like the iridescence of dragonfly wings. It rumbled with contained power as the door closest to Cait came open.

"Step inside yourself," Rose said from behind the wheel. "Preston's visiting his mother in Hoboken."

Cait looked inside at the car, better appointed than any house she'd ever lived in.

"I don't make enough to sit in here," she said.

"Neither do I, dear. But we do what we must. Move along. I have to be selective where I park this behemoth."

Cait climbed in and slid onto the bench seat, realizing she was uncomfortably close to Rose. Maybe the car was bigger on the outside.

"'Behemoth?' Not much of a name for a car."

"People and pets and horses get names," she said. "This is a car."

"But what a car."

The leather of the seats was yielding to the touch but felt like it could turn any knife short of the white obsidian blade tucked into her clutch. And maybe it could stop even that.

She was rocked back in the seat as Rose pulled away from the curb, door barely latched. She muscled into traffic, taking space more than asking for it. The other cars gave no argument, not even horns.

"What, exactly, do you know about the Cinderhaus?" she asked. "By the way, good choices in dress. Pretty, a little rough. Your makeup's overdone, though."

Cait didn't know what to think. She was being buffaloed, but she was also letting herself be. Rose was the boss, but how far was that supposed to go?

"Cat got your tongue? That won't do. Not where we're going. Can't just get by on a batted lash and knee and cleavage. You better be able to talk."

"Hold on. I'm just settling in."

"You've got about ten minutes to put all that behind you and be ready," Rose said as she pushed the car into a lurching long turn on Los Feliz towards Hollywood.

"Ready for what? It's an auction."

"Girl, you say auction when it's really <u>court</u>. We're at court with lords and ladies and people who would just as soon flick us away like flies."

"'Us'? That's crazy. You and I aren't even from the same world. You're driving a goddamn Duesenberg and I'm… Well, leave off my car." The Mercury was sitting in her garage, though it shouldn't have been. It should've been resting comfortably near the pilings of Fisherman's Pier in Venice. Instead it was in the covered garage of Cait's apartment, just daring to be driven. Cait hadn't gathered the nerve for that yet.

"Oh, you recognized the make?" Rose said with an approving grin. "Most folks would just say it's a Rolls and that really grinds my gears."

"Says so on the plaque on the dash and the inset on the wheel."

She tore her eyes away from traffic for a second and glanced to where Cait had pointed. "So it does. And you and I are closer together in class than you might think. I just happen to have money. Some. Now. Cinderhaus."

Cait tried to compose herself but her insides felt like a cracked sea cliff road ready to give way. She hadn't needed to put up a front since her job before Third Hand, the one she'd set fire to and was the best decision she'd made in months.

"Need to get you some spurs, Cait."

"Spurs? Oh, right. I was gonna ask."

"Ask away. And yes, I'm wearing them. Especially now."

"Okay, what's with the spurs?"

"To remind me that I better be leading the horse or by god the horse will lead me."

"And horses don't have any sense?"

"They have more sense than most people. But you ride or you are ridden. There's no in-between."

Cait took a breath and braced herself against the upcoming at the yellow light. Instead, Rose just hammered the gas and the car roared through the intersection and the was blood red behind them. Vertigo and surprise flushed through Cait as she caught her breath.

"The Cinderhaus. What do you know?"

Cait flummoxed in place of answering until she got a hold of things. "Cinderhaus is exclusive, art and books and–"

"The Unique. Nowhere else will you see these things."

"I was getting there!"

"Well get there! Who runs it?"

"Don't know. Nobody knows. They don't have a physical address. I've only seen an invitation once."

"Twice," Rose said as she whipped her hand up, traffic light filtering through the parchment oblong, gilt edges catching light and looking like forgotten embers, writing ornate and nearly unreadable.

Cait snatched the card from Rose's fingers and started reading it as best she could. The type owed more to Belle Epoque than the Bauhaus, somehow unexpectedly so.

"Okay, it says you and one guest. But I still don't get why you picked me."

"Because my pocket forger and I are no longer on speaking terms," Rose said grimly. She shot a glance at her directly. "Oh, yes, I know."

She felt diminished somehow, hollow as the first time she'd tried to dress up like a grownup, only to be treated like a kid. "I'm going to guess Valerie told you."

"Mmm-hmm. I asked around after Roy hired you. Not that I don't trust him, but I am curious." The oncoming lights made Rose's face hard-edged and wiser, all the wrinkles bought and paid for with experience. "If this is even something you're still doing. I couldn't catch wind of it. Don't feel bad. I know how to keep a secret."

Only because you don't know what my secret really is. Only because you don't know about the book that I didn't forge but wrote and how it came true anyways. At least I could enjoy books now. There were months that I couldn't open one.

"Besides, we wouldn't have much of a business without forgery. There's only so much actual rarity to go around."

"So, you want me to spot fakes for you? I'll do what I can, but I'm rusty. Gave it up, remember?"

"Oh, but fakery never gave up on you." Rose slashed over and the nearly three tons of iron flowed like mercury down the boulevard. "Don't worry. Just put on your spurs and get ready for the show. You'll know what I need when I need it."

"Well, that's a relief. Now if only I could do that for myself."

"Don't be hard on yourself. You got this far."

The doozie pushed on like a China shop bull, shouldering ahead until the lights looked a little more like Hollywood. Spotlights stabbed up, beacons to something otherworldly, telling them it was okay to land here no matter how freaky they were. They'd be at home.

INVITATION ONLY, the marquee at Grauman's Egyptian theater read in tidy translucent red lettering. A brace of bruisers stood at either side of a purple-carpeted walkway. Their suits fit so perfectly as to pass into the realm of fiction and impossibility. They wore expressionless faces, immovable until shown the invitation or lack thereof. Lackers were sent packing without anger or umbrage, but sometimes a subdued glee. Cait watched the two of them bodily remove a pair of would-be gatecrashers, smiling gorilla smiles as they flexed muscle beneath silk jackets that defied the pricing of mere currency. She couldn't help but think of another pair of bouncers that were probably at their post at the Last Prayer Club, just up the street a ways. Though maybe not. Rumor was that the club's best days were behind it and maybe the queen's death took more with her than No Tomorrows or her followers were going to admit to themselves.

"Oh, good evening Miss Gill," one of the gorillas said in a caramel-smooth baritone. "So lovely to have you join us tonight." There was a faint trace of an accent to it, something old and of the continent.

"So good to see you, Otto," Rose said as she offered the invitation.

He held it in front of an unassuming candle that glowed with the most golden flame Cait had ever seen.

"A formality," he said by way of apology.

"I'd insist if you did not," Rose said. "This is my associate and guest for the evening, Cait MacReady."

The bouncer took her in at a glance. "Will she be returning with you to future events?"

She glanced back and gave a wink. "Jury's out. And you're assuming there will be future events."

"One must always plan." His voice was a booming rumble, even in resignation. "Please do go in."

His partner and he stepped aside, far enough to permit both Rose and Cait to pass with a respectful distance between their massive shoulders.

"Thank you, boys," Rose said.

"Why the muscle?" Cait asked after she thought they were well out of earshot.

"Not everyone gets inside. And there has been… trouble over that."

The Egyptian's atrium was bordered by faux sandstone walls and escarpment cut and shaped to mimic the proportion of titans, of time long past, offering a taste of grandeur that was once sought after and today only seemed kitschy. Strings of lights went from wall to wall overhead, making a luminous webbing. No bugs circled the pinpricks of light or the lit torches that made a processional alongside the purple carpet. Something in its fibers glittered like tinsel embedded in the floor long after Christmas, something special.

Firelight threw rippling shadows of the palm trunks against the walls, evoking a feeling that nothing was fixed. Cait found herself watching the light and shadow, swallowed up by it. Bas-relief faces of pharaohs took on life, lips pursed as if to speak but held back.

"I feel a little weird," she said.

"Then you'll fit right in. Everyone's a little weird here."

Rose took Cait past columns shaped like ancient urns, over which cuneiform-seeming neon burned and opened a gateway to another place.

The inside lobby was done up like Cleopatra's tomb in neon and 30s glamour with some of the shine rubbed raw. After the glow of the lights and gleam of gilt paint and wall frescoes, she was hit with the clean and pungent smell of burning white sage. Underneath that was tobacco and weed and something else, more floral.

"Guess the new smoking laws don't apply here, huh?" she asked.

"Old habits will die hard. Besides this isn't a public space tonight. I don't think anyone will complain."

They passed a man in an embroidered suit at the ticket taker's space. His skin was layered in gold, everywhere that Cait could see, metallic sheen turning colors in the building's interior lights. He collected the invitations without a word, nodding and smiling as he did. Beside him was a sign indicating that cameras and recording devices were strictly verboten, using that word with an underline streaked out in gold so as not to be missed.

"I hope you're ready," Rose said as she took Cait into the crowd.

Music strung through the room, punches of urgent drum and sinuous organ tones with overlapping singers, almost tuneless. The voices of the crowd blended into white noise, a language beneath whatever was being spoken, becoming the snatches of speech heard on the edge of sleep. Everyone there had stepped out of an Erté drawing, pulled from life but made unreal. The glamor came out not in drips but a flood, dresses custom and outrageous, suits terminally sharp and adhering to their own sense, their own fashion. It wasn't even like what Cait saw on the magazine stands, but an alien set of standards and superlatives.

"Surviving?" Rose asked. "Maybe you need a drink."

"That's probably a bad idea," Cait said. "I'll be okay. It's just a lot."

Rose pulled her to one side, in the glow of a concession stand filled not with popcorn and candy, but jewelry and gemstones laid out in glittering arrangements. Other artifacts were there, staked out on the ripples of black velvet, as enticing as a book with a page torn out. Just their presence aroused a desire, a need to have, simply because they were there with the glass between you and them. They'd been elevated form object to obsessional, to fetish.

Cait's eyes flicked to the crowd again, their panoply, united only in the fact that they were human plus, removed from the mundane. Of course they were. They were rich. And she was hopelessly out of place. Even more than she had been at faculty and fundraising functions, where the school and it representatives would go out with hat in hand. She hadn't been on their level for being there. She had been nothing more than a potential tax write-off or perhaps another set of lights to get a name hung in. She wished for a familiar face besides Rose, whom she hardly knew. Instead she was swimming in a world that was rarified, where the air was only mostly breathable.

It was then that she saw Alondra, dressed not for her station as queen of No Tomorrows, but as they'd first met, in black denim and a tightly-cut motorcycle jacket that was smooth as an asphalt kiss. She locked eyes with Cait for a moment and then smiled, bringing up a single finger to her darkened lips and making the sign for silence. She, too, was wary. Her braids were tight and she was polite and restrained in her movements. She was on guard. She had her spurs well on.

That was a comfort that Cait couldn't even begin to describe. She had gone head to head with Alondra and Ariela before her and at least had survived it. If even Alondra was not relaxed and easy here, Cait could feel that way and be in good company.

It's just Hollywood. Nothing you can't handle.

"You ready to do this?"

"Yeah, just. Straight into the deep end." Cait waved her hand, so as to encompass the clothes and the weird light and the holdover Egyptian décor like a Disneyland of the deranged.

"Only way to really know if you can swim." Rose patted her on the shoulder gently. "You should have seen me at my first. Couldn't have been any much older than you. Was brought here by a friend who was even more a fish out of water then than we are."

"That's pretty tough to imagine."

"Oh, it's not so bad now. Used to be that class was a solid wall that you couldn't hope to climb over. Oh sure, you could have an affair, but only on the QT. Back then, well, things were different."

"I won't pretend to get it."

"Good. Knowing that you don't know anything is a good place to start. Come, let's look over the catalog before the action begins."

The catalog was not a printed book, a fact that did not surprise Cait, given the admonishment against recording and cameras. The Cinderhaus was a place that only existed for a short time, temporary as sidewalk ice. Permanence did not suit it. Nor did leaving a written trail. Though it hadn't always been like that, or so Rose had said. There had been catalogs for a short time in the thirties, rumored to have come from the very first years, when the auction had been started by expatriate Europeans fleeing the rise of fascism and the fall of the world they'd known. Same as the expressionists, artists and writers like Brecht who left home and ended up in wildest Hollywood, surely as out of water as any fish had been.

The offerings for the evening were set up in a room off to the side, a modest space filled with most immodest treasures. At least that was the sense that Cait picked up. The lighting was less curatorial and more reverential, not merely illuminating the collection. Instead, it was gauzed like the old-time movie cameras, given a glow and indistinctness that made the mundane seem more than that, more than mere.

Men and women suited like the ticket taker, each of them daubed with gold makeup, whether on their cheeks or eyes or lips, stood by every catalog item. All of them wore white gloves of felt or some other matte material, without dimension or depth. They had clouds for hands, moving like cirrus over the desert when the land thirsted for rain but could offer none. They danced with dryness and would answer questions but not engage in conversation or chit-chat. You were expected to inquire, not to gossip. Various buyers drifted past the exhibits. All of them ended up stopping at their own prize, pointing and maybe even allowing an expression of glee or awe.

Cait had seen that look in the face of men and women, when their desires had been laid bare and presented to them, whether it was at Third Hand or the book fair or the library or even face to face at a place of their choosing, where a copy of the *Darrab Althabean* could be found, sold by Cait. Sometimes even made by her.

They were selling personal dreams here. To only the people who could afford them.

"Do not touch," Rose warned with a weight to her voice. "If you wish to see a different view, please ask the enablers to hold the item for you or turn the page."

"Touching is reserved only for the purchaser?"

"And sometimes not even then. Often the item is bought and whisked away into a case or a shelf or safe deposit box never to be seen again. Collectors are an odd lot."

"Is that what you are, Rose? A collector?"

"You make it sound like a dirty word."

"I didn't mean to."

"I'm teasing."

"Just that, I understand wanting a thing, but it makes people do weird stuff. Paying outrageous sums is the least of it."

"One woman's outrageous is another woman's trifle. Come, let's look. But no more talking. You are allowed to question each Enabler once if you like. Twice will mark you as a rube or indecisive."

"We wouldn't want that," Cait said with light gravity.

"Remember I'm your sponsor, so what you do, I did."

"I'll behave."

The first table was violet velvet-draped, almost the same color as the carpet-way outside. On it, in a pool of light cast by an unseen lamp was a dirty bottle of whiskey, Bart's Bug Juice by brand. The liquid inside was clear and amber and Cait was made thirsty just looking at it.

"Blessed by the priest?" Rose asked the maroon-jacketed attendant.

"The very same. Would you like to look closer?" The woman held her hands just short of the bottle, perfectly still.

"Thank you, no. I wouldn't want you to cloud it with sediment."

The bottle was rough, hand-made and blown, label slapped on carelessly as a Saturday night after a row of shots. But the liquid inside fairly glowed.

It's just the light. Just old hooch. Nothing holy about it.

Just a ways down was a table where a squat videotape sat, one of those professional jobs, not VHS for the home. Written on the label in fat red ink was the word AIRBURST with double underlines beneath it. They drifted past.

Not an antique so why is it here?

Another table with a light amber jug, squat and round with a paper label that said PUREX on it. The liquid inside was cloudy and seemed to swirl of its own accord. The type on it was old, not Art Deco, but a sturdier and more workmanlike block printing. The contents turned and whirled. Inside shoals of glittering dust and what looked like disembodied teeth were the bones of fishes that Cait could not name. Some part of it touched her, not in thirst, but in sympathy.

"When did you get this?" Rose asked. "Someone's been hiding it."

"I'm not at liberty to say, Miss Gill. If you rephrase, I might be able to help you." The Enabler, a heavyset Black man spoke with a voice that seemed to rumble from beneath him.

"That's all right. Still, a marvel to see."

Cait tried to understand the significance of it. Maybe it was part of Thing That Wants, but then all water was. Her thoughts turned to it and whether or not it had found the peace it thought it was seeking or if it would keep its promise.

Surely it has to.

They passed a table with three pyramidal chunks of either glass or metal or something in-between. Pausing before it, Cait could feel them humming, a sound that was palpable but not audible. An eerie magnetism passed between them, shivering and tentative. Cait felt gooseflesh go up her arm and right to the base of her skull. Beside that was a double helix of thorny vines, intertwined upon one another like snakes in mating.

Rose wiped away a tear at that, not one born from love or from mourning, but something that Cait couldn't find a word for and maybe Rose herself could not.

Cait looked away and gave her a moment, even if she would never have asked for it. Scanning back, Cait saw another familiar figure, this one a man in a dark blue suit, cut for him some fifteen pounds ago. His skin was well-tanned and wrinkled more from the sun than from actual age. He was another faker, just like Cait had been once, only a different flavor.

Ehmet Khan looked up and saw her, his dark eyes twinkling with not mischief, but superiority, glowing with smugness. He went from a surprise to a smile and leaned over to the man he stood beside, an older white man, thin and deliberate and patient. The other, clearly the superior, nodded and gave a dismissive wave. Khan left with a supercilious bow and then walked towards Cait.

Oh goddammit. I am not in the mood for his bullshit right now.

"Miss MacReady," he said with a frictionless smoothness. "Why what a pleasure it is to see you here at the Cinderhaus. Finally. Would you like me to show you around?"

Ughhhhh.

"No thank you, Mr…" Cait pulled back a half-step and brought a finger to her lips. She stroked them thoughtfully. "What *is* your name again? I know we've met."

Khan's face went long. "Ehmet Khan. Why, not a year ago, you sold me some books."

Over which you later tracked me down and accused me of being fake. Yeah, I remember you just fine.

"I've sold a lot of people books," she said, trying to keep with insouciance instead of the rudeness he deserved. "You'd have to be more specific."

"Why, the *Darrab Althabean*, the 1812 edition."

"Mr. Khan, can I call you Mr. Khan?"

He opened his mouth to make it more familiar and Cait cut him off.

"That book that you were so enamored of, is one that was sought by a number of potential buyers."

Come on. Take the bait. Let's see if you have the guts to do this in public.

"But this one was special. I believe it to have been hand-made," he said with a grin. "It's actually part of a lot that Mr. Bergeson is offering up for sale tonight."

"Well, I wish you the best of luck on the sale," she said. "Is there something else that I can help you with?" Cait realized her attitude had parked itself somewhere between customer service and go fuck yourself. About where she wanted it. "I'm not really in the field anymore, just a guest of—"

"Rose Gill!" a hollow yet insistent voice declared. It was Bergeson. "Why it's been ages!"

Rose, composed, turned to regard him and barely suppressed a shudder, just enough to maintain propriety. "Oh, Hal. How delightful."

Cait admired the both of them saying one thing, but clearly meaning the opposite. Yet to a casual onlooker, it was two old friends seeing each other after some time.

"Cait, this is Hal Bergeson, who I've known for too long a time, really. Please say hello."

Bergeson was a slight man, built on the frame of a jockey perhaps, half a head shorter than Cait herself. He was possessed of an insistent and acquisitive energy, eyes taking in things keenly.

"A distinct pleasure, Miss MacReady," he said with something that approached warmth. As practiced by a shark perhaps. "Oh, I overheard you and Khan. I'm not a psychic."

"Well, that's a relief. Don't need mind-readers around." Cait did not offer her hand when he moved to take it. "I'm just getting over the flu, so let's wave our hellos at a distance."

"Flu is no laughing matter," he said gravely.

"Miss MacReady helped get-" Khan tried to interject.

"I'm aware," Bergeson said with irritation. He showed too much of his teeth in speaking, seeming to bite the air. "I'm old, Khan, I'm not an imbecile."

"Apologies." Khan tried to shrink out of his suit and disappear.

"Rose, where have you been keeping yourself?" Bergeson drew the knives back out. "Our circle hasn't been the same since you departed."

"Oh, here and there. I spend time in the desert. A lot of time, really."

"Really, we should get back together for drinks soon. You know how to reach me. RE-1955. However they do that now."

Rose sighed. "You've had the same number since forever, Harold."

Bergeson smiled thinly enough to slice a man open. "So good to see things haven't changed. Good evening Miss MacReady."

"Mr. Bergeson. And Mr….Khan. Right." She grinned.

Bergeson nodded slightly, like he got the joke. "Come on Khan. We don't have all night."

Khan himself said nothing, only staring rubber daggers at Cait for a moment before disappearing to Bergeson's side.

"Wow, what a corny character," Cait said as she turned back to Rose. "Khan and his master." She stared at Rose who was shaking in her spurs, white as bleach. "Hey, are you okay?"

"I just need a moment," she said through gritted teeth. "I wasn't expecting that. Bergeson."

"I could tell that you and he would be happier knifing each other in a street fight. But it's not my business."

"It's not. Just watch him carefully if you ever wander into his world. Well, any closer to him than you already are."

"Anyone who's a friend of Khan is not a friend of mine."

Rose grinned weakly. "Oh, Ehmet is fine. You have to know exactly who he is, then he'll always behave the way you expect." Labor strained at her, aging her or perhaps revealing what she'd striven to hide. "Let's look over the rest of the catalog."

The next table was empty but for two glass vials about as long as Cait's index finger, both stoppered with what looked like ivory or maybe Bakelite, a hard and shiny substance that wasn't quite white or quite yellow. Inside the vials were what looked like locks of hair, one set a graying auburn and the other a much more dazzling platinum silver.

"Mansfield or—?" Cait started to ask before Rose squeezed her hand abruptly.

"<u>Very</u> quietly, if you're going to speculate," she whispered.

"Respect for the dead?" Cait asked.

"Something like that."

Cait wondered about the hair. She'd seen Victorian-era antiques, where the survivors saved locks of the loved one's hair, or their tears. The feeling was both endearing and ghoulish.

There was a table with a sweating metal cup that should have been in the hand of a soda jerk. The top of it was open, but Cait was reluctant to look inside. Condensation ran down the edge and to a thin ring of dark on the velvet.

"Since November 11, 1962," Rose whispered. "I've seen it several times here, never owned by anyone more than a year. And they always lose money on it. Still, a powerful temptation."

"If you say so."

Cait stopped at the next table. She had thought Khan had been joking with her, trying to get her goat. But he'd been telling the truth. There was a copy of the *Darrab Althabean*, the 1812 edition, with the maroon fabric cover, the color of a mummy's blood. There were others too: *Between the Whispers*, *The Sun is the Moon*, and *Green is the Color*, all books that Cait had forged at one time or another. She'd have to look inside to know for certain if they were her work. But then she thought about it a moment and knew.

Blood rushed up her neck and scalp and then she felt the same chill that she'd imagined Rose had when Bergeson crossed her path.

"No," she whispered. She tried to calculate the odds of these books being grouped randomly and stopped counting after a moment and the number was approaching the count of grains of sand. "Not possible."

"The not possible is what the Cinderhaus traffics in, Cait."

"But how?"

"I stopped asking myself these questions some time ago."

"But those books, I…"

"You shouldn't say what you think you want to now. If you must, sell your secrets but never give them up for free."

Cait could remember stitching the signatures together, aging the pages and scuffing the covers so as best to sell them for what they pretended to be. Maybe they'd become more than that since then. They were, after all, still handmade books.

"Is this why you brought me here?" she asked, wondering if she should be angry or just exhausted.

"Partly. It's not to tease you or call you out. Just to show you something."

"I want them back," Cait said. "I want them gone."

"Nonsense. They're beautiful books. The world needs more of them. If they make someone happy looking through them or just seeing them on the shelf, they're every bit as real as any other book."

"Yeah, what if you make a book that makes someone unhappy?"

"Hard to see that it's your fault."

"Hard not to see that."

"What happens to a book, to someone reading one, that's co-created. There is no one book, just whatever happens in the reader's head and heart when they read them."

Cait stared at them, trying to take them apart with her mind, imagining the covers unraveling and the pages flying out, like moths trying to batter themselves out of a mason jar. She tried to understand how and why and nothing she came up with made her feel any better.

"If you want, I'll advance you the money to buy them," Rose offered. "But you'll probably be working for me until you're half my age."

"Maybe more."

A tall woman tightly followed by two bodyguards passed by. She wore a jacket over a long dress, green like the sea in the lights of the pier. Her shoes were silver, nested and intertwined straps covering her feet in metallic vines. Her face wasn't quite visible, hidden by two layers of mesh, one thick-threaded but loose and the other that seemed like it should be all but invisible. Instead it was as concealing as smoke, baffling and making her face utterly unable to read. Red-brown hair beginning to go silver was tied neatly at her neck and then splayed out beneath that, struggling to get free of a scarlet bow that contrasted the color of her dress like roses thrown overboard. Her bodyguards were not much taller than her, unlike the gorillas at the door. These were more subtle, noticeable only by the way they stuck to her like shadow sticks to sunshine.

Her walk was refined, practiced. Cait could imagine a red carpet beneath her feet, even though the rest of her was trying for camouflage. Only her proximity had given her away. She disappeared into the crowd ebbing towards the room's single doorway.

"Come on, Cait. More to see."

They passed a table with a collection of gilded rubble, bricks from something that looked like Liberace's sarcophagus.

"All that's left of the building," Rose said. "A pity."

There was a collection of poker chips, old enough to be actual clay, colors faded to a sun-blasted approximation of red white and blue. They were laid out like a pastel flag of a country long forgotten.

There was a table with nothing on it but a square of carmine cardboard, a little smaller than a playing card. It was marked with symbols that were vaguely familiar and the letters OTO with the name Jack Whiteside Parsons stamped out in tiny capital letters. Over at the next was a collection of photos and newspaper articles, all faded, and a 7" record from a band called Carousel that was arranged in such a way that Cait felt like she should have known who they were, but she hadn't a clue. Next to that was a chandelier shaped out of chunks of broken glass all somehow stuck to a flowing organically-shaped metal armature. It was jagged and beautiful, red candles jammed into the light-bulb sockets that had been there.

Cait stared at the next table. On it was a piece of antique watercolor paper. Painted on that was the figure of the Devil and a multi-headed beast intertwined into a shape that was erotic in and of itself, red fingers stroking and caught up in a mane of snakes, eyes closed in raptured completion.

"It's by Blake," Rose said quietly. "They've been trying to destroy it as long as they've known about it."

"Who they?"

"Just they."

Finally, they stopped at the last exhibit. On the table was a double-barreled shotgun, breech broken open to prove that it was unloaded. Two hammers, two triggers. It had seen a lifetime of wear and use, muzzle and barrel chased with weird prismatic burnishing like the sheen of oil on water. At the butt end of the stock, the whole works was chased in sturdy silver, not for decoration but some other purpose. There was nothing even about it, as if the butt end had been slammed into uncounted targets over the years.

"I didn't believe it when I first heard about it," Rose said with awe hushing her voice.

"I don't know much about guns, Rose."

"That's a Parker Brothers shotgun, based on their 1878 model with modifications requested by the owner."

"I thought they made Monopoly."

"You're not so funny as you think you are."

"It wasn't a joke. Same name."

"Parker Brothers made guns in the late eighteen hundreds until the thirties. They were bought out by competitors who liked the name and wanted to own more of the business."

"You knew the man who owned this gun?"

"Yes. I did. Years ago." She paused. "He lost this one before we met."

"An old flame?" Cait blurted out without thought. She wished she could pull it back just as the words escaped her lips.

"I was young once," she said. "Foolish, too."

"I'm sorry I asked."

"Don't be. It's an honest question. We're all people here, we all have lives even though you're only seeing the merest fraction of any of us tonight."

"Why… Why does it have that silver on the butt? Wouldn't that hurt like a son of a bitch when you fired it?"

"You know anything about firing guns, Cait?"

"Just a little. My dad took me out shooting with cousins a couple times."

"It should always hurt some when you pull the trigger. Just to make you not quite so happy to do it, is all. That's what he'd said."

"Good, 'cause I thought you were going to say something like 'werewolves' and I'd lose it."

"Like werewolves would be enough to upset you."

"I'd have to see one to know. I've seen… Well, I've seen some things."

"Just means you've started to live a life." Rose pulled out a timepiece from her small bag and narrowed her eyes. "Could you please? I haven't my glasses."

"Ten thirty."

"Oh, we should get to our seats. Come on. We don't want to miss the action."

They passed out of the catalog and through the lobby, neon-glowed Anubis with his jackal head watching as they passed into the underworld of buyers and sellers. The theater's auditorium was not huge, not by the standards of the CinemaScope screens that Cait had grown up with. Its grandeur was more subtle and unexpected. Instead of modernist and minimal interiors, the Egyptian was done up with column and scarabs carved from stone that was old when the pharaohs walked, ushering the viewers to another place entirely. Maybe it was just the work of the Cinderhaus and the weird, dry weed that everyone must have been smoking, maybe it was like this every night.

Directly above the screen, at the center of the room was a metallic scarab braced on either side by three interlocking swans, all rendered out in a style that fell between deco and classical, old and new somehow.

Cait and Rose took their seats in the seventh row, almost at the middle. Pairs were seated next to one another with a single, empty seat between them. There were exceptions, though. Alondra sat with the two door girls from the Last Prayer. Cait couldn't tell what they were wearing but it was shiny, glistening. They braced her like an oiled shield. For once they matched and Cait wondered why.

The woman who Cait had seen in the catalog room was in the third row, her two bodyguards each a seat away, the rest of the chairs clear. The fourth and second rows were left vacant entirely. Whoever she was, she was being treated like royalty, even if she was sitting with the commoners. The woman looked straight ahead as if no one else was there.

The last attendants were seated and the lights dimmed down, ebbing as if bleeding out. Music was playing, something modern and minimal, chord changes coming only grudgingly, trying to express everything with timbre or pitch or vibrato. The lights went dead for a second and then a muted blue spotlight fell on the scarab ornament, dancing over it, suggesting shape and form and texture more than merely illuminating it.

"Ladies and gentlemen, meine damen und herren. Good evening and welcome to the Cinderhaus." The voice was male and refined, with Marlene Deitrich's pacing and languor.

The screen lit up with an icon of a flame over an equilateral triangle, two mirrored slanting lines marking off either side. Muted applause followed, rippling through the place like water over stones.

Then the spotlight flicked down to center stage, where stood a carved wooden lectern, its upper half shaped like a chimera or eagle or dragon. Behind that stood a tall Black man in a suit with vest, single-breasted, broad shouldered. The tailoring spoke of wealth and taste and more than a little showing off, old but not antique. A derby hat was balanced rakishly on his brow. He then removed and tossed with a flair to one side. A showman.

"I am Lucius Sturm and I will be calling the auction tonight. Do not expect the rapid-fire delivery of other auctioneers. I was raised to take my time in all affairs, with ladies, gentlemen or those who are both, neither."

The audience chuckled sensibly, though no wolf-whistles or catcalls followed.

"So wonderful to be in a room with adults. And please permit me to introduce our escrow for the evening, Les Freres du Vienne."

Sturm extended a hand towards stage left and there stood two pale-skinned men in costume, broad collars, big buttons, frills and tricorne hats almost as wide as their shoulders. One wore feathers in his, the other a long strip of purple silk that trailed down all the way to his hips. Revolutionary war musketeer new romantics.

"Adam Ant did it better," Cait whispered.

Polite applause followed.

"The management compels me to remind everyone here of the rules. Rule one." He held out his left hand with the thumb extended.

"Cash payment only," the audience, including Rose said.

"Rule two." He raised his index finger.

"All sales are final," replied the crowd.

"Rule three."

"Provenance is not the house's problem." There was some grumbling and discontent in this one, a few voices ringing sour.

"That's right," Sturm said. "Rule four."

"Have some fun, dammit." The synchronization of the crowd enveloped Cait, making her feel part of it even if she didn't understand what was going on, not quite.

This last line was followed by cheers and applause. Sturm bowed at this, graceful and easy.

"We have, as you've seen, some lovely items to admire and pursue. Choose wisely and may you find relief in your purchases."

The Freres du Vienne half-walked, half-glided to the side of the stage and then wheeled in a silver service cart draped in the now-familiar purple velvet that was Cinderhaus' hallmark. Upon it was the chandelier of broken glass, its profile looking like a swan rendered out in hesitation cuts.

"A true piece of history, and a sad one at that. Formerly hanging at the Last Prayer Club and with us tonight," was all that Sturm said of the item.

Cait wondered if that meant the club had been closed or were they simply redecorating? She hadn't seen that fixture in her trips there, but that was only twice and she had hardly been there to take in the atmosphere.

"What am I bid?"

Cait found herself watching the crowd as much as the bidding from the audience. Each started with "A single dollar," as Sturm would say for every lot. It was odd, unlike the rapid-fire adrenalin-driven almost dervish trance of the auctions she'd seen. In those, the auctioneer seemed to be there only to fire up impulse buying and drive the prices higher and higher. Sturm questioned each bid, gave people every chance to reconsider, as if he was examining their own desires more than they did.

The chandelier only had three bids, one from Alondra and from the tone of her voice, Cait was convinced she'd buy it only to smash it to bits. Alondra didn't walk out with it, but someone named Robert Higgins did. Each bidder raised their hand and when the bidding was concluded, they identified themselves by name. It was not mere formality, but part of some ceremony that Cait could only guess at. The transfer of an item was more than that; it came with a price and it came with giving one's self up, even if just for a moment.

The clay chips came up an there was some jostling over those, though Cait couldn't begin to guess at their significance. A blonde woman in a flapper's dress went to battle with a man in a wheelchair over them, waging reputational war across the aisles. The man pushed himself to his feet at his last bid, more than ten thousand dollars, calling out the figure with an operatic finish. The woman said nothing when Sturm passed the bid to her. He identified himself as Horace Ginley from Trenton. Anyone could come see the chips once they paid an admission fee.

"No advertisements," Sturm warned. "Common courtesy, please. Self-promotion is so unbecoming."

The three stones, that Sturm had called 'tektites' were bought by a man in a sharp blue uniform covered in silver and gold insignia that felt more Hollywood than real.

"Your name, sir?"

"General Addison Lye," the man in the uniform said, silver eagles glinting.

Sturm raised an eyebrow at that.

"Honest."

"Fair enough."

The twisted braid of thorns came up and Cait caught herself watching Rose's reaction, but she had none this time. Maybe it was enough to know that they existed. The bidding fell between Bergeson and two others who made moves but were quickly fended off when he doubled his offer to more than a hundred thousand.

"I am capable of managing the bid, sir," Sturm warned.

"Does the figure stand?" Bergeson demanded. "Or will we play games with this?"

"Games are all we have sometimes. But yes, the bid stands. Remember rule four, please."

"The fun is in the winning."

"So you say."

The lot of Cait's books came up and she felt herself clutching. The mute brothers wheeled them out to the auctioneer, seemingly hunched. The cart had developed a squeak that went from piercing at first to somehow comical, as if everyone was compelled to note that yes, something was wrong, but that saying anything about it before anyone else was unthinkable. The cart squealed and scratched out to the stage to a couple of dry coughs from the audience, perhaps attempts to cover up snickers and laughter. The thought of that stabbed at her.

"Four infamous books," Sturm said with a tone that conveyed doom. "Notorious might be a better word." He looked the volumes over, appraising them, then turned back, satisfied. "A single dollar."

There were no bids. Only the sound of rustling in seats and low whispers amongst the crowd like the ghosts of children hushed at church. The low figure hung in the air like shame. Cait's heart pounded at it, pacing with the power of a caged tiger hungry for the keeper to drop his guard if only for a second.

"Can I bid?" Cait whispered to Rose.

"What?"

"I'm just a guest."

"You're here, aren't you?"

"A. Single. Dollar," Sturm said with pity, but offered no defense for the items, no assertion of value.

Cait raised her arm. "One dollar," and her voice cut through the shuffling and echoes.

Sturm looked her way without smiling. Then he scanned the audience. "No others, then?"

There were sounds of shifting in seats and maybe even bracelets and jewels clinking against one another but not a word.

"A single dollar. Your name, miss?"

"Stand up," Rose whispered.

Cait's head was swimming so much it was drowning, but she stood anyways. "Cait. Cait MacReady."

"Well then, miss Cait MacReady. They're yours."

But they already were. Guess you can't win them all, right, Khan?

Her face was flushed as she sat down and she fanned herself, raising then lowering the collar of her dress to blow cool air across her throat.

"I guess people just don't know the value of these things," Rose said.

"Or a dollar is harder to come by than you think."

The cart wheeled back without a sound. The other items followed but Cait could hardly be bothered to notice them, thinking instead of what had just happened. Were her books valueless or priceless?

The haunted milkshake cup came and went without even a bid, evidently the crowd tired of it passing amongst them or fearing whatever specter followed it. The Carousel fanclub material was bought by an effusive man with a distinctive British accent who identified himself as "Paul Silver," and Sturm wagged a finger at him. "No more pseudonyms, sir" and the crowd laughed at that.

Rose bought the shotgun for a figure that would have kept Cait in her life for the rest of her life and then some. The whiskey bottle and the bricks and other items went for sums that felt modest but were perhaps ruinous for the buyers. The Blake watercolor was sold to a man of the cloth named Sark who was made to promise that it would not ever be destroyed, the only time Sturm had felt compelled to offer an editorial as to an object's disposition. The round-eyed clergyman nodded.

The final lot. The twins carried the two vials out not on a silver cart, but instead a satin pillow. They held it beside Sturm in a strangely mirrored recollection of Gainsboro's Blue Boy with the hues shifted, fleshtones bled out.

"Our final item for the evening," Sturm said with emphasis, so as to calm the crowd, made restless by time and duration. "Two vials, hair from the same head in different aspects. We need not name, need not dwell on the details whether salacious or sordid.

"A single dollar."

The bids went out like seagulls picking at a shark carcass on the shore. Once the predator, it was now not even prey but food for scavengers. And the scavengers themselves relished in that reversal. All those teeth and tough skin and relentless appetite only to be washed up on the sand and made helpless. The shark would keep feeling the bites and pecks long before it ran out of breath.

Ten, twenty, fifty thousand. The crowd demanded more, each taking another chunk.

The woman up front, the one in the veil, had been bidding, calmly, with restraint. At first. Her whole body was tensed, shaking almost visibly.

"One hundred thousand," Sturm said after a break in the bidding. He surveyed the crowd, judging their interest and intent and quite nearly their worth.

There was some hesitation in the bidding, where before there had been flocks of arms like leafless branches reaching out. Only the serious remained. Perhaps ten or twenty bidders from the more than a hundred before persisted, each ratcheting of the bid found fewer coming to it. The crowd had found their limit where the real collectors were just getting warmed up. As more dropped off, the electric anticipation of the crowd swelled.

The veiled woman and Bergeson and a handful of others were all that remained as Sturm pushed the bid to eight hundred thousand. She remained stiff, her right hand up, propped on the arm of the seat, fingers working, reaching for something not quite yet in hand. Her skin was ghost pale and bloodless.

Bergeson was twitching in his seat, calculating figures in his head. If Cait were betting, she'd say that he was getting near the end of his rope.

Perhaps the thorns had cost him more dearly than he wanted to admit. Perhaps he was always like this, always dissatisfied, always ruled by what he did not yet have.

At nine hundred and eighty thousand, he tapped out, throwing up his hand in disgust. Had he miscalculated or merely wanted the impossible at a bargain price?

"Too bad, Harold," Rose whispered with a grin of satisfaction.

"No love lost, huh?"

"When I run out of things to say, I'll tell you his story. And I'll finish it, even if you beg me to stop."

"I can hardly wait."

"Ladies and gentlemen, that concludes the bidding at nine hundred and eighty thousand American dollars." Sturm clapped his hands together and over the mic they sounded like a shot going off. "The Cinderhaus thanks you for your patronage this evening."

The twins beside him bowed, removing their hats in a flash of threaded sheen.

"She should identify herself," someone shouted. It was Bergeson, his voice strained tight from anger and bruised ego. He all but stood and pointed. "It's custom!"

Sturm waited at the lectern, shaking his head almost sadly. "We hardly believe it necessary--"

"No pseudonyms! You said that yourself!" Bergeson snarled.

Sturm's head dipped in recognition or was it defeat. "I did at that. Madam, I'm afraid I must ask you your name."

"Those don't belong to the Cinderhaus. They were stolen." The quiet anger in her voice made Bergeson's seem all the more childish in comparison.

"I'm sorry, madam. Rule three. We all abide by them."

The woman stood up, fist clenched tight, said nothing and stalked out of the theater without saying a single word.

"Hah!" Bergeson crowed. "Those are mine!"

"Mister Bergeson, must I remind-"

"Quiet, lackey! Do your job!" Bergeson vibrated not with triumph, but rage, one that would never quiet.

Sturm swallowed hard and said "This business is concluded. Successful bidders are invited to the stage. All others, including invited guests, are required to retire to the lobby or wherever the night takes you. Adieu and auf wiedersehn."

Cait watched as Ehment Khan made his way out, with the rest of the newly-made hoi polloi.

Who belongs now?

The pale brothers stood to either side of the lectern, now supporting an open ledger, antique and yellowed. One of them held a quill pen in one hand and a crystal vial of ink in the other, passing the pen to buyers in turn as they recorded their name, their purchase and how much money traded hands over it.

"I thought no records," Cait said to Rose as they waited.

"The Cinderhaus keeps its own records, just nothing that can be made public."

"Sounds like blackmail."

"It would be extortion, I think. Though I must say, I'd give quite a bit to peek at some of the names on those pages. And here, you should go ahead of me. It is your first Cinderhaus after all."

Rose and Cait switched places and they both watched General Lye sign for the tektites. He then placed them in a briefcase that was filled with foam cutouts just their size, snug and tight.

"Let's go home," he whispered to the case as it shut and locked.

"Our boys in uniform," Rose said with a laugh. "Bless 'em."

Cait took the quill and it felt like a bone from some alien bird, its color indescribable, between known hues. She printed out her name as if she was at kindergarten, taking care to be open and legible, only later noticing that some buyers had just left a scrawl or even a symbol. The verbal self-identification seemed sufficient in some cases. She wrote next to her name "my books" and "a dollar" in the appropriate columns.

She returned the pen to the pale and waiting fingers then she heard some kind of ruckus from behind the screen.

"You cannot go back there! Ma'am! Ma'am!" The voice was polite and accented and more than a little flustered.

A sound of leather on the hardwood floor, scuffling in a quick and brutal soft-shoe routine, slid out and a door opened. From somewhere off the stage, the veiled woman in her green dress and her two slim and compact bodyguards materialized in the wings. One of them was dusting his hands off, as if he'd just taught someone a lesson.

"I'm sorry that I have to do this, but you've all forced my hand." The woman stood there, arms crossed in front of her, one foot forward. She shook her head with defiance. "I've come for what's mine. I'll pay. I have it all here."

She pointed to her bodyguards, who each opened an opposite side of their jackets, bundles of bills hanging in straps sewn into the linings.

"It's all there."

"I'm sorry, ma'am," Sturm offered. He was so beautiful up close, broad and sharp cheekbones, a chin made to hold and eyes made to stare deeply into. His voice, however, was stone. "The deal has been done."

"But not entered. Isn't that right?" she demanded of Bergeson, who was a couple spots behind Rose in the line. His expression wavered between horror and triumph.

"You're too late. I won. They're mine."

"One of those was stolen and you know it," she said, scowl visible underneath her veil. "You'd destroy this whole thing, the Cinderhaus, all of it."

"Provenance is not--"

"Shut up! You think you've found a loophole that lets you steal from one side and launder it in the other." Her fingers shook, trembling rising to her shoulders.

"Please, madam," Sturm said. "The deed has been done. Making a fracas of it will help no one."

"Ask him what he's to do with it." She pointed at him.

Something about her voice was familiar to Cait but she couldn't quite place it. It was steely, not breathy, all resolution and no flightiness. The fact that she couldn't place it gnawed at her.

"That's not the Cinderhaus' business," Bergeson gloated. "They sell. We buy."

"I bought," she said. "I won it fairly, you germ."

"You had your chance. You could strip naked and it wouldn't make a difference."

"Everyone's already seen that," she nearly spat. "You think that scares me?" She shook her head then turned to Sturm. "He's going to give me away. You know that, right?"

"That's really not the Cinderhaus' concern."

"It had best be. Because it won't stop with me." She moved, just to break the full-body rictus of outrage she'd held. "Tell me, what do you know about the work of Glassberg and Jeffrys?"

"Sturm, do something about her! She's obviously delusional!" Bergeson looked pale and precious, sweating for no reason at all. "Take her away, you two!" he said to the brothers.

"You, Harold Bergeson, are not in a position to give orders. You are a buyer and welcomed here at the Cinderhaus' discretion. This is irregular, yes. But then so are we." He squared his shoulders and turned back to the woman, standing so still she must have been exerting herself to do so. "Elucidate, ma'am."

"I keep up on this. Glassberg and Jeffrys are the first, but they will not be the last. They're geneticists over in the UK, working on a way to identify criminals by way of their DNA. The unique code in everyone's cells. Yours. Hers," she pointed at Cait here. "And even mine."

"I don't follow you."

"I do," Cait said. "They're finding a way to track down not just criminals, but anyone, from traces left behind, right? Like skin and hair?"

"Hair." The woman nodded, the line of her mouth flat and biting. "She gets it. You can too." She indicated the vials. "Those are mine. One's old. One's new. Stolen from my home."

Bergeson's thin lip quivered as he spat "This is ridiculous. Provenance-!"

"There's provenance and there's *thievery*," Sturm said.

The older man spluttered and then contained himself. "Cinderhaus traffics in personal relics all the time. Kirchner's last breath? Valentino's left hand? John's scalp?"

"Oh the scalp. Nothing but trouble, that," Sturm said with a groan. "But all those are from persons no longer with us, and *not* stolen."

"He's going to use those to identify me, to package and sell me personally," the woman said. "And it won't stop. Not with criminals, not anywhere there's a penny to be made."

"Ridiculous," Bergeson said, only making it more so in the saying. "What if I just want the thing? I want it. I bought it. It's simple."

"I can't take that chance. And the Cinderhaus shouldn't either. Before long, there won't be any mysteries left. Everything will be collated and catalogued. There'll be no room left for the almost, the not-quite or in-between."

"It's mine. Those are mine. And what I do with them is my business." Bergeson's hand darted inside his jacket pocket and snaked back out with a short-barreled gun of blue metal. It had four very small barrels.

By the time he had it out and level, the bodyguards had stepped in between him and their boss in the veil. One of them had his own pistol drawn squarely on the older man.

"I won. It's mine." His face was a skull with skin barely stretched over it, tight in anger and envy.

Sturm's eyes went from one to the other and back again, desperately trying to find a way out of this, bound by both propriety and lack of arms. Behind him, the brothers feigned disinterest but watched from the corners of disaffected eyes.

Cait tasted bile crawling at the back of her throat. "Can I say something?" she asked, glass-fragile, afraid to bend the moment into snapping.

"I doubt it can hurt at this point," Sturm said, stabbing at a joke.

"Mr. Bergeson, might I offer that you think you want a thing."

"I don't think. I do want." His words grated out of teeth grinding on one another. "Stop this moronic game."

Cait took a hesitant step away from the lectern and the book, feeling like she'd drawn the spotlight onto her in the middle of a stage-crashing. "It's not dumb at all. You're chasing a thing. But you're really chasing a feeling. Believe me. I used to be in the business of things and feelings. We complicate them, fortunately for business, unfortunately for everything else."

"Nonsense. I want it. I won it. That's not feeling."

"It's okay for this to be weird. You're not used to--"

"Shut up!" The barrel of the gun shook in place, more than a little. "This isn't about emotion. It's about ownership."

"And _that_ isn't emotional? Denial doesn't look good on you."

Bergeson reddened.

"I used to make fake books, Mr. Bergeson. I was very good at it. And it didn't really matter if they were fake at all, so long as they made the buyer feel like they were real. Most everyone was just looking for an experience, right? They wanted the feeling but the feeling didn't happen from looking at in a shelf or knowing it was in a lockup somewhere."

"This is bullshit."

"The truest kind. If you really want those objects, you want what they make you feel, and that's already happening even if you don't own them. Unless you just want to deprive everyone of that." She took another step, kitty-corner in his direction. "Just put the gun down. Nobody wants to hurt you and I'm pretty sure that if you were going to shoot, you would have already."

Bergeson shook his head slowly, uneasily. His suit looked ill-fitting, as if he'd shrunk within it. "Gun stays here, but you can talk."

"You want a thing that nobody else can have. A unique thing. I don't get it, but I get it. What if I propose a trade?"

"That's not your place to decide," the woman in green said, all but hissing.

"Look, I don't know you, but you've thrown us all in some soup, so please let me finish." She turned back to Bergeson. "A thing for a thing. Assuming that everyone here can keep a secret."

"I like secrets," Bergeson murmured. "Keep talking."

"Something of value that won't track back or can't be tracked back to the Cinderhaus or to her. For the locks."

"Like what?" the woman asked.

Her veils broke up the profile of her face, but not entirely. Cait could almost pull out something familiar in it, but not in the silhouette.

"I don't know. There must be something. Something memorable."

"Better be pretty damn memorable. That's money on the table there."

"You can keep it," the woman said.

"What about…" Cait stopped herself. "No."

"What? Speak up," Bergeson snapped.

"I can't. She's right. It's not my place to offer." Cait flushed carmine feeling it burning her cheeks and ears. "I'll kiss you. How's that? A good one, too."

"No sale," he said.

"Gods, I'd kiss him if I thought it would move the needle," Sturm said.

The woman's head turned towards the table with the locks and back to Bergeson for a moment. "How about a favor from a goddess? Is that enough?"

Bergeson's eyes went wide as if he'd seen the oncoming train and was stuck in place. "What?"

The woman took a deep breath, deep sea-green satin rising and falling with her as she became someone else. Her hip cocked and she balanced on her silver shoes differently. Breath filled her and she leaned forward slightly as her arms came up with slow care and she made to remove the veils at a clasp on the back of her head.

The fabric fell away and she revealed her face and her name and why she would not just give those away.

"Marilyn," Bergeson said, only just above a whisper of awe.

Cait's heart stopped and flipped over in place. It was her. One of the few who'd surpassed mere celebrity, who could claim that divine title, the goddess.

"You only guessed, didn't you?" Marilyn said, not airy or cute at all, but unbendingly. "You'd hoped, but didn't dare dream. You wanted a machine to tell you."

The room, even the brothers jaded as they were, all stood riveted to the floor in disbelief, unable to make what they were seeing line up with expectation or even mere knowledge. They'd acted like they'd known, but hadn't.

She was Marilyn Monroe, older, proud in that. Made up with sharp cat's-eye line and subtle rouge, eye-shadow with the same scintillation as her dress. Unexpected lines creased her face, folded near her eyes, revealing a lifetime of laughter or worry, of private emotion that had necessarily been hidden away while she wore her other face.

"You sicken me, Bergeson. And the rules of this goddamned house, too."

"Ma'am," Sturm moved to say. "The traditions have served us so far."

"That's easy for you to say."

Cait's vision swam. Her skin went clammy and she shook herself to bring her focus back. "My god," she said, far too loud.

"So nice that I can still make an impression," Marilyn said with a half-laugh. "Back to the matter at hand. This," she held up the veil and it drooped like a dead black bird in her hand "was not easy. Everything will be undone and I'll have to start over. But that's nothing compared to what will happen if anyone walks out with those locks but me."

"Bergeson?" Sturm asked.

"Not enough. You said 'favor.' And you said you'd kiss me," he said, pointing at Cait. There was no lasciviousness, no lewdness, just cool transactionality and expectation.

It nauseated her to her core. It had become control.

Me and my goddamn mouth.

"You didn't agree to it," Cait said. "You said--"

"I said 'Not enough,'" he snapped. "I didn't say 'No.'"

"Put that stupid gun down, then."

"Not until I get what I'm after."

Cait sized him up in the moment before she was going to approach him. Who even knew how old he was. She should be stronger than him? But then the psycho need to control probably gave him an edge and even he couldn't miss at the range she would be in.

"Fine. But tell me how much you hate me first."

Ugh.

"Man, I've only known you for ten minutes, but it doesn't take long to recognize a sucking wound with a skin stretched over it. Does that fucking count?"

"How lovely. Step up." He waved her in, moving the gun aside for the moment.

Cait took her disgust and shoved it down hard enough to keep it from boiling back up. She could taste it anyways.

His teeth were too big and there were too many of them, lips pulled back slightly in a not-smile, but a dominance display. They were not papery or ragged like she expected, instead vital and unexpectedly strong. He was not as he seemed. He sucked in a little and parted his teeth.

She pushed back as strong as he had come forward. "And that's that."

He clamped his jaw shut as she pulled away. The click she heard was already in her nightmares.

"As for you," Bergeson said, already discarding whatever he thought he'd taken from Cait. He turned towards Marilyn, looking her up and down in open appraisal. "You look better than I thought. I'd figured you were going to go all crazy or mushy like a bag of cottage cheese."

"Isn't it nice not even pretending to be human?" Marilyn asked him. "Do we have a deal?"

He licked his lip slowly with a tongue that was too pink. "I want something I can take home and show."

"You can tell people the story," Marilyn said, summoning the ghost of her old self, sneaking practiced female impersonation into the performance. "Maybe if you tell it well enough, they'll believe you. But that's all you get."

He frowned, lines scalpel-deep around his mouth and across his brow. "I'm not such a good storyteller."

Scorn deadened her face and then she smiled. "It's not my problem that you can't work with the material of a lifetime." She stepped towards him, achingly impossible and real, goddess and human both. "Now say it."

Anticipation shivered in him and on him, radiating off his being like heat on a summer street. "I withdraw my bid."

She turned to Sturm and glared at him "And I have revealed myself. I'm Marilyn. You don't need a second name from me. Restore my bid and the Cinderhaus gets its cut."

"I'll enter the transaction myself," Sturm said with an unfamiliar humility. He dashed out a few lines in the ledger, strokes both jagged and fluid as an earthquake reading. "It's done," he near-whispered as he set the pen down.

Marilyn sighed faintly then nodded to one of her bodyguards to collect the vials and leave the money behind. When he finished, he pulled out a pistol and the other replaced his in the same motion, as if there were only the one weapon between them, passed by means of sleight of hand.

"Pay attention," Marilyn said, goddess-voice in full power.

In spite of himself, Bergeson was losing control. His eyes fluttered closed and his gun dropped to his side.

Marilyn flashed the briefest of smiles after looking him over, seeing he'd dropped anything resembling defenses. He was wide open. Her left hand went back and flattened out in a motion that was almost too quick to see, just the flashing of the jewelry on her wrists in the stage lights, etching out a brilliant scrawl. Her hand came across his cheek with a sharp crack followed by the sound of his gun going off, little more than a child's toy, too high, too diffuse.

"Aaah!" he cried, lifting his foot suddenly, reeling from the impact of the slap at the same time. He pitched over onto his opposite hip and fell to the ground with another yelp.

Rose snickered for everyone.

"Oh, dear. I'm sorry. That must have hurt," she said, laughing behind her hand.

"My foot. You bitch!" He snarled as he struggled to his feet.

"You should have packed a gun with a safety."

Without motion or anything else, one of the brothers had his hand around Bergeson's wrist and was shaking it sharply, relieving him of the weapon. The pale man took it and held it as one might hold a dead rat that had gone to necrosis, fingers pinched in disgust. He walked it over to Sturm, over Bergeson's spluttering protest.

"Oh be quiet," she said. "I doubt those pellets could even get through the shoe leather. You'll just have welts."

"That wasn't the deal!"

"The deal was a favor and I just did you one by letting you walk out of here. You should thank me, and her," Marilyn said, pointing at Cait.

Cait bubbled over with a thrill that she could not put a name to.

"My guards wanted to simply dispatch you on the way back to your car. And I had half a mind to do it," she said bitterly. "Oh for god's sake, someone help him up. I hate talking to the floor."

The pale brothers took the command and Bergeson tentatively tested putting weight on his foot. The two twins smoothed out the wrinkles in his jacket and dusted him off. He growled soundlessly.

"This isn't finished."

She touched him on the tip of his nose with an insouciance that was enraging. "It is. I'm not coming back here. And if you value that skin that you're wearing, you won't go seeking me out."

She said it to him, but she meant it for everyone in the room. The words cut through the awe and humor and shock, down to the bones of all present.

"You think you've seen something, but you don't know what. Keep it that way," she said with both chill and charm. "You can think me a goddess if you like, but that means you'd best not trifle with me. Come, gentlemen."

Her guards were at her side and before any other questions could be thought of, she disappeared offstage, only the clicking of her heels fading behind the screen left behind.

Cait rolled the side window down so she could feel the velvet and smog of the night air as the Duesenberg pulled onto Hollywood Boulevard with a lurch of power. She watched the lights bleeding past, neon marquees and club signs, even the pink and green of the grandest thrift store on the strip.

"You okay?" Rose asked. "That was something else, even by Cinderhaus standards."

"It's not the craziest thing I've done, but it's in the neighborhood." The shape of the crowd, like so many cutouts and silhouettes all blending together into new geographies on the street, rippled and moved like one thing alive.

"Well then I want to hear about the craziest thing you've ever done."

"Gonna be hard to narrow it down," Cait said.

"Spend some time thinking about it. Tell me the story then."

"Only I won't stop, even if you ask me to."

"Deal."

The phaeton flooded down the streets, through the history that persisted even into the now.

KICKSTARTER BACKERS

Here's a list of the brave folks who put their money and faith behind this project. Most were backers of All Waters Are Graves, some not. Special shout-to those who went for all three books not having read one of 'em.

Edward Abbott	Constantine Koutsoutis
Corinna Bechko	Kevin Lama
Russell Borogove	Algie Lane
David Brothers	Steve Lieber
Devin Bruce	Ken Lowery
Don Cardenas	Andrew McClure
Christopher Cinq-Mars	Jason R Merrill
Mathew Digges	Derek Moreland
Cielyn-Gizmo	Jacki Myers
Matthew Carpenter	Eric Newsom
Larry Clow	Kirk Pennak
Jeffrey Coleman	Chris Reid
Aleph Craven	Rhiannon R.S.
Mike Davis	Jessica Ritchey
John DiBello	Eric Schuster
Nate Dryden	Steve Sears
Joshua Dysart	Ekaterina Sedia
Philip Flores	Siegfried
Marc-Oliver Frisch	Randall Sims
Justin Greenwood	Bill Smiley
David Harper	Eric Trautmann
Adgee Harville	Jeff Treppel
Conrad Heiney	Jason Urbanciz
Andrew Hickey	Tim Utsler
Yvette Hines	Mark Wandra
Alan Hughes	Evan Waters
Dan Johnson	Andrew O. Weiss
Mary Jones	Matthew Wilson
Jared Kahanek	Dorian Wright

AFTERWORD

The stories from Fake Believe were all written a couple three years ago, for the most part. Back then I thought this would be a book called *Asphalt Tongues* and someone else was going to be publishing it. I'd been done with self-publishing and didn't think I'd return.

I should have been a touch more flexible. At any rate, after a few changes and rearrangements and substituting one story for another, I got it out into the world with some help.

This is the second book I've ever Kickstarted. That campaign is still in progress, with nearly two weeks left as I write this. There's still room for growth in the audience and I'm trying to be patient about that.

As for the stories themselves, they're mostly self-contained. That said, it's not impossible that some of these characters might show up in the background of things again. I've already got some thoughts as to where Luxe/Lucille might appear. Maybe Glorietta and Pecas. Maybe even Trudy. I'm not sure about Roscoe and Greg. Their luck might've run out.

Cait and Grace will of course be appearing in *The Missing Pieces*, which should be the next Hazeland book and should be up for funding in early 2026. If we're all here. I dunno sometimes. It's getting wiggly, getting squirrelly out there.

I'm not supposed to do this, but I hope you enjoyed your visit to this weird little corner of the world. It wasn't just me that brought it to life. I had help from copy/editor Kyle Marquis who wouldn't take money for the job which I'll respect even if it goes against my nature. Thanks to early readers Costa Koutsoutis, Corinna Bechko and Jamie Delano for their feedback on things. Sometimes a simple "It's good, keep going" is good to hear.

Maybe even necessary.

BIOGRAPHY

I was born in California, sometime between the JFK assassination and the moon landing. Lived there my whole life. Learned to drive stick shift in the parking lot of the ziggurat that you see in Roger Corman's *Death Race 2000* and went to school where they filmed all those soft brutalist sets in Battle for the *Planet of the Apes*. I've worked in video arcades and think tanks, been an animator, taught sociology, thanatology and ethnomethodology.

My past writings include work for Blizzard Entertainment, stories in both *Tomorrow's Cthulhu* and *Welcome to Miskatonic University* from Broken Eye Books. Broken Eye was the original publisher for *The Queen of No Tomorrows* as well, recently re-published by Highway 62 Press.

I've self-published a number of books, both nonfiction/commentary and short/long fiction works. I was also the writer and publisher of the weird western comic series *Strangeways*.

Hazeland will be the bulk of my work for the forseeable future. Unless someone wants to pay me to do something else. It's not like there's a lot of money in this. Sorry, high priests of success. It's true.

Sure. I'd love to be on your podcast.

http://highway62press.com
@highway62 on Bluesky, not Twitter
Not really anywhere else

www.ingramcontent.com/pod-product-compliance
Lightning Source LLC
Chambersburg PA
CBHW071605110726